AS YOU
ICE IT

AS YOU ICE IT

USA TODAY BESTSELLING AUTHOR

EMMA ST. CLAIR

To the Dallas Stars for giving me all the inspo but please next time have a less exciting Game 7 in the playoffs when I have work to do.

And to the DLLS Diehards for helping fuel my obsession. #stanleycone

CONTENT WARNINGS

This is a light and funny romcom, but I want to help readers feel safe! Here are some topics that are touched on in the book:

- Parental conflict
- Early-onset dementia (of side character)
- Hockey talk
- Text messages without proper punctuation
- Some pinching

Spoiler alert: No one dies. There is no sex in this book. You will get a happy ending with no cheating and minimal angst.

ABOUT THE APPIES

THE APPIES IS a fictional AHL team located in the also fictional town of Harvest Hollow. We wanted to create a hockey team with the vibes of the Savannah Bananas. (If you don't know the Bananas, do yourself a favor and look them up. You're welcome.)

All of the Appies books can be read as standalones, but if you'd like to read in order, this is the reading order: *Just Don't Fall, Absolutely Not in Love, A Groom of One's Own, Romancing the Grump, Runaway Bride and Prejudice, When Alec Met Evie,* and *As You Ice It.*

While these are hockey books, they are primarily romance books, so at times, some liberties may be taken with some details, hockey and otherwise.

CHAPTER 1

Naomi

FROM THE BACK seat of my little Honda, my dear, sweet, wonderful son pipes up with yet another hockey fact. "Hockey players weren't required to wear helmets until 1979. Did you know that?"

I'm pretty sure the question is rhetorical, as the only hockey things I know are the ones Liam has been telling me. I answer anyway, trying to make it sound like the words aren't coming through clenched teeth. "I did not."

Nor do I particularly care, but that seems irrelevant.

"But players who signed contracts before that year could choose whether or not to wear one. The last player who skated without a helmet was Craig MacTavish, who retired in 1997."

"Playing hockey without a helmet sounds dangerous. Like riding your bike without a helmet," I say pointedly.

Liam ignores my comment and goes on to tell me what year visors on helmets were mandated (2013) and to list the only four players who don't wear a visor now.

"Jamie Benn is known for his visorless death stare."

"Good for Jamie Benn," I mutter. *Whoever that is.*

On the seven-and-a-half-hour drive from Oakley Island, Georgia to Harvest Hollow, North Carolina, I've been forced to listen to my son share no less than one thousand three hundred fifty-seven hockey facts with me. Approximately. Which, according to my best mathing, is an average of one fact every two minutes.

Somehow, it feels like more.

Liam's stupid hockey kick, which started months ago but is currently at a fever pitch, is all my fault for (briefly) dating a hockey player last summer. Except I'm choosing to blame the aforementioned hockey player for Liam's obsession. Because it's far more mature to shrug off your own responsibility and dump it on someone else's shoulders.

Someone else's broad, sculpted shoulders.

No! Bad Naomi. We are not even thinking about his shoulders. Even if they are—

Nope. This train of thought ends now.

I force myself to picture Liam's first-grade teacher from a few years back. The one who always had a little bit of spittle in the corners of his mouth and who talked to my chest—insignificant though it may be—rather than making eye contact. This mental image always helps exorcise any unwanted romantic thoughts, even if it's rude and shallow.

Actually no, I think, remembering the way Mr. Gull's gaze always fixed a few inches below my collarbone. *I'm not the shallow one.*

"Goalies are also known as netminders," Liam continues.

"Or goaltenders. They have a different kind of stick with a wider paddle to block shots."

Facts number one thousand three hundred fifty-eight and one thousand three hundred fifty-nine.

"Marc-André Fleury is my favorite goalie, even though he retired."

"Mm-hm. And why is that?"

Do I sound convincingly like I care? I sure hope so.

This is the part of parenting no one tells you about. It wasn't included in the well-meaning but unsolicited advice I received from friends and strangers alike or the books or blog posts I devoured as a nineteen-year-old trying to prepare for a surprise baby. I was prepped for late-night feedings and having a sick baby while I was also sick and trying to keep Liam from ingesting common household chemicals. Knowing didn't make it easy, but it was eas*ier* since I had some level of expectation.

But I was wholly and woefully unprepared for the emotional weight of feigning an interest in a sport you'd like to see wiped from the face of the earth. The strain of having to talk about hockey has my eye twitching.

"They call him Flower. He's one of few players who's loved by everyone. He was known for pranking people."

"Don't get any ideas."

"I won't." Liam pauses, and I can hear the smile in his voice when he continues. "Probably. He talked to the goalposts and thanked them in both French and English. And he's the only goalie in NHL history to record a shutout as a teenager and after the age of forty."

"He sounds ... neat."

And I sound dorky. Who says *neat* anymore?

But I'm struggling through this conversation and feel like the little meter showing my emotional regulation is teetering swiftly into the red zone. The one that says *Hit the deck! She's gonna blow!*

"He's a legend," Liam says, then rattles off stats I don't follow regarding save percentages, goals against average, and career shutouts.

Give him an iPad for the car ride, my brother's wife suggested. *It will make the trip go a lot easier.*

Eloise might have been correct—*if* Liam were a more typical ten-year-old. I should have known he wouldn't watch movies or play games with headphones on. Instead, he's been learning everything he can about his new favorite obsession —hockey—and then mistakenly thinking I'm also interested.

In case it's not already clear, I'm not.

I've never been a big sports girl, generally speaking, and anything I do know is about the more mainstream sports: football, baseball, basketball, soccer—the general American sportsball sports. When it's either a summer or winter Olympic Games year, I become a temporary expert on figure skating or swimming.

Hockey, however, is what I consider a fringe sport, like MMA or Formula 1 or rugby. There are definitely obsessed fans—just in smaller numbers than the American mainstream sports. I am not one of the obsessed or even mild fans. Before last summer, I knew hockey existed. Liam's facts notwithstanding, I still only know the very basics: ice, pucks, skates, fights.

After last summer, however, I am not simply *dis*interested in hockey or hockey neutral. I am actively *anti*-hockey.

But I am very *pro* Liam. My kid is brilliant and amazing, and I'd never trade him and his penchant for hyperfixating for a kid who'd watch seven straight hours of *Bluey*. Even if I personally happen to love *Bluey*.

Unlike hockey players, *Bluey* would never ever break my

6

heart. Even if I cry in some—fine, *most*—of the episodes I watch by myself. (I will accept zero judgement for watching *Bluey* alone or crying about it.)

The point is: I love Liam. And right now, Liam loves hockey. So, pretending I care about hockey is my current lot in life. I'll do whatever is needed to make Liam feel loved and valued.

Even if it means gritting my teeth and finding ways to respond as he starts reciting more goalie facts.

"Their pads and gear can weigh up to thirty-five pounds," Liam says.

"Seems like it would be hard to move carrying that much weight."

"It takes a lot of athleticism," he agrees, and I feel a tiny bolt of pride for contributing something he deems useful to the conversation.

Look at me—contributing to the conversation! Then, I remind myself that *I do not care about hockey*, and Liam continues onward.

"Shots can launch the puck at speeds of almost one hundred miles per hour," Liam says. "So, goalies need the protection even if it's bulky. Pucks can break noses or the orbital bone—"

I tune Liam out with a shudder as he starts listing off gruesome hockey injuries. I am easily nauseated by talk of blood and guts. If I actually *witness* any of those things? It's all over for me. I love this turn of conversation even less than I did hearing about goalie pads.

"Hey! It's our exit! We're almost … home."

The word feels strange and wrong in my mouth, and maybe it does to Liam's ears, too, because he stops talking and turns to the window.

Harvest Hollow is a small city nestled in the hills of

North Carolina. Not typically the kind of place you'd think of as teeming with jobs. Had I known the office administrator position at the title company where I've worked for six months was *here*, I wouldn't have applied. Just about any other geographic location in the continental United States would have been okay with me.

But the listings on the company's job site were all vaguely arranged by state, not city. North Carolina sounded not too far, but just far enough for the escape I felt I needed from Oakley. I assumed the job would be in a more significant city like Charlotte or Asheville or the Raleigh-Durham area.

Not ... here.

The size of Harvest Hollow is not my issue. Heck, I grew up on Oakley Island, which is tiny *and* an island. It's not far from Savannah, but when you have to cross a bridge to leave, it creates a kind of dome effect, enhancing the small townness.

Harvest Hollow is at least ten times the size of Oakley. It's also not too far from the larger Asheville to the east and a little further to Knoxville to the west. From what I understand, this area of North Carolina is also dotted with little towns nestled into the hills and hollers, adding to the population.

So, it's not the size that has me gripping the wheel so tightly as we exit the highway.

It's also not because I'm trading the ocean for the mountains, though I *am* a beach girl at my core.

"Mom! There's the Summit!"

Liam practically has his face pressed to the window, iPad forgotten in his lap. "Can we stop?"

I glance out the window at the stadium building Liam is gesturing at wildly. The Summit, which houses the Appies,

Harvest Hollow's AHL team, is a physical manifestation of the reason why I would have chosen any other place to live.

Because my ex, the one from a short summer relationship that was supposed to stay casual and fun and, above all, temporary, plays hockey for the Appies.

And if Camden finds out I've moved here, he'll probably think it has to do with him. It seems a little too coincidental.

So, I just need to make sure he doesn't know I'm here. Ever.

This shouldn't be too hard, considering the fact that the Appies are basically low-key celebrities. When Camden and I first met, I did a little reconnaissance—a.k.a. curious social media stalking—and the man has two hundred thousand followers. Not as many as some of the other players, but way beyond normal-person level. Even beyond typical AHL players. Camden's comments may be turned off, but every post has thousands of likes and shares. It's honestly a little unnerving.

But it makes my point: He's busy. Kinda famous. Our paths are very unlikely to cross.

The challenge would actually be getting in touch with him if I wanted to. Which I don't. But knowing how geographically close we are to Camden—I mean, he could be in that building over there *right this moment*—combined with the reminders from Liam's constant stream of hockey facts, is like massaging salt into very open wounds.

I thought I ended things with Camden before Liam's heart got tangled up as badly as mine did. I *thought* I made the right choice. The smart choice.

I mean, Camden as a long-term, serious boyfriend or possibly *more* was a pipe dream. Which is why we talked about keeping things casual. He's a hockey player, and any professional athlete comes standard with a whole slew of unpleasant side effects like constant travel, weird schedules, fame ... and stuff I don't know about because I barely know hockey. Plus, his home was off Oakley, and I told myself a long-distance relationship—assuming Camden might even want the same thing—would be impossible.

But it wouldn't be long distance now ...

Shut up, inner voice, I silently tell the voice of *unreason.*

Because all other reasons aside, there is also the little factor of the boy in the back seat, who, despite how quickly he stopped asking me about Camden after the breakup, was clearly impacted by my short-lived relationship. Hence the hockey facts.

I'm only grateful Cam's name hasn't come up. Not in relation to our move or included in the litany of information he's been fire-hosing at me. I keep waiting for the other shoe —or in this case, skate?—to drop. But between the two of us, Camden has become like the boogeyman or, to use a more current analogy from *Encanto,* a movie Liam obsessed over and I couldn't stop humming for months, like Bruno.

We don't talk about him. Even if he might still be present, living quietly behind our walls.

"I think the Summit is closed right now, bud."

"The gift shop in the lobby is open," Liam says. "The hours today are from twelve to five."

He memorized the Summit's hours. Just swell.

I draw in a slow breath and remind myself how much I appreciate my child's unique brain, even if I don't know where it came from. Certainly not me. My brain is a combo of a pinball machine with half a dozen balls going at once and a sieve, all connected to a mouth that's at times a little too smart for my own good. And Liam definitely didn't inherit his smarts from his biological father, an absolute nothing of a man I'd regret if not for the amazing kid I ended up with.

"I want to get to the house before it's dark," I tell him. It's January, and now we're in the mountains, which means at three thirty in the afternoon, shadows are already stretching long, the sun dipping below the mountains, and leaving a ribbon of gold along their peaks.

This will take some getting used to. I'm lucky there's no snow or ice at the moment. I am completely ill-prepared for that. We don't even own coats. It's on the list. Along with fifty thousand other things. At least the house we're renting came mostly furnished. One small thing.

"We should settle in," I continue gently. "Unpack the car and all that."

"Oh," he says, and the disappointment in his voice is a backhand to my heart. "That makes sense. Okay."

As we pull up to a stoplight, I lift a hand and press two fingers right between my eyes where a headache is forming. Too little sleep lately. Too much caffeine today on the drive.

Too many NHL facts.

But what do I hate more than thinking about hockey and especially hockey players?

Disappointing my kid.

"I promise to take you another time, okay?"

"Really?" Liam's voice rises with unbridled excitement.

"Sure. Yes." This is the kind of promise that kills me to make, but I'm making it anyway. "We'll go to the Summit."

"To a game?"

I swallow around what feels like a handful of sand. "Sure."

Unless I can somehow switch his interest to some other topic first.

Saving the rainforests, if they still need saving.

Quantum physics, whatever that is.

Even the life cycle of dung beetles would be preferable.

Or maybe I could bribe him with a dog. He's wanted one forever, and I've said no every single time. Would I prefer having a dog to hearing about hockey?

Definite food for thought.

"A hockey team's home arena is also called their barn," Liam says, and this fact is recited with a little less excitement than his others.

"So, the Summit is the Appies' barn?"

"Yep."

"Do people also call hockey players horses?" I ask, hoping for a laugh.

Instead, I get a derisive snort. It makes me smile anyway. "Mom, *no*."

"Just asking."

I love horrifying my child. I'm really looking forward to his teen years when I can google all the current teen slang and then casually throw those terms into conversation. He'll *hate* it, and I'll *love* it.

I'm so grateful when the Summit passes out of view without Liam bringing up Camden that I don't realize how quiet the car has become. A mother knows her kid better than anyone else does, which is why, when Liam's silence stretches for longer than it has this entire car trip, I know something is up as I turn into what will be our new neighborhood.

"You okay?" No answer. "What's wrong?" I ask, turning to glance back as we reach a stop sign.

Liam doesn't look hurt. Or even sad.

He looks ... guilty.

Dread rises, clawing its way up my throat until I can taste the panic. Guilty means he's done something. Something bad enough to stop his parade of hockey facts.

"Liam, talk to me."

12

"I'm glad you said you'd take me to the Summit," he says, his words carefully measured. The gears in his head are turning at a rapid rate.

"Why are you saying it like that? With that tone, and with such specific wording?"

"I did something." Liam sounds miserable. "I know I shouldn't have. I know I should have asked you. But I was afraid you'd say no."

I miss the turn to our new street, and the GPS interrupts, rerouting us. A perfect pause in which to collect myself. I breathe deeply and attempt to settle my nerves.

Don't freak out. Whatever it is, be cool. You're a good mom. Mostly good. Just because you're a very emotional person doesn't mean you need to unload on your kid when he does something awful. It's probably no big deal.

"It's fine. Whatever it is, we'll deal with it. But you have to tell me."

"You promise not to freak out?" he asks. "You promise not to be mad?"

"I promise I'll *try*. And even if I'm a little upset, you know nothing you could do could make me love you less. It's you and me versus the world, right?"

"You and me and Uncle Jake and Aunt Eloise and Grandpa Ned," he adds stubbornly.

Hearing Liam list off names of the family we've left behind, my hands reflexively white-knuckle the wheel.

For years, I've gone back and forth between living in Savannah and living on the island with my family surrounding me—those Liam mentioned plus all the more recent additions he didn't: Merritt and Hunter and Sadie and Benedict. And the one I'm shocked he didn't mention, Hunter's daughter, Izzy, who is Liam's age and a good friend.

It won't be easy. I knew this going in. But the reality right this exact moment is a sucker punch.

I like to think of myself as an independent woman. Capable. Smart. Brave. And, sure, I am those things. Just the fact that I've managed to raise a really decent kid on my own is proof of that. But even while living in Savannah, I was, at most, thirty minutes away. I've never lived this far from a support system. I was never truly alone like we will be here.

Like we are now.

I'm struck with a sudden and painful homesickness like I've never known. The excitement I've felt about change and a fresh start is quickly collapsing into something a whole lot more like panic with a side of *Oh, no—what have I done?*

I swallow. "Right. You and me and all our people versus the world."

The GPS informs me that our destination is on the right. I recognize the house from pictures and pull up to the driveway. It's a cute little craftsman bungalow with a wide porch, emerald-green paint, and fresh white trim. It restores my excitement temporarily. But then I realize Liam is still quiet in the backseat.

Right. I almost forgot that he was about to confess something.

Whatever it is, do not start yelling, I tell myself. *You are an iceberg. A veritable city block of chill.*

I park in the driveway, then glance in the mirror to see Liam biting his lip. "Spit it out."

"You promise you won't yell?"

I drop my head to the steering wheel, wishing I had a paper bag to breathe into. What could he *possibly* have done?

"I won't yell."

"You won't ground me forever?"

"Definitely not *forever*. But with the way you're talking, it sounds like maybe whatever this is might require some kind of consequence. I promise I'll be reasonable. How's that?"

"Deal," Liam says. Then hesitates some more.

I swear, I can feel individual hairs turning gray while I wait and worry. Shifting, I take off my seat belt and twist uncomfortably to face him.

"Liam," I practically growl. "Come on. Let's get this over with. It can't be that bad."

Please, please *don't let it be that bad*, I silently plead with no one in particular.

I try to be thankful. Liam from a few years ago never would have done whatever it is he doesn't want to tell me. I'm not happy about whatever it is, of course, but it's a by-product of the good changes that have taken place. He used to be more socially awkward and a whole lot more serious. Now, he smiles more, jokes more, and is slightly less of his uncle Jake in a smaller body.

It also happens to mean he gets into normal kid trouble in a way he didn't before.

After another few excruciating seconds, Liam says, "I took your credit card and signed up for hockey skating classes at the Summit."

I totally forget all my promises and I shriek, "You did WHAT?"

CHAPTER 2

Camden

I'M WAITING outside Coach's office, trying not to worry about why I've been summoned or how long this will delay me getting home. I'm also trying not to eavesdrop, but it's hard with all the yelling leaking out from behind his closed door.

I don't catch every single word, since Coach, the Appies' team owner, and someone else are yelling over each other. But I do get the gist, and it's not good. Sounds like there's trouble between the Appies and our NHL team. A rift is not good because when push comes to shove, players are assets. Not people. We can be moved around at will. Even with contracts and agents giving some semblance of security, I've seen a guy dress for a game only to be pulled out of the locker room because he got traded.

But serious tension between an NHL team and their affiliate is *not* good.

Before I can put together any concrete details, the door is thrown open and the Appies' owner stomps by. Larry is followed by the head of the Appies' legal team. He winces when we make brief eye contact.

Definitely not good.

Stepping forward, I knock lightly on the doorframe. "Hey, Coach. You wanted to see me?"

Coach Davis is staring down at his lap, elbows on the desk and both hands clutching his bald head. "Camden Cole," he says. "Come in and close the door."

I take a seat across from his desk and wait. My hair is a little longer than I usually like it, and right now, it's dripping onto my collar since I came straight from the showers after our optional morning practice. It's the first time I've ever been in this spot, and I don't like it. It reminds me of a few principal's office visits from so many years ago. Especially when he's calling me by my full name and not just by Cole like usual.

I might be in trouble—if only for playing like half of me is somewhere else this season. Which is … accurate. Nothing so far has helped me fix it, though, and I doubt a heart-to-heart with Coach will change that.

Finally, he sighs and sits back in his chair, assessing me with tired eyes. He looks almost worse than he did at the end of last season when he realized his daughter had married Van, the one guy on the team who loves to push Coach's buttons.

"I need help and thought you might be a good guy to ask." When I don't say anything, he continues. "You might have heard we've started a new set of classes for youth and—"

"No."

He rears back. Probably because I didn't let him finish. Or maybe it was the hardness in my voice, surprising even me.

"No, *thank you*," I amend, but it doesn't soften my delivery.

"You didn't even hear what I was going to ask," he says, a furrow appearing between his brows.

I shake my head. "If it has to do with working with kids, ask someone else."

Coach's face is an understandable mark of confusion. "Do you not like kids?"

A muscle in my jaw tics. "I'm just not ... good with them."

"I find that hard to believe." Coach narrows his eyes.

I hold his gaze, though what I want is to get up and walk out the door. "It's true."

It's *sort of* true. I don't have a ton of experience with kids, but I failed hard enough recently to make me want to stay away altogether. Disappointing one boy was enough. And I'm not sure I could work with kids without the very painful reminder being thrown in my face.

"You don't have enough guys to help?" Now that he's bringing it up, I remember hearing some of the guys talking about this earlier. Like most of the locker-room talk lately, it floats around me, never quite landing.

"We did. And we're rotating Saturdays when we don't have games. But we had a record number of kids sign up." He scrubs a hand down the side of his face. "And then, a few minutes ago, Tucker and Dumbo had a little ... issue."

My lips twitch. Those two guys are the Tweedle-Dee and Tweedle-Dumb(o) of our team. "What kind of issue?"

"They taught a group of five-year-olds the lyrics to 'Baby's Got Back' while they were gearing up."

I choke back a laugh. "Why? How?"

"It's Tucker and Dumbo." Coach throws up his hands. "I don't question anything when it comes to those two. It did *not* go over well with the parents, as I'm sure you can imagine. The point is, I could use one more person. Dominik is helping—"

"You asked Dominik?"

"He offered." Coach smiles at this. "The Kid's come a long way."

Even though Dominik is no longer the youngest on the team now that we've acquired the eighteen-year-old twins from Texas, people still call Dom "the Kid." It's even started catching on with our fans. And he *has* come a long way. Dominik arrived in the middle of last season with an attitude larger than his homeland of Russia. I'm not sure if there was one specific turning point or just the continuous influence of a team with no room for attitude or ego, but he's definitely matured.

Still. I'm surprised he volunteered to help with the youth classes. And more than a little bit chagrined now that I'm refusing to do the same. If Dominik is willing, then I should—

No. This has to be a no.

In addition to the fact that I am not someone who should be working with kids given my current headspace, I need to get home. I don't *want* to get home. But I *need* to.

I'm still getting acclimated to this twitchy feeling of worry when I'm not home. And since I haven't told Coach or anyone else about my new houseguest and my new reality, no one understands my sudden need to hurry out of the building and back home. Probably because I've been like a ghost all season. They might not notice a difference.

"What about Theo and Carter?" I suggest. "The twins are high energy."

"They're helping next week." Coach pauses. "I'm not sure you know this, but the guys look to you as a leader. Especially with Alec gone."

I almost laugh.

Alec, our captain, retired midseason after injuring his knee one too many times. Coach has been giving different guys the opportunity to be captain or alternate for games. I've worn the C on my jersey twice. We lost both games, and I had nothing to say in the locker room.

Logan speaks up, and Felix always has something smart to say when he wants to. Van's always running his mouth, though not in a captain kind of way. There might be a bit of a power vacuum going on, but I am not the one to fill the void.

"I don't think that's true."

"It's hard to see in yourself what others see in you."

"Maybe, but you're wrong about this."

Coach sighs heavily. "I don't need you to believe it—not yet. I just need you to *do* it. Help out today, Cole."

I stand. "I wish I could help out, but I can't."

Coach sizes me up for a moment, like he's trying to read what is a very closed book. I haven't talked to anyone about anything since last summer, no matter how much they've all pried. I'm not going to crack for Coach.

I'm not.

He keeps staring.

I'm probably not going to crack.

Thankfully, he speaks before I do. "I know we don't need to talk about this until the summer, but are you thinking you want to stick around?"

My contract is up this summer, and my agent has been

20

asking the same questions. I've been dancing around an answer for a while now.

I like it here, but … I don't know. It's been two years, and signing a contract to stay longer feels like such a commitment. I'm honestly surprised Coach is even asking, considering how I've played this year. But he doesn't make the final decision, so he's probably just getting a feel for where my head's at.

Too bad my head is miles away. On the same island where it's been since summer.

"I'll have to think about it," I tell him.

"Sure. You've got time," Coach says, but I can see his disappointment.

Time for a topic change. "That meeting seemed pretty intense. Everything okay with the bigwigs?"

Coach's lip lifts in the smallest of sneers. I've yet to meet anyone who genuinely likes the Appies' owner, Larry Jenson. Instead of hiring a general manager to handle the business and team, he's a control freak of the highest degree and has insisted on acting as both. Which wouldn't be terrible if *he* weren't terrible.

The Appies' success has very little to do with him or his decisions, though he definitely gives himself all the credit for it. And the past year or two, he's been running the organization into the ground, insisting on all kinds of extra events to capitalize on the viral social media success the team has had.

Like this youth hockey thing, which normally would not be run by pro hockey players.

"Nothing new," Coach says, then mutters, "And nothing good."

As I remember the snatches of conversation—yelling, really—I heard when I walked up, the uncomfortable feeling that's been swirling in my gut intensifies.

21

"Do we need to be worried?"

"Honestly," he says with a heavy sigh, "I don't know."

Maybe I don't need to worry about signing an extension after all.

Coach's words and the defeated look in his eyes hang over me as I head through the locker room to grab my bags. Despite the urgency to get home still pounding like a drum in my head, I take the long way and pass the rink. Maybe because I'm curious or because I feel guilty about saying no.

Whatever the reason, I find myself on our bench, glancing out at the chaos. Kids from toddlers to pre-teens are skating or falling or holding onto the walls. Some have sticks and are clearly familiar with hockey while others appear to be on skates for the very first time. Cones and long black pads break the rink up into stations, though there is little order. Groups of parents watch from the stands, some pressed close to the glass, phones up and filming.

Eli, one of my teammates, catches my eye from where two little kids are whacking him on the shins with their hockey sticks. *Help*, he mouths.

Grinning, I shake my head. It's clear saying no was the right call.

There are half a dozen of my teammates plus most of our assistant coaches out there. Even Parker, our social media manager, is on skates with a group of kids. It's an all-hands-on-deck situation.

But my hands aren't needed; they've got this.

Probably.

I'm just turning to go when two of the more advanced pre-teen skaters zoom by and then both stop, spraying a snow shower of ice on a kid a little younger than them who's barely keeping himself upright.

Punks, I think, as I watch the older boys laughing.

The younger kid got a face full of ice, which isn't easy to wipe off because of the cage of his helmet. I don't catch what they're saying, but I don't need to hear it. His cheeks turn red as he tries to unbuckle his helmet with his gloves on then almost eats it. The other boys start imitating him, pretending to lose their balance.

"Hey!" I'm already making my way down my bench.

Three heads whip my way, and I wince when the smaller kid falls to the ice. The other two try to skate off, but I hop over the low wall, blocking their exit.

They stare up at me, mouths open. I'm not sure if it's because they recognize me or because the look on my face is so intense. I take a breath and try to remind myself that I once had a punk-kid period too. I never forgot how some sharp but true words made a lasting impact on me. There's time yet for their little brains to shift and grow.

"Hockey is a team sport," I grit out, barely holding my temper in check.

"He's not on our team," one boy sneers. "He's with the baby skaters. They've got stuffed animals instead of pucks."

Okay, maybe I was a little too optimistic about being able to make any headway here.

To his credit, the other older boy doesn't laugh. He still looks like he's about to pee his pants.

Good. There's a shred of hope for humanity left.

I narrow my eyes at the unrepentant one. "You want to play in the NHL?"

He scoffs. "I don't want to. I *will*."

"You know what coaches want to find in recruits? You know what they tell scouts to look for and ask about when they're watching up-and-coming players?"

"Yeah," he says, and I swear I can see his little chest

inflating with misguided pride. "Goals. Points. Wins. And someone who can skate."

He throws this last line to the younger boy still trying to get his feet under him.

"Sure. They look at those things. But those aren't the only things, and there are a thousand kids out there just as good if not better than you." He looks ready to argue, but I turn to his partner in crime. "Do *you* know what coaches want to see?"

He shakes his head. "No, sir."

I retrain my gaze on the first boy. "Coaches will ask your coaches and even sometimes other players about you. Not just how you conduct yourself on the ice. In the locker room. If you're polite to your mom. If you show respect for your coaches and others in authority. And"—I lean forward, using my height to tower over him—"how you treat your fellow skaters. This kind of behavior will *not* have teams and coaches fighting over you or even looking at you. This is going to ensure you're passed over again and again, kid."

"Whatever," he mutters.

His sneery little face as he starts to skate away backwards is the kind that will become very punchable in a few years.

"You're just an AHL player. Couldn't hack it in the NHL," he says, laughing as he spins and skates back to his group.

Not the kind of insult he may think it is. Some guys, guys like me, are career AHL. They might dabble in the NHL, have a decent two-way contract, but mostly stay in the minors. And it's not a bad life. Less pressure. I still get to skate, and the money is fine. Especially with the Appies.

No use explaining any of this to the kid. He's gone anyway.

To my surprise, the other little instigator has actually

helped the younger kid up and is saying something in a low voice that sounds an awful lot like an apology.

Warmth starts to swell in my chest, like maybe it *wasn't* stupid of me to jump in and pretend I had any business jumping in. But then the younger boy, the one who looks as wobbly as a newborn giraffe on skates, glances up at me.

Every muscle in my body tenses with shock. Because I know this face. And it belongs to a kid who absolutely shouldn't be anywhere near Harvest Hollow and definitely not here on my rink.

CHAPTER 3

Camden

I'M STILL STANDING stock-still when the older boy skates away, giving me a little nod I can't return. Hell, I can hardly breathe.

"Hey, Mr. Cam," Liam says. His tone is funeral solemn, and I know that's my fault. Same with the flat look in his eyes.

"Hello, Liam."

He's grown since last summer and has the look of a kid who hit a growth spurt and is still trying to figure out how to manage newly longer limbs. Still shorter than the other two boys who were picking on him, but they also were a few years older, I think.

How old is Liam, again—ten? Nine? Eleven?

Has he had a birthday since I left?

A sudden tightness clutches my chest at the mental image

of Liam and Naomi sitting at a table with a cake and birthday candles. Just the two of them.

But no—she would have her whole horde of extended family from Oakley Island with her. I met most of them, then promptly forgot everyone's name. Except for Jake, her lawyer brother who looked at me like he'd find a way to either murder me or sue me into bankruptcy if I hurt Naomi or Liam.

I can feel the searing heat of that gaze now, a few states and a few hundred miles away. Jake is probably plotting my demise right now.

"Mr. Cam? Or should I call you Coach Cam now?" Liam asks, his face so bright and open.

"Yo! Cammie! Get your skates on, bro!" Eli calls. He's overrun with little kids who look like they're trying to fell him like a tree. Stuffed animals litter the ice around him. "A little help here?"

"Is that your group?" I ask, remembering what the one kid said about pucks versus stuffed animals.

Liam's head dips, but not before I see color rise in his cheeks. "Yeah."

He's at least five years older and six inches taller than everyone else in the group. Apparently, he's the only kid his age who truly looks like he's never been on skates before.

"I'm taking this one!" I call to Eli, whose face falls.

Liam's head snaps up, but he looks away again so quickly I can't read the expression on his face. I ignore the voice of protest in my head telling me this is a bad idea—a very bad idea. Because if Liam is here, his mom can't be too far away. I don't allow myself to scan the groups of parents who stayed to watch. Not yet. "You've got it!"

I'm not so sure that's true, though, as a moment later, the

kids take Eli down and swarm over his body like locusts on a fresh crop.

He'll live.

"I've got my gear over on the bench," I tell Liam, not meeting his eyes. In truth, I'm ashamed to look straight at him.

I don't know what his mom told him about everything that happened. Or how he processed our last conversation, the one I wonder if he told Naomi about. But considering the way he rode his bike to my hotel on his own without permission, I suspect not.

And more than anything—more than what I said to Naomi in our last conversation, more than the way I packed and left the island so quickly, severing any and all ties—I feel terrible about how I left things with Liam. I hate remembering the look of disappointment on his face. I know what it's like to have adults let you down. To be crushed by their choices.

At the time, standing in my hotel doorway, my bags halfway packed and Liam staring expectantly up at me, I told myself I was doing him a favor. Making a difficult choice now to save him from more heartache later. I blamed the distance, an easy thing to blame.

"I have to go home," I told him. "My whole life is there."

Before the words left my mouth, they seemed like a pretty basic explanation. Toothless. But once I saw the way Liam's face fell and then how he tried to draw himself up, absorbing the words and pretending they didn't crush him, I realized how they must have sounded to him, what he might have heard.

My whole life is there; you and your mom are not part of my whole life.

But he was gone before I could repair the damage. Not

that I would have had any idea how to begin fixing the hurt I caused. My last view was of him pedaling away, back stiff and legs pumping as fast as they could go.

I wouldn't blame the kid for hating me.

But Liam's face looked happy moments ago, not bitter or hurt or angry. Which almost makes it worse somehow. Anger I could take. Forgiveness, on the other hand, I don't know if I deserve. Even if the way things ended between his mother and me was her choice.

At least, she started the end. I simply finished it.

"Come on. It'll only take me a few minutes," I tell him.

"Okay," he says, his voice unsure. But there's the smallest spark of hope in his eyes that wasn't there moments ago.

When he doesn't move to follow me, I realize that he may not actually be able to navigate to the bench. At least, not quickly. He's still gripping the low wall for support.

"Grab on." I face him, holding out my hands, palms up.

He hesitates, then takes one of my hands in his gloved one, clutching the wall until the last second. Even after I've got both of his hands, he almost goes down.

I bite back the urge to say *steady*, because obviously, if he had any choice in the matter, he'd *be* steady.

"Keep your weight over your legs. Don't lean forward. That's it. Bend your knees a little—like that. Trust your legs. Feel the difference?"

He nods, which throws him off-balance. This time, though, he doesn't pitch forward or use my hands to hold him up. I can see him straining, working to keep his weight in the right place.

"Good."

He beams at the praise, but then he almost goes down and the smile falls. "I can stand here, but I don't know how to move," he admits.

I wish I could remember how my dad taught me to skate. But he pretty much threw me on our backyard pond in Wisconsin almost as soon as I could walk. The memory brings a swell of uncomfortable emotion, like a hiccup stuck in the base of my throat.

I've often wondered if my father regrets teaching me to skate and setting me on this path. If he knew how things would end up, would he have given me a basketball or a baseball bat? I'd ask him, but that's not the sort of relationship we have now—the kind where I can ask honest questions about the past.

These intrusive thoughts are replaced by another: I need to get home.

A sliver of worry zips up my spine. But an extra hour away should be fine. Just in case, I'll send a text saying I'll be late once we get to the bench.

"For now, I'm going to pull you," I tell Liam. "Just focus on keeping your knees bent, your toes facing me, and don't lean forward. Got it?"

He does, mostly, and I pull him back to the bench where I dropped my bag a few minutes ago. I wonder what would have happened if I hadn't come down to the rink. If I'd just gone home like I told Coach I needed to do. Now, I'm stuck.

But maybe ... I'm glad?

Time will tell. And it will depend on someone other than Liam. Because I can't imagine Naomi being pleased about this.

Now, as Liam sags onto the bench and I drop next to him, I let myself scan the crowds, seeking out a head of wavy brown hair and piercing blue eyes. Naomi isn't the kind of woman who can disappear into a crowd. She's a woman who—

"She isn't here." Liam's voice jerks me back into the

30

moment. He's taken his helmet off, revealing sweaty hair sticking up in a bunch of directions. He stares at me intently, like a challenge. "My mom. She had errands to run, but I think she was just avoiding any chance she'd run into you."

Man. I'd forgotten how direct Liam is. No thought of holding back. Liam says the things he's thinking. And he's always thinking, which means he's always talking.

I wonder what that's like.

"I mean," Liam continues, talking a little faster now as he clearly realizes he might have said a little *too* much, "not that she said anything about it. I'm just guessing. Because of, well ... you know."

"Why are you here?" I ask, desperately not wanting to talk about the *you know* Liam hinted at. But my question is a little too abrupt.

This is why I told Coach I shouldn't work with kids. Well. It's *one* of the reasons. The other is the kid sitting beside me. Though I was thinking more about avoiding *memories* of him (and his mother) rather than actually avoiding *him*. This was definitely not on my bingo card. Because Liam and Naomi live in another state. Or ... they *did*.

"I'm here because I want to play hockey," Liam says simply. A little bit of *duh* in his voice. Also a fair bit of stubbornness. Which is good. He'll need it if he wants to play hockey.

I'm also glad to see him warming up, opening up. Makes me think that maybe I didn't ruin everything before I left.

"I mean, why are you here in Harvest Hollow?" I ask patiently.

"Oh. We moved."

"You moved? Here?"

"A week ago. Mom's new job had an opening, and she applied and got it before she realized it would be in Harvest

Hollow. Then she tried to tell her boss she actually didn't want a raise if it meant moving here, and her boss said no, and then Mom threw her phone and said a lot of words I'm not allowed to repeat because she didn't know I was listening. And now, here I am!"

There's a lot to unpack there, and I store away most of my thoughts and questions for consideration later, when I'm alone. Needing something to do, I unzip my bag and pull out my phone, shooting off a quick text about my delay. I get a response quickly, assuring me it's not a problem. I tuck my phone away and start pulling on my shin guards.

"Is that all your gear?" Liam asks.

An obvious question, but I can see his curiosity as I pull out my gloves.

"Just my practice stuff. I like to keep it with me. Just in case."

Liam's grin is fast. "Just in case of a hockey emergency?"

I smile. "Yeah. I guess so."

Every guy is different in how they handle their equipment. My preference is to lug my practice stuff back and forth and keep my game day gear at the Summit to be washed and handled by the equipment manager. My practice pads are still damp and in need of a wash, but I don't need to put everything on now. It's not like Liam is going to be knocking me into the boards or hitting pucks at my face. He's not even ready to have a stick.

"So, how did you convince your mom to let you try hockey?" I ask.

I don't think I need to add, *Since she didn't even want to move here because of me.* The implication is clear enough that it might as well be sitting on the bench between us. It doesn't make sense that Naomi would let Liam sign up for a sport at the very facility where I spend all my time if she wanted to avoid me.

"Uh," Liam says. He takes off one glove and scratches his nose. "I didn't tell her. I borrowed her credit card and signed up on my iPad."

I can't help the laugh that booms out of me as I pull on my hockey pants. "I bet your mom loved that."

"She said some other words I'm not allowed to repeat."

"I'll bet."

Liam watches with interest as I slide on my hockey socks and start taping them up. Honestly, I could probably have just put on my skates and no pads, but it feels weird enough to leave off my shoulder and elbow pads. Plus, there's something inherently calming to me about the routine of getting geared up.

Right now, calm is what I need.

After the summer, I thought about Liam a lot. Hard not to, with his mother always on my mind. I wondered how he was doing and if he was okay, generally speaking. I hoped he wasn't too hurt by what I told him, that it wasn't some kind of formative dark moment—like the ones that haunt me when I let them.

Naomi kept a careful distance between her son and me at first. It made sense to keep things slow in that regard, considering Naomi and I were vague about how or even if things would end when I left Oakley. It was the conversation we constantly pushed off. Even when I didn't leave after my planned week-long vacation on Oakley and instead booked my room all the way up until the day before training camp.

By the second week of us dating, she asked if I minded Liam tagging along on a beach day. I didn't. Though I *was* nervous. I'm not around kids much, other than hockey meet-

and-greet events. Which is no preparation for meeting the child of the woman you're seeing.

I didn't want to mess things up. Didn't want to be too standoffish, but I also didn't want to do the opposite and form a bond when I didn't know what the future held. Naomi warned me ahead of time that he was on an ancient Egypt kick.

"He will tell you disgusting facts about mummies, and I'm very sorry," she told me.

And true to fact, within two minutes of being introduced, Liam told me that when preparing the mummies for burial, embalmers would pull the brain out of the nose with a hook. Naomi looked like she was going to throw up.

I laughed.

I'm not sure why, as there is nothing humorous about the mental image I got. I think it was more just the shock of it and the matter-of-fact way Liam said it. When I laughed, he grinned and asked if I knew how to ride waves. We spent the rest of the afternoon doing just that, with Liam critiquing my form. Any awkwardness I'd felt dissolved quickly and never returned.

At least, until now.

Now, I'm feeling unsure for a lot of reasons.

First of all, we have a secret between us. One I've kept from his mother and assume Liam did too.

Back then, I probably should have told Naomi that Liam came to see me. If I were a parent, I'd want to know. But I was—and still am—torn, not wanting to betray Liam's confidence, especially after sending him away.

Now, I've been blindsided by Liam's appearance and the knowledge that Naomi is in Harvest Hollow.

I don't have a playbook for this.

But then I realize I don't need one; I have hockey.

34

"How do those skates feel?" I ask Liam while lacing mine up.

His are clearly borrowed, scuffed with dull blades and mismatched laces. Possibly the wrong size. His hockey socks are sagging because he didn't do a good job with the tape.

"Fine, I guess. How *should* they feel?"

"They should support you. Tight but not too tight. Did you lace them up yourself or did your mom help?"

For most younger kids, getting geared up is a two-person job. But I'm not surprised when Liam tells me he got ready by himself. His mom *really* must not want to see me. I swallow down the lingering discomfort I have about this.

At a glance, I can tell that Liam's laces are too loose. Kneeling before him and keeping my gaze firmly fixed on his skates, I say, "Let's tighten these up, get some fresh tape, and then we'll get you back on the ice."

———

Half an hour later, I'm watching Liam shove his mismatched gear into a duffle bag. I'm not sure where Naomi found all this stuff, but it's all heavily used and ill-fitting. Without meaning to, I've made a mental checklist of his size and what he needs.

Not that I have any business even thinking about buying Liam new gear.

I don't want to assume it's a cost issue for Naomi, who never mentioned financial struggles in our brief time of dating. From what Liam said, moving to Harvest Hollow related to her getting a raise. Maybe Naomi told Liam she'll buy him his own gear if he sticks with it, which sounds like a Naomi thing.

Hockey is the most expensive youth sport besides any

sport involving horses, so it's a practical choice to start with used gear. Even though some of Liam's looks like it's falling apart.

There are hockey players who keep wearing their old gear until it looks this bad, but that's more about superstition. Dumbo's shoulder pads are the same ones he's been wearing since he was seventeen and are held together by duct tape and—according to him—*good vibes*. But that's different from Liam's ill-fitting, worn-out gear.

He doesn't seem to care, though, and beams up at me after zipping up his bag. "Thanks, Camden. I mean, Coach Cam. That was awesome. Will you be here next week?"

"Yeah, Cammie." Eli appears, draping an arm over my shoulder. His floppy blond hair tickles my neck. I shove him off. "Will you be here next week? I could use another set of hands. Did you see those little kids? Bloodthirsty monsters, I tell you."

I don't answer quickly enough, and Liam's face falls. Eli's hand gives me a painful squeeze.

"Yes," I say finally. "I'll be here. But not to help with your group." I shake Eli off and give him a playful shove. "Just Liam."

Bad idea, a little voice in my head warns. I ignore it, as you're supposed to do when you hear voices in your head.

"Really?" Liam's voice pitches high with excitement.

My chest constricts, thinking about how, in a few years, he'll be entering into the too-cool teenage years when guys seem to think they have to hide their enthusiasm for anything.

Even while trying to keep his skates underneath him, Liam was stoked to be here. Concentrating with all his might, celebrating every little victory, and rattling off hockey facts. Between the last time I saw him and now, he's grown

36

two inches and become a veritable piñata stuffed with hockey information.

Is this … because of me?

Last summer, Liam's knowledge of the sport went so far as to know that it's played on ice with skates. Now, he's here in Harvest Hollow, sneaking his mom's credit card to sign up for hockey training, and knows Sidney Crosby's current number of assists. Not for the season. Sid's *lifetime* number of assists.

Maybe it's unrelated, but this sudden interest—fixation? —seems a little too pointed to be coincidental.

I shouldn't feel so happy at the thought.

Eli narrows his eyes at me, letting me know he's going to have a lot of questions later. I ignore him, the same way I will when he asks all the questions.

"See ya, kid," he says, ruffling Liam's sweaty hair before walking off toward his group of little guys. "You looked good out there."

He did—at least compared to how he started. I mean, he's still wobbly and barely able to take more than a few strides in a row without falling. And he can't turn. Or stop. But he's no longer holding onto the wall or to me for support.

"Thanks, Coach Cam," Liam says.

I shake my head. "That was all you. Way to put in the work."

We stand there for a few seconds, Liam still grinning and me trying not to watch the door for his mom. Long enough that Liam stops smiling and picks up his bag.

"I should wait outside," he says.

"Want me to go with you?" I hope I don't sound as desperate as I feel for even just a glance at Naomi. Not that a glance would be all I want. But at this point, I'm a bear coming out of hibernation. I'll take what scraps I can get.

Liam hesitates. "Um."

"Ah. I can't walk you out because your mom won't want to see me, right?"

"I'm sorry." He looks miserable.

"It's not your fault, Liam. It's just ... grown-up stuff."

And to explain it, I would have to understand it myself. I'm still honestly confused about how it all went down. One minute, Naomi and I were together and I was trying to find the best way to talk to her about what would happen when I left my unexpectedly long stay on Oakley Island for training camp.

The next minute, she was telling me we were done.

And any thoughts about trying to convince Naomi to at least talk about what things could look like with us long-term or long-distance, all that vanished when Liam came to my hotel. Which is a dark kind of irony since he came to convince me to stay.

"Mom said that too," Liam says. "It's not my fault. But ..."

He doesn't finish whatever thought is in his head—a rarity.

"Liam, it wasn't your fault. Sometimes with adults, things just get ... complicated."

His smile has a bitter edge, one that looks too old for his young face. "Funny how you and Mom say all the same things. I thought breakups happen when two people *don't* agree."

I don't have a response to this. Not a good one anyway. Normally, when I don't have things to say, I don't say them. It's why I'm often accused of being too quiet.

Now, I need to say something.

What to say is the question.

I decide to go with brutal honesty. "You know, I'm sad about your mom."

I probably shouldn't say this. I don't want to give him false hope. But I don't know what the protocol is with kids. Not in general situations, and especially not in this one. But I can't not say *something*. And this is the something that comes out of my mouth.

Liam nods, his jaw clenching. Again, he looks older, giving me a glimpse of the young man he'll turn into.

"Yeah. Mom's sad about you too. She pretends, but she's not very good at it. See you next week."

And with that, the kid hoists his bag with the broken zipper and walks out the door like he didn't just pull the pin from a grenade and then drop it at my feet.

CHAPTER 4

Naomi

"HOW'S THE JOB?" Eloise asks in her most annoyingly chipper, patent-pending Eloise voice. My brother's wife is the happiest person I've ever met. I love this about her.

I also sometimes want to shake her and see if any of the happy will fall out of her proverbial pockets like loose change.

Covering the mouthpiece of the phone, I whisper "thanks" and take the box of gluten-free apple cider donuts from the smiling woman behind the counter.

Her smile is ... disconcerting. Friendly, but with a knowing edge. I have the very strong suspicion she has just become my new donut dealer. I'm not sold on this apple cider flavor, however, which she assured me is a Harvest Hollow favorite. Bonus points for having gluten-free options, which means I can share these with Liam.

We'll see how they taste, I guess.

With my shoulder, I hold the phone to my ear and push through the door, precariously but successfully balancing the box and my latte. Outside, wind whips straight through my hoodie and down into my bones. Immediately, my eyes start to water.

I hate winter. And I hate it more in the mountains where it's not buffered by the mildness the ocean brings.

"The job is ... fine," I tell Eloise.

Fine would be a glow-up for my current position.

On career day in elementary school, I guarantee that no child ever says, "When I grow up, I want to be an office administrator." Because what even *is* an office administrator? It's the position Pam Beesley invented out of thin air in *The Office*. That's how they should have described it on my company's website: a made-up job from a fictional TV show.

Back on Oakley, I was an administrative assistant, which meant loads of paperwork, making copies, and sometimes fetching coffee. With my oh-so-glamorous office administrator upgrade, I still do some of that, plus now I order the paper and coffee. Technically, I think I'm also supposed to oversee the administrative assistants, but no one has explained what that entails, and the women in my new office don't seem to *want* to be overseen. At least, based on the way they clump up together and shun me.

All in all, it's unpleasant at best. The raise that looked good on paper somehow translates to only a few hundred more per month. Nothing life changing, and hardly impactful in the end.

"In other words," Eloise says, her happiness now sounding a little bit more like sage smugness, "you *don't* love it, the raise isn't worth making the move, and you should have kept working at the bed and breakfast right here on Oakley with your family. Got it."

She's right, at least about some of it. But it would take actual torture to make me admit it. Or the threat of torture. Because all someone would need to do is pull out a pair of pliers or show me a sharp blade and I'd sing like a canary auditioning for *American Idol*.

But no one is threatening me, and I refuse to cave so quickly and admit to Lo that she's right about anything—especially after only a week. It would invite a huge *I told you so*.

Even if she'd never say it, she'd *think* it.

Because Eloise *did* tell me the job I took at a real estate title company four months ago wasn't going to make me happy. And she repeated it when I told her I was moving for a job with the same company. Before that, I'd been working at the bed and breakfast that Lo and her sisters started out of their grandmother's old house, and things were good. Family and friends as coworkers can be a challenge, but not with Eloise and her sisters. I liked the hours and the ability to look out almost any window and see the ocean.

I can't fully explain why I became discontented. I've never been able to put logical sounding words together in a way that adequately describes the restlessness that seems to live underneath my skin. It goes dormant sometimes, though I'm always aware of its presence inside me, waiting, building, humming like an electric razor. When the hum becomes a persistent and unignorable buzz, I have to find a way to get it out of my system.

Usually through a new job. A new apartment. Sometimes picking up a new hobby will suffice. This is usually when I try a new hairstyle or color. It just depends how loud the noise becomes, how strong the buzz.

Had I been born in a different time period, I would have really rocked the nomad life. Hoisting all my belongings into a bag I'd sling over my back, ready to pull up roots like tent stakes.

But I wasn't born in another age, and in our current cultural climate, my urge to cut bait and run makes me look irresponsible and flighty.

It also wreaks havoc on the ability to maintain a relationship, as one might imagine, though Jake says my bad luck is more about the quality of men I pick. He's not wrong, though I'm self-aware enough to know there's a heavy dose of self-sabotage thrown in there. I have a hard time imagining myself in a serious, committed relationship. At least while Liam is young.

It's so much work to find a good guy to date, but I'd also need someone who could do double duty as a dad or father figure. The idea is so intimidating to me, that I feel like I've essentially given up and resigned myself to short-lived relationships until Liam is out of the house. They're too risky, too much pressure.

There's also the memory of Liam's biological father and the way his whole face went feral when I told him about Liam. Not that I knew Liam was Liam then, so it was more me telling him about the miraculous kumquat-sized human we had unintentionally created together the one and only and regrettable time we slept together.

Christopher's eyes went wide, his mouth went slack, and I'm still shocked he didn't dive straight through the glass window of the coffee shop where we met in order to escape the truth. I guess he did the figurative version, which was backing away from the table, hands up like I had a gun trained on him. I guess that's how it felt to him.

"It's not mine," he said first. "You need a paternity test."

I sipped my decaf peppermint tea, which wasn't half bad even if it wasn't coffee, and declined to answer. What was the point? Christopher was the only guy I'd slept with, and only the one time. No paternity test needed on my end.

More than once I've thought about taking money to Vegas since I clearly am good at beating the odds.

Christopher took my silence as some kind of threat because then he moved on to point a finger and tell me he wouldn't pay for anything without a test and that he would call the family lawyer—his family was one of the old Savannah kinds who likely had a lawyer on retainer—and that we were done here.

Then he left. And that was that.

While I wasn't sad about Christopher, the moment did leave me with the impression that my newfound growing baby made me part of a potentially undesirable joint package for men. And I know Christopher was a tool—which I realized long before that conversation—and shouldn't get to represent all men, but it's hard to shake the sense of doom I felt at his visceral reaction.

Sitting alone at that coffee table, swiping the whipped cream from Christopher's untouched white mocha, is the first time I ever told Liam, "It's you and me versus the world, kid."

Even if I ever decided I was ready for something serious, I'm not sure anyone would be good enough to earn my big brother's approval. The only one who came close was Cam. But since I never explained the breakup to Jake, I'm pretty sure my brother blames Camden.

Just as well. Not like it matters now.

Anyway. The restlessness leading me now to be freezing my butt off while carrying a box of apple cider donuts is just the way I'm wired. I need to go, to move, to try new things.

My theme song is U2's "Still Haven't Found What I'm Looking For." But it's hard to find a thing when you don't know what the *thing* is.

The one constant in my life is the consistent, persistent ache for new, different, and *more*, which sometimes explodes into a crescendo of discontent I have to act on.

And then there's Liam.

As a person who's supposed to be a stable, functional member of society, my restlessness is inconvenient at best. Being a single mom? It's an irreconcilable difference without having a divorce. Two unlike things forced to coexist: my need for frequent change and my son who needs some semblance of stability.

Sometimes I wonder if having a kid so young is what caused the restlessness, but I don't like that train of thought. Sounds too much like blaming Liam for my issues.

In this particular instance, with the biggest move of my life, I know a good portion of the restlessness stems from what happened with Camden. It hasn't been easy the past few years watching everyone around me fall in love while remaining the lone singleton on the island.

For half a second last summer, I thought I might be joining the falling-in-love club. And it actually sounded like a club I finally wanted to be part of.

But then I panicked, broke up with Camden, and after months of regret and hurt and rehashing this in my mind, I accidentally took a job where he lives.

In order to pull off the lie that it's not a big deal, this move to my ex's town, I've had to pretend I'm still stoked about this whole misadventure instead of terrified. My well-meaning family and friends—not just Eloise—would say *I told you so* but quickly follow it up with offers to help me move home. Frankly, the offers would be tempting.

"Where are you right now?" Eloise asks. "It sounds like you're inside of a wind tunnel."

It *feels* like I'm inside a wind tunnel. I'm hustling to my car, cheeks wet with cold-induced tears. "I'm picking up donuts and coffee. It's freezing here. Disgustingly cold. But … refreshing," I say, once again feeling the need to sell this whole thing.

"Ew," Eloise says. "It's a little colder than when you left, but the sun is out, and it feels amazing. I just got back from a walk on the beach."

I'd like to kick her in the shins with my pointiest shoes.

I get my car door open and throw myself inside, immediately jamming the key into the ignition to blast the heat. "Stop gloating. You think me moving is a mistake, blah blah. I can outlast the cold," I say. In all honesty not sure I can.

Eloise hums. Even her stupid hum is happy. "But you don't *like* the cold. Or your job. You don't need to stick this out as a way to pass some test no one gave you."

I take an angry bite of donut to keep me from snapping at Eloise and almost moan at the taste. That woman inside is definitely going to be my new donut dealer. This town is onto something with these apple cider donuts.

"How do you know how to read me so well?" I demand. Eloise has only been in our lives a few years. A permanent fixture now, being married to my brother. But still. It's a little scary how she can hear my lies even through the phone.

"Jake gave me a Naomi decoder ring for Christmas." She pauses, like this is some kind of *gotcha* moment. Honestly, a Naomi decoder ring sounds great. I'd like one myself. "Just kidding! Obviously. I just *know* you. Remember—I grew up with two older sisters. It's impossible to survive without picking up some mad observational skills. This just so happens to be one of mine."

True. Especially true thinking about Merritt and Sadie. Mer, the oldest Markham sister, has chilled a lot since moving to Oakley and taking Hunter, the island's hottest single commodity, off the market. But she is one of those hyper successful, driven, type-A kind of women. I can only imagine growing up with her as top dog.

Then there's Sadie—every bit as headstrong and opinionated as Merritt, only usually running in the opposite direction. It's practically a nuclear combination. I've witnessed Lo smoothing things over between her older sisters almost effortlessly, heading off budding arguments and steering them toward a greener pasture where everyone gets along.

Eloise is every bit as strong as her sisters, just in a different way. Less combative and more sneakily coercive.

I lick my sticky fingers clean and put the car into gear. It's almost time to pick up Liam from the Summit. "Ugh. Your logic is impeccable, per the usual. What was your degree in, again—psychology?"

"Literature. How's Sir Liam?"

I could not be more grateful for the conversational switch. Eloise has been calling Liam that ever since he had to dress like a knight for a school thing. I mean, sure, he was adorable. But Eloise said he really looked like he *was* a knight. Look—I'm biased toward my kid. Trust me. But I don't know what she was seeing. The chain mail I found in a costume shop was missing whole chunks, like it belonged to a knight who definitely didn't make it through the battle or was fired by a dragon. Not to mention that it was an adult size, which meant it came down to Liam's knees.

Still—Eloise persists with Sir Liam.

"School is good so far. I mean, it's only been two weeks, but he's doing well academically—no surprise there. And I think he's made a few friends already."

This is a huge relief to me. Liam's tendency to hyperfixate on topics, not understanding why no one else cares, can be like his own scarlet letter, setting him apart in negative ways. Through no fault of his own, he spent a lot of his early years around adults. He didn't ever speak like a kid or relate to kids. But he can sit through a conversation about inflation or work-life balance and totally track. He's kind and loyal and fun, but he doesn't color in the lines or always act like the other kids.

In the last year or so, he finally started to make more friends outside of Izzy, Hunter's daughter. I wasn't sure how his fledgling social skills would translate off the island though, and I was more nervous about this than running into Camden. Even last week coming out of the Summit, a few kids waved and one boy who looked a little older gave him a friendly looking slap on the back.

I swear, I got teary-eyed watching it and had to work really hard to recalibrate my face by the time Liam reached the car.

Just as hard? Not asking if Camden was there. But that would be the kind of news I'm not sure he could have kept to himself. I think I would have seen it in his face or body, a sense of sadness weighing him down like a heavy cloak.

I was both relieved and disappointed that he said nothing. At least, not about Camden.

Liam had plenty to say about hockey and talked of nothing else for three straight days. Three. Days. I've gotten used to him talking hockey, but it hits different when he's talking about it in relation to himself.

It was even *worse*.

Telling me about how to stand with your weight over your feet, not leaning too far forward, while I made dinner. Describing the sound of the ice when someone does a hockey stop when he should have been doing homework. Talking about finding the inside and outside edges of the blades while I was setting up his school lunch account online.

The one thing he *didn't* talk about was Camden.

I should be relieved. I am, kind of. But I'm also disappointed. Somehow the constant hockey talk and the notable lack of Camden talk made my mind spin out with questions and worries even more wildly than before.

But I don't want to be the one to first break our unspoken vow of silence regarding Camden.

I can only assume this means Liam didn't see him because he absolutely would have told me. Wouldn't he? Before we moved, I would have been sure. But now, I'm dealing with the new Liam—the one who stole my credit card to sign up for hockey classes. I can't be sure what to expect now.

But surely he would have said *something*.

After meeting Camden, Liam latched on. Hard.

You and me both, buddy.

In fact, it was *this*—seeing Liam get starry-eyed over Camden—that made me realize I needed to end things. Because it wasn't just my heart on the line. At the end of the summer, no matter what wishful thinking kind of talk Camden and I might have, he would leave me. And leave Liam.

I didn't think either Liam or I could take the heartbreak if we attached any more to Camden. Fear made the restlessness start humming under my skin until I just blurted out, "I think we should stop seeing each other" in the middle of an otherwise perfect date. Not my best move.

Hearing about the breakup was the first and only time Liam has ever yelled at me. He shouted *Why would you do that?* and *Something is wrong with you* (that one stung) and called me stupid, which didn't hurt but did get him grounded. He took off on his bike before I could enforce his first-ever grounding.

When he came back, he was no longer angry but resigned and sad.

Drooping shoulders. Red eyes. Trembling lower lip he bit so hard it bled.

I hugged him, ungrounded him, and we went for dinner at my dad's place. A pirate-themed bar isn't normally the place to cheer up a kid, but Liam has always loved Bard the parrot and my dad's grilled cheese on gluten-free bread he stocks just for Liam.

Watching him perk up slightly as Bard quoted Shakespeare didn't reassure me I'd made the right choice breaking up with Camden before things got harder. It made me imagine what things could be like if I hadn't. Because I could suddenly see Camden in the kitchen with us, being present in his quiet way. Bringing his steadiness into my chaos.

I started to do something I rarely do: second guess myself. I got a feverish case of whatever the breakup version of buyer's remorse is.

Is breakup remorse a thing?

A legitimate illness or not, it led to me making a mistake I'd rather not think about right now, parked in the shadow of the Summit. I'd rather stuff another apple cider donut in my face, so I do, while Eloise catches me up on Oakley gossip. I turn the engine off to save on gas, hoping the heat in the car lasts until Liam comes out.

By the time Eloise is finished with her updates, I've decided to tell her about Liam and the hockey classes. So far, I've managed to keep it from everyone back home (namely, my dad and Jake), and our schedules haven't lined up for Liam to talk to them. I'm sure it would have been the first thing he said.

So, Eloise *will* find out. It's shocking she hasn't used her built-in Naomi radar to guess already.

"You want to know what stupid thing your Sir Liam did?" I ask, heart beating a little more wildly than it should.

"Is that even a question? Absolutely."

"First off, he *borrowed* my credit card."

"No! Liam? No. Not Sir Liam. Wait! Was it to fund a nonprofit or donate to an animal shelter?"

"No."

"Did he ... buy a set of vintage encyclopedias to read when he's bored?"

"No, but only because he's hoping you and Jake will get him one for Christmas."

"Ooh, good idea. So, what did he do?"

"He signed himself up for"—*just say it. Just say the word, it's not like Beetlejuice*—"hockey. Some youth training classes for six Saturdays with the Appies."

"The Appies, as in the team where your ex plays?"

"Yes," I grit out.

There's a beat of silence. Then raucous laughter.

"Laugh it up, fuzzball," I mutter.

"You've watched *The Empire Strikes Back* a few too many times with Liam," she says.

"Yeah, well. If the Wookiee comparison fits ..."

"That took less time than I thought," Eloise says, wheezing.

"What did?"

"Liam trying to get you and Camden back together."

"That's not what he's doing," I say quickly. And quite defensively, despite my efforts to hide it. "He's just hockey obsessed, and we moved to a town where hockey is, like, a whole thing."

"Sure. Tell yourself what you need to tell yourself. He's absolutely going to Parent Trap you."

"He absolutely is *not* doing that."

Is he? What if the lack of Liam talking about Camden is actually some kind of surreptitious long-game plan?

No. It couldn't be. Liam couldn't have known we'd end up moving here, since I didn't even know until a month ago. And back to the Bruno thing, Liam hasn't so much as uttered Camden's name since the night he yelled at me and rode off on his bike. A ten-year-old isn't crafty enough to mastermind something like that.

I dismiss the idea entirely. It's preposterous.

"Also—Liam on skates," Eloise says. "How's that going?"

I give her credit for not actually commenting on Liam's lack of athleticism. He comes by it honestly. I enjoy the occasional yoga class—child's pose is my personal favorite—but anything involving running or throwing or kicking balls is beyond my skill set. The most athletic thing Liam does is ride waves at the beach. He's a strong swimmer, but anything on land or involving hand-eye coordination? Nope.

It's honestly why I didn't nix this whole thing—the non-refundable payment aside. I figured after the first week, he would realize ice skating wasn't his thing and maybe it would kill off his whole hockey obsession.

Sadly, we're back for week two, and he practically dove out of my moving car when we got here.

"I haven't seen him skate yet, but he's apparently doing fine. He loves it, anyway."

"What do you mean you haven't seen him skate?" Eloise demands.

"He's old enough that I can just drop him off."

The silence on the other end of the line is like a loaded

gun. Then Eloise says the words I've been hearing echo in my head all week.

"Naomi. You can't *not* watch Liam just because you don't want to risk seeing Camden."

The guilt I've been trying to ignore rises up, clogging my throat.

She's right. She's absolutely right. It's been killing me to not be inside that building, watching over my very uncoordinated child as he tries to navigate a sheet of ice with blades on his feet. Even though I'd be a different kind of nervous wreck actually watching him.

Last Saturday I couldn't even eat until I picked him up and saw him in one piece, smiling.

The coffee I've been sipping turns to acid in my gut, and I hope I can keep those donuts down.

I *should* be in there. I know it.

While I'm well aware of my shortcomings and imperfections as a mom, I also know I've mostly done well by Liam. He's a good kid on his own merits, but I haven't screwed him up. I've supported him and given him freedom to be himself and encouraged him to chase after his interests. Even this one, while gritting my teeth the whole time. But this is the very first time I've honestly felt like I'm making a poor choice —the *wrong* choice—as his mother.

Still, the idea of possibly running into Camden is a strong enough deterrent that I double down.

"I'm just using the time to run errands alone," I lie. "Camden's possible presence here is irrelevant."

"No," Eloise says, finally sounding serious for a moment. I like it way less than when she was laughing at me. "No, it's *very* relevant. Not just to you but to Liam. Naomi, why did you break up with Camden? And don't give me the whole story about how it was just casual. I saw you with him. You were anything but casual."

She's right. Of course she's right. But it's hard to articulate the breakup when, in hindsight, it's so dumb.

"Did he do something?" Eloise presses, her voice a little softer.

"No," I confess in a choked voice. "It was me. I ... panicked. Liam started to get attached, and when I thought about how it would work long-term dating someone who lives in another city and has such a weird career, it just seemed like cutting ties sooner would save Liam disappointment later."

And save me heartache, I don't add, though I'm sure Lo knows me well enough to know this too.

Spoiler alert. It didn't save either of us from anything.

"Oh, Naomi." Eloise sighs.

"Plus, I had no reason to know if Camden was thinking about moving beyond the casual summer dating we agreed to. As it turns out, he wasn't."

"How do you know?"

I swallow, prepping myself for the humiliation of this next admission. "Because I tried to walk it back. I called him and told him I messed up. Asked if we could talk. He said ... it was for the best."

"I'm so sorry," Eloise says.

I really don't like the way her words or the kindness with which she says them dig way down deep and make me squirm.

But what I like even less is what I see out of the windshield. Or—*who* I see, striding across the parking lot with purpose toward my car.

My mouth goes dry. All the oxygen in my lungs is

suddenly gone. For a beat or two, my heart seizes up, pausing mid-beat.

"I'm so sorry," Eloise repeats, "but I think you were both lying to yourselves and maybe to each other. And I know you didn't ask for advice but—"

"I need to go," I say, interrupting her.

I stopped listening fully the moment the Summit doors opened and a tall man walked through them.

"We're not done talking about this," Eloise is saying as I hang up.

No, we're definitely *not* done with this subject. There will be even more to say.

Because Camden is now standing by my car window, staring in at me with the intense brown eyes that have haunted my memories for months.

CHAPTER 5

Naomi

THE VERY FIRST time I saw Camden, my reaction was similar to the one I'm having right now. I froze. Simply froze.

I don't know what it is about him.

With his brown hair and brown eyes, there's nothing overtly arresting about Camden at first glance. He has the build of an athlete but is not linebacker big or basketball tall. Cam is the kind of well-muscled height that's more subtly noticeable in the way he moves and carries himself. He's handsome, but his looks aren't *loud*.

For me, though, Camden has an inexplicable but *very* physical impact.

Our first meeting was in Gator's Groceries, Oakley Island's tiny local grocery store. I was swinging a basket in one hand, humming under my breath. A Miley Cyrus song, which I only remember because I hated the song, but it earwormed its way into my head without permission and wouldn't give up residency. I also had the hiccups, which were almost as annoying as the song looping in my head.

A man I didn't recognize was blocking the aisle, crouched down and reading a label—a habit I personally find very silly. Don't we all know most food is filled with preservatives and chemicals that are going to kill us? Might as well eat, drink, and be happy, for tomorrow we die—thanks to food dye.

Case in point: I was there to grab some instant ramen for me, Kettle Chips (his favorite gluten-free option) for Liam, and a Diet Dr Pepper to get me through the afternoon. Not to say we live off that kind of food on the regular, but you'll never find me taking up a whole aisle reading ingredients before making a purchase.

I paused for a moment, waiting for the most-likely-a-tourist to notice me and move. He didn't. I cleared my throat. Still no movement. The guy was reading this label like it just hit the NY Times bestseller list and this aisle was the most comfortable reading chair in the world.

"Excuse me," I said, trying to channel fake cheerfulness to cover up the annoyance I was actually feeling. A hiccup punctuated my words. *Awesome.*

The man took his time putting back whatever he was looking at—his body blocked my nosy eyes from seeing what it was—and stood, turning to face me.

That's when I froze. Well—I froze after my fingers opened, dropping my basket to the floor. My hiccups instantly evaporated. *Poof!* Gone. Along with thoughts, rational and otherwise.

Just like now.

Whatever I was thinking moments ago, whatever Eloise had been talking about when I hung up on her, whatever planet I'm on—all of it's gone.

There is only Camden, standing outside my car, staring intently at me. His eyes might be a medium brown, but the heat in his gaze is scorching hot.

So much for staying out in the car to avoid any possibility of running into him.

Even though I'm looking right at him, when Camden knocks on my window, I jerk, dropping my phone. It falls somewhere between the seat and my center console, the no-man's-land of every car, never to be seen again.

I throw open my door, inadvertently slamming it right into Camden. He groans loudly and stumbles back, bending over. I jump out of the car, instinct making me reach for him. But since I absolutely can't go around casually touching Camden, I stop short and wave my hands ineffectively in the air like I'm trying to fan him.

"I'm so sorry! Are you okay?"

"You hit me with your car," he grumbles.

"My car *door*. You make it sound like I mowed you down in the street with a moving vehicle. And why were you standing so close to my car?"

He glares at me, finally straightening up to his full height. "Why didn't you just roll down the window when you saw me standing here?"

"The car isn't running!"

"You're sitting in the parking lot during winter without the car on? Aren't you cold?"

I am, now that he mentions it. But I hadn't been or at least hadn't noticed. Now that I'm standing outside, my teeth are already starting to chatter.

Camden's frown intensifies. "Why aren't you wearing a coat?"

"I wasn't planning on getting out of the car. I'm just waiting for Liam."

But also ... I don't own a coat. I mean, I have some hoodies like the Oakley Island one I'm wearing, a scarf, and a hat. With all the expenses from the move, which were unfortunately not covered by my employer, I only had enough to buy him a coat. It hasn't been pleasant these last two weeks, but my plan is to go coat shopping later today.

I have a feeling if I mention this, the frown on Camden's face will only get frownier, and it's a good look on him. So, I swallow down the words before I nervously babble a confession about not owning proper winter wear while living in the mountains.

His expression shifts. "I need you to come inside with me," he says.

"No, thanks." I cross my arms, a move that does double duty. I'm cold, but it also bolsters my words. It's body language that communicates strength and determination I absolutely don't feel. I'm about ready to buckle like a belt.

"Naomi, please."

There was a time when a *please* from Camden would have dismantled any resistance. I can feel the one word attempting to melt my already pitiful resolve. But I bite the inside of my cheek and remind myself of how hard it was to hide the sound of my sobs from Liam in the months after Camden left Oakley.

Nope. Not going there again.

I start to get back in my car. "That's okay. I'll just wait here for Liam. He's taking hockey classes."

Camden's expression doesn't change, and I swear, somewhere, Eloise is laughing at me.

"But you already knew that."

Man, Liam and I need to have a talk about honesty.

Camden reaches out, his big hand cupping my elbow lightly.

It's the gentleness that does it. If he'd grabbed my arm, I might have yanked myself away and actually tried to hit him with my car. But the softness from this strong man has me hesitating. The touch of his hand, even through layers of fabric, sends a confusing cocktail of neurological signals through my body. I'm drunk on memories.

Longing, heat, regret, longing, confusion.

"What do you want, Cam?" I ask, my voice coming out in a pained wheeze.

His eyes do a quick sweep of my face before he drops his hand. "It's Liam. He's fine," he adds quickly, though my heart is already racing with panic, "but he got hurt during practice."

It's pure reflex when my fist swings toward his face.

———

Before Liam, I never really understood the term *mama bear*. Now, I know what it's like to instantly go grizzly in defense of my kid. It is a nuclear option. A burn the world down, whole body reaction. It is me in feral beast mode.

Which is why, ten minutes later when I'm in some kind of medical room with Liam trying to brush off my hand and my concern, Camden has an ice pack held to his face.

I didn't shoot the messenger; I decked him in the eye.

I know I'll feel bad about my knee-jerk reaction later. It's not fair to Camden, who did nothing but tell me what happened. He didn't cause the accident.

He's likely the reason Liam got interested in hockey, but even that isn't something Camden did on purpose. It's more a by-product to his very brief but apparently impactful presence in Liam's life. Proof that I shouldn't get involved with a man until Liam is older. My heart—my hope—isn't the only one at stake.

So, Camden did *not* deserve to be decked. I'll apologize—and probably feel a lot worse—later.

For now, I'm still buzzing with the BMBE—Big Mama Bear Energy. There is no room for apologies or regrets or anything other than the need to protect my cub and tear the limbs off anyone who stands in my way.

"It's fine," Liam tells me for what is probably the fifth time, but he shuts up when I glare at him.

He might be hurt, but that doesn't mean he's above getting the stink-eye from me.

"It's not fine. You need *stitches*," I seethe from between clenched teeth. I narrow my eyes, making sure to send silent threats to every man currently in this room. By the way they all shift on their feet—everyone but Camden, that is, who doesn't react—they sense the danger and smartly keep their mouths shut. "How did this happen?"

I'm not even sure who I'm asking, but I glare at every adult in the room. Liam, apparently giving up on trying to mollify me, doesn't say a word.

"It was an accident," says one of the men. A trainer or medic—I'm not sure.

I wasn't really listening to introductions when I flew into this room somewhere in the depths of the Summit. It looks almost like a large room at a doctor's office with a few exam tables bearing the Appies logo and glass-fronted cabinets with bandages and other supplies. Everything looks shiny and expensive and professional. Maybe it should put me at ease, but I'm not sure that's possible right now. I'd happily take a pair of surgical scissors to the vinyl exam table right now.

"A little kid got going too fast and couldn't stop. He

tripped over a barrier and tangled up with Liam," Camden says, adjusting the ice pack on his face. "The boy's skate blade made contact with Liam's forearm."

The thought alone turns my stomach. Thankfully, I haven't seen the injury yet. The blood on the cloth Liam has pressed to his arm is bad enough. I immediately looked away when I saw it, my stomach turning inside out. One of my biggest weaknesses in the mom department is my inability to stomach the gross things.

When Liam barfs, I barf. And when he bleeds, even if it's a simple skinned knee, I get nauseous then woozy. I have been known to pass out.

Which I *refuse* to do today. I will show zero weakness in front of Camden.

Thankfully, my BMBE is keeping me steady. For now.

"It didn't do any serious damage to the muscle or tissue underneath," the same trainer or medic says. "Just a superficial cut. Nothing to worry about."

The man clearly doesn't value his life. Before I can lunge at him, Camden anticipates my move and his hand curls around my shoulder. He holds me in place with the same gentleness he used in the parking lot outside. I like his touch too much.

Maybe I should punch him in the other eye. But I think I'm the one who needs punching. Or ... to tamp down my violent instincts.

Shaking off Camden's hand, I say, "A superficial cut needing *stitches*. How often does this happen?"

"Not often," the trainer says, then pauses and scratches his head. "Actually, there was a time in the youth program last year when something similar happened. But it's unusual."

I've had enough. Of the surprises, of the excuses or explanations for my kid getting hurt, of the hockey. I take Liam's good hand and give him a little tug.

"Come on, bud. Let's figure out where the nearest ER is."

"Mom, they can just do it here," Liam says.

"*Who* can do *what* here?"

Again, I glance around the room. The room might look like a fancy medical exam room, but this is no hospital. None of these men are wearing a white doctor's coat. And other than the one with the blue eyes and a head that's shaved to cover baldness, they barely look older than I am. "You want the people responsible for your injury to Frankenstein your arm? No, thanks."

"Ma'am." I zero in my gaze on the bald man, who steps forward. "I understand your concern. But these are the trained professionals who handle any of the injuries to my players during a game or practice. Dr. Samuelson"—he gestures to the second man, not the one who kept talking to me—"is more than capable of stitching up your son. With your permission, of course."

"And who are you?"

"I'm Coach Davis," he says, holding out a hand, which I do not have any intention of shaking. After a moment, he slides it into his pocket and gives me a tight smile.

"Thanks for the offer, but I think we'll take our chances at the ER. Liam, let's go."

"Mom," my son says, using his most reasonable voice, the one he uses whenever I'm overreacting to something. "It's fine. They know what they're doing. Plus, it's free."

"I'm not worried about money. And it's only free because they're worried we'll sue."

The only reason I haven't sent Jake a preemptive text asking about a lawsuit is because he'd blow up my phone—which I managed to fish out of my car after I punched

Camden. Jake might even get on the next plane if he hears Liam got hurt.

But suing is an option. Probably. Not one I'd likely do, but it feels like a piece of armor I can wear right now. I'm sure Liam signed some kind of waiver online pretending to be me, but *I* never signed. And even with waivers acknowledging the risks and responsibilities, lawsuits still happen all the time. That's why the coach looks so nervous.

Liam levels me with a very grown-up look. "Mom. We're not suing anyone. It was an accident. And you know you don't want to pay for an emergency room visit right now."

He's right to appeal to my cheap side. Normally, I don't want to pay for an ER visit, even if I don't need this room full of strangers—and Camden—knowing that. While we do have insurance, the deductible is massive, and it's the start of the year, so we haven't touched it yet.

"Your health is worth any cost," I tell him. "*You* are worth it."

"Naomi." Camden sets down the ice pack, and I force myself not to wince at the redness around his eye. I'm the tiniest bit surprised I landed such a punch, though my knuckles are throbbing and regret is starting to seep through me like the cold air outside. "Please let them take care of Liam. I promise you, they'll do a great job. It will take less time and far less hassle than going to the ER. Since it's non-life-threatening, the hospital would make you wait hours there with all the germs. It's better to take care of this here."

"Come on, Mom. It's fine." Liam reaches for my hand. The towel he's holding on his wound falls to the floor in the process, revealing his arm for the first time.

I draw in a breath. I don't care what the guy just said about it being superficial—the cut on Liam's arm is long and open and immediately starts oozing blood.

Sparks dance across my vision as my stomach lurches and dives.

"Oh, shoot," I hear Liam say. His voice suddenly sounds very far away. "I forgot Mom can't handle ..."

Blood, I think as I feel my legs give way. *I can't handle blood.*

Then there's only a soft, dark tunnel and a warm body surrounding me as I fall.

CHAPTER 6

Camden

"THAT'S the woman you've been hung up on for months, Cole?"

Without even understanding the specifics of Van's implication, I smack the back of his head. He barely reacts. Probably because he's used to it. Occupational hazard of running his mouth.

Van might mean that Naomi is too good for me, and I would agree. She's the kind of beautiful that needs no makeup, as evidenced now by her fresh face. She even looks good when furious—though I'll admit I prefer her smile.

Or maybe it's because she has a kid? Our team is still pretty young, and only one or two guys have families. They're the ones too busy to hang out much outside of required team events. Of the guys I spend the most time with, only Alec is dating someone with a kid. And Juno is still a baby, which feels different than someone Liam's age. Though Alec is smitten—both with Evie and with Juno.

I have a sneaking suspicion Van's comment is more about the hostility emanating from Naomi, directed straight toward me.

"Yes." A one-word answer is all Van—or anyone else—is going to get about Naomi and me dating. "Now stop staring at her."

"I'm not staring—ow!"

I'm not about to apologize for smacking Van again, though this time, it was a little harder.

Naomi is currently sipping a glass of orange juice and half listening to Eric, our head trainer, while fully glaring at me through the glass window of the medical suite.

I'm with a handful of my teammates in the pool room that houses our ice baths, small pool, and sauna. The chlorine is burning my nose, but I'm not about to leave. Not until they're done stitching up Liam. He's sitting behind Naomi on one of the exam tables, watching Dr. Samuelson with interest.

Naomi, meanwhile, sits by Liam's legs with her back turned to the action. She clutches Liam's foot with one hand while sipping orange juice with the other. Her posture is rigid, like she's fighting the urge to turn around. Which would probably make her pass out again.

Naomi's squeamishness around blood isn't something I knew about her, and it makes my gut twist. What else don't I know? There are so many things I never learned and probably never will.

"You're still staring," I point out.

"I'm a married man." Van flashes his wedding band, which he still does every chance he gets. "I'm not checking her out or anything. I'm just curious about the woman who's

67

had you tied up in knots all season and why she looks like she wants to murder you." He pauses, maybe waiting for me to hit him again. I don't. Yet. "I'm just surprised. She's not what I would have expected."

I turn the full weight of my gaze on Van. He's taller than I am, broader too, but I think he can tell I would take him out right now because he holds up both hands and backs a few steps away.

"I don't mean anything by it," he says.

"What *do* you mean?"

From his spot leaning against the wall by the sauna, Eli snorts. "Keep talking, Vanity. You're providing a lot of entertainment right now. I'd like to see Cammie's careful control snap."

Eli's smile falters as I swing my attention his way. He is what you'd get if you crossed a golden retriever with a ball of sunshine. His wild blond mop of hair only accentuates his personality. Glaring at him feels like kicking a puppy. But right now, I don't care.

The only person whose feelings I care about punched me in the face less than an hour ago and looks willing and ready to do it again.

"Sorry, man," Eli says. "Carry on."

"You know you can leave at any time. All of you," I say, glancing around at my teammates, all of whom suddenly appeared moments after Naomi passed out, like sharks smelling blood in the water.

Besides Van and Eli, there's Logan—who at least has the good sense to stay silent—and then Dominik, which is a bit unexpected. He's taking after Logan, mirroring his silence and his casual posture, so right now my ire is trained on Van and Eli. Felix, our goaltender, is also here, though he's so quiet and still I almost forgot. All of them were helping today

68

—I guess some of the guys are on rotation because Logan, Van, and Felix weren't here last week—and so now I'm subjected to having them here.

As soon as Naomi regained consciousness, she asked me to leave. But I'll still hold onto the brief moment while she was still coming to when she sighed and nestled into my chest.

I can tell Coach is doing his best to navigate the situation, but his cheeks are flushed and his bald head, which he's kept shaved for the past year, is shiny with sweat. He keeps checking his phone, probably waiting for someone from our legal department to get back to him. Every so often, he shoots me a look as if he's asking for help, but I'm definitely not wanted in that room.

Liam lifts his good arm and waves, his smile wide.

Okay, I'm not wanted in that room by only *one* person. Very strongly not wanted.

I think it's irrational and probably part of a defense mechanism of some kind. She's scared and upset about what happened to Liam. And I already know from him that she didn't want to see me. So, I've become the focus of all that negative energy—the fear, the concern, the shock of seeing me.

I can handle her misplaced anger.

Ignoring the laser heat of Naomi's glare, I nod at Liam. I'm glad he doesn't seem bothered getting stitched up. He handled everything today like a champ, even going so far as smiling at the smaller kid who accidentally pinwheeled into our practice area, his skate slicing right through Liam's shirt and into his arm.

"Not a big deal," Liam told the sniffling boy who looked ready to burst into tears. Liam somehow managed a smile while holding a glove over the cut. "It's just hockey."

I honestly wasn't sure until that moment if Liam would continue with hockey. Usually by his age, kids are well acclimated to the ice. He's starting at a deficit. It will take work. Commitment. Heart. And though he's incrementally better today than last week, it's clear he's not the most coordinated to start with.

He told me himself last summer that he's more into academics than sports, though he was great at riding waves. Guess that's what happens when you grow up close to the beach. If I had to bet after last week, I wouldn't have put money on Liam continuing after this six-week intro class.

But today, watching him try to make the younger kid whose skate cut him feel better changed my mind. Liam's arm was dripping blood onto the ice, even as he smiled at the kid and said, *It happens. It's just hockey.*

Coordination can come with determination and practice. But the will and the heart to succeed in hockey is harder to come by.

In that moment, Liam showed that he has the mental fortitude he needs in spades.

"Why didn't you tell us Liam was your ex's kid?" Eli asks quietly, though I know they can't hear us in the medical suite.

I shrug.

"Because Cole doesn't tell us anything," says Van. This time, I don't hit him because it's true. "He doesn't tell us when he's working one-on-one with his ex's kid, or that his ex is here in town, or about whatever has him rushing home lately." When I look at him, surprised, he adds, "Don't think we haven't noticed."

I definitely thought that.

But him even bringing it up has me pulling out my phone to check the time. I still have about an hour but send a quick

70

text just in case I run late. I'm not leaving until I feel like Naomi and Liam are okay.

No response. I could call, but it probably wouldn't do any good. It's probably fine. But now my worry splinters, extending in two separate directions—here and also there. I drag a hand through my hair as I realize every guy in the room is watching me.

"Like right there," Van says, pointing a finger at me. "Secretive texts."

"You could talk to us, you know." From the other side of the room, Logan finally speaks. "We're your team. You can trust us off the ice, you know."

"We trust you," Eli says.

"If you want to talk, some of us are good at listening," Felix says, giving Van a pointed look.

"Hey, I can be a good listener," Van says.

"When you're not talking. Which is ..." Eli trails off, pretending to be thinking hard.

"Almost never," Dominik supplies, shrugging when Van glares.

The tiniest pinprick of guilt needles its way into me as I watch the easy way the guys engage with each other.

I know Logan's right. I could trust them. From the moment I got here, the guys brought me in. Or—attempted to. They even added me to the group chat, which most days I regret. But even if I don't engage as much as most of them, I've made it a habit to at least read through all the messages at night. I usually find myself smiling. I just happen to lurk more than I text.

This season, I've found myself ignoring the group chat and talking more in a separate text thread with Wyatt. He left last summer to play for Boston, and maybe that's the key— Wyatt isn't here. It's easier to open up with a guy I don't

71

have to make eye contact with or see in his briefs—or *less*—almost daily.

Not that I've opened up very much to Wyatt. But I've said more to him than to the guys currently in this room.

I assumed they showed up here for curiosity's sake, and maybe that is partially true. But I realize now they're here because they're trying to support me.

Meanwhile, I'm doing my best to push them away.

It doesn't feel right or good to be called on it.

Connecting with people has never been my strong suit. Chemistry on the ice—no problem. But off … it's never come easy. Especially after my teenage years and how things changed with my family. The rejection I felt—still feel—left a crater inside me. I'm self-aware enough to know this, but it doesn't necessarily help me know how to move past it. The rare times I've attempted to open up with other people, I regretted it.

Naomi and I lock eyes through the glass. One beat. Two.

Something passes between us—a wordless exchange that makes my heartbeat quicken and a tiny bubble of hope inflate in my chest. Her expression softens slightly, the sharpness dissipating like fog. But then Liam says something, and she turns away.

"That," Van says in his most punchable voice, "is the face of a woman scorned. Dude—what'd you *do* to her? Must have been bad."

I swallow. "It's complicated."

I don't tell them my theory that she's scared and feels a lack of control, which is manifesting in frustration toward me.

"You cheated?" Van sounds incredulous, which is good. I guess it means he thinks it would be out of character.

"No. I'm not a cheater."

"Left without saying goodbye?" Eli suggests.

I shake my head.

Logan frowns. "You ... dumped her?"

"No. Like I said, it's complicated." I pause and decide to tell them something, offering up even a small bit of truth. "She broke up with me. But I didn't fight her on it. Or fight *for* her. I should have."

I did more than give up. When she called me after the breakup, saying she might have been hasty, I told her that it was the right decision. Liam's expectant face had still loomed large, reminding me how much was at stake. I didn't want to let either of them down, so leaving before things got more serious seemed like the smartest choice. The last thing I wanted to do was disappoint a kid the same way I'd been let down by my family.

Turns out I ended up doing so anyway.

"You know, a heartfelt apology can go a long way," Felix offers.

Eli drags a hand through his hair. "I second that."

"When do you ever screw up, golden boy?" Van says.

"Constantly," Eli says. "Ask Bailey. Although she's probably too nice to say anything bad about me."

Van rolls his eyes. "I don't buy it. You treat that woman like she farts rainbows."

"Maybe she does." Eli grins. "I've never heard her fart. So, I don't have definitive proof."

"Are you kidding?" Van yells. "Everyone farts!"

"So, you're telling us Coach's daughter is extremely flatulent?" Felix raises an eyebrow at Van. "Got it. I'll be sure to tell Coach you said that."

"Come on, man," Van whines. "I just got him to stop hating me. Mostly. Don't ruin it."

"Clearly," Logan says, once again turning back to me as he

raises his voice, "we're all a bunch of idiots just trying our best. And sometimes failing."

"Or farting," Felix adds. It's an oddly out of character quip from him, and a laugh bursts out of Eli.

Van pulls up his sleeve and flexes. "Speak for yourself. About failing, anyway."

"I was speaking for *you*," Logan says. "Specifically."

Dominik says something in Russian. We don't need a translator to get the gist, which is something like, *You're all idiots*. Or maybe he's saying something about farting. Dom speaks very good English, but at times, he prefers to toss out things in Russian that we all just nod along with like we understand.

"Looks like I'm walking in on something fun."

Parker, Logan's fiancée, strides into the room, pausing to drop a noisy smack of a kiss on Logan's cheek. She tries to spin away, but he hooks an arm around her waist and we all groan as he kisses her for real. Much longer than necessary in a public space, but I think that's the point.

"Don't forget little eyes are watching," Felix says, and Parker yanks back from Logan, wiping her mouth as she glances through the window where both Liam and Naomi are staring. Coach, even, is glaring.

"Oops," Parker says, smoothing back her ponytail. "Coach texted me a 911. What happened?"

I should be the one to explain, but Van jumps in first. "To sum up: the woman in there glaring at Cole is his ex. Her son got hurt in the hockey camp today. Oh, and he didn't tell us either of those things."

Parker's eyes are wide. "Wow."

"And we're all idiots who make mistakes in relationships," Felix says.

"Got it," Parker says, taking all of this in stride. "Is he okay?"

"Yes," I say.

"Not as bad as the injury we had last year," Felix says. "Similar, but not as deep."

Parker shakes her head. "I wish we could afford to outfit all of them in Kevlar. Or bubble wrap. And for the record, women make mistakes. Maybe not quite so idiotic, but we mess up, too."

"Logan, it's a trap," Van whispers dramatically. "Don't agree with her."

"Wasn't about to," Logan says. Parker beams and pats him on the shoulder.

"One more important point: everyone farts," Eli says, then holds up both hands. "Allegedly."

"So much ground covered in so little time," Parker says slowly. "Exes, idiots, and farting. Busy few hours for y'all. So, why did Coach send for me?"

"Because Camden's ex threatened to sue," Felix says.

Parker angles herself to look through the glass. Seeing Naomi, she waves. Naomi does not wave back. "Ugly breakup, huh, Cambo?"

I only grunt. At both her question and the new nickname, which I hope doesn't stick. I can't decide if it's better or worse than Cammie.

"Don't bother trying to squeeze info out of him," Van says. "He won't tell us anything."

"We'll see," says Parker. "Anyway, potential lawsuits sound more like a Summer problem. I'm not the lawyer."

"But you're very good at smoothing things over," Logan says. "I'd bet that's why Coach called you down."

"Thank you." Parker smiles at him, then swings her gaze to me. "Anything you want to add?"

"Her brother is a lawyer," I say.

She rolls her eyes. "I didn't mean like that."

"Then what would I have to add?" I ask.

Parker gives me a look as if to say, *You really are an idiot.*

"Context," Dominik says in his crisp, accented English. "Some idea of why your ex is angry enough to punch you."

"She punched you?" Parker says, sounding somewhere between shocked and impressed. She wrinkles her nose when she looks at my eye.

I glance at Naomi again. She's still looking at me. With slightly less venom than before. "I think the punch was more an involuntary reaction to finding out Liam got hurt."

"Keep telling yourself what you want to tell yourself," Van says. "Sounds highly unlikely."

Now it's Parker who smacks the back of Van's head. "Sorry," she says, not sounding sorry at all. "Mostly. Will you let him talk? Camden, go on."

I stare blankly. "What?"

"You were about to tell us why that woman looks like she'd happily boil your bunnies."

Logan and Eli burst out laughing, Dominik covers his mouth, and Felix chuckles. Parker glances around, clearly confused.

Van looks horrified. "Is boiling bunnies some kind of ... euphemism? It sounds dirty."

"No!" Parker shouts, her hands going to her suddenly pink cheeks. "Oh my gosh, no. What even would that—never mind. Ugh! It's a reference to *Fatal Attraction*. Classic movie—Glenn Close as a stalker? No one's heard of it?"

Felix raises a hand. "I knew what you meant. It was funny, Parker."

"Thank you."

"Oh, look," I say. "They're done."

Liam is no sooner on his feet than he's bursting through the door connecting the two rooms. Naomi, looking torn, is caught talking to the medic but keeps her eyes on her son through the window.

He bounds over to me and holds out his arm, grinning. "Check it out! Wicked, yeah?"

I have no idea what the right response is. The sight of the long, neatly stitched wound on his forearm doesn't make me feel woozy, but it turns my stomach a little. Because I care about Liam. And though this was a relatively shallow injury, it could have been worse. Had the kid's skate sliced through the other side of his arm or gone deeper, it would have been a hospital situation like Felix mentioned had happened before.

I'm far too emotionally invested in the relationship—or lack thereof—I have now with Liam and his mom. Part of me wants to roll him up in bubble wrap and return him to Naomi. The other part wants to give him a high five and tell him he handled it like a champ.

I do neither. I just stand here, nodding.

Van steps up and gently takes Liam's hand, giving the wound a good look. "That's a beaut," he says. "You'll have a really good scar, but nothing too gruesome. Ladies love scars."

"He's a little young for the ladies, don't you think?" Naomi asks, walking into the room and going straight to Liam. She puts an arm around his shoulders and pulls him back a little from Van.

"You're never too young," Van says, holding up a hand to high five Liam.

Parker steps between Van and Naomi, who looks about ready to explode, this time at Van, not me. Logan drags Van away, putting a hand over his still-running mouth.

"Hi! I'm Parker." She thrusts a hand toward Naomi, who shakes it quickly, looking wary. Parker shakes Liam's hand next. He looks thrilled, but that may have more to do with the other players in the room. They're all helping with the class, but I'm sure he hasn't gotten a chance to meet most of them aside from Eli, his original group leader.

"I'm Naomi. This is Liam."

"Great to meet you both! I handle the team's social media," Parker says. "I heard we had a little bit of an issue at the class, and I just wanted to check up on things."

"You could say that," Naomi mutters. But she looks a little less murdery than she did a moment ago. Parker has that effect on people.

"I got twenty-seven stitches," Liam tells her proudly. "But I need to go back in there and let them put a bandage on it so Mom doesn't pass out again."

Parker's eyebrows shoot up, and Naomi rolls her eyes. "Way to throw your mom under the bus, kid."

"Do you want to meet all the guys first?" I ask Liam, and his eyes go wide.

"Um, yes?"

I make introductions, Liam's smile growing wider and wider while Naomi seems to shrink back more and more. Parker notices, too, and steps forward, linking an arm through Naomi's and whispering something to her. After a moment, Naomi nods, her eyes skating briefly over me before landing once again on Liam.

"Go get your bandage so we can get out of here," she tells him. "Remember, we've got big plans today."

"Right. Big plans." Liam laughs. "Mom's buying a winter coat," he announces to the whole room, though he's looking at me. "We didn't need them where we lived before."

He heads back into the medical suite, and I turn to

78

Naomi, remembering how she was shivering out in the parking lot in just a hoodie earlier.

"So, you *don't* have a coat?" I shouldn't have spoken the words out loud. I know this even without the searing look Naomi gives me.

"I don't have a coat *yet*, not that it's any of your business. Also, speaking of things that aren't your business, it didn't escape my notice that the gear Liam has in there isn't what I bought him. Know anything about that?"

I cross my arms. "I bought it."

"I can buy gear for my kid," she seethes, and I can see the self-reliance I respect so much bubbling up and boiling over.

I bite the inside of my cheek so I don't say, *Says the woman who hasn't bought herself a coat.*

"I saw a need. I met it. Not a big deal."

Naomi's eyebrows shoot up. "Not a big deal to you, maybe. But all of this is a big deal. Liam signing up for this, you coaching him without either of you thinking I might need to know, him getting hurt. Big deal."

I belatedly realize I probably should have messaged Naomi last week when I started working with Liam. Just to give her a heads-up. The same way I should have told her that Liam came by to see me after our breakup.

Now I'm holding onto several large secrets, and the knowledge makes me distinctly uncomfortable. Her anger feels a lot more justified, taking all of this into account.

An awkward silence descends on the room for a few seconds, and suddenly, the guys are apologizing and making excuses as they shuffle toward the door. Parker hovers, glancing between Naomi and me. I swear, I can smell her getting ideas. Parker is always getting ideas.

Thankfully, whatever she's cooking up gets interrupted when Liam bounds back into the room, his arm wrapped neatly. "Look, Mom!" he says, waving his arm in her face. "Now you don't have to see it."

Naomi still looks slightly woozy, and I bet she's imagining or maybe even remembering what's underneath the bandage. She takes a step back and gently guides his arm away from her face. "Um, yes. That's great. Now we can go."

"Actually." Parker steps up, I guess not fully deterred from whatever ideas she has. I wonder if I should stop her, but Parker is somewhat of a bulldozer when she gets excited about something. A cheerful, happy bulldozer. But she'll plow through you, nonetheless. "I was thinking maybe we could do something nice for Liam after having such a rough morning."

He frowns. "My morning was awesome. I got stitches! And I got to see cool places like this that no one gets to see in the Summit. And I met some of the Appies."

Naomi looks far less pleased by each of these things.

"Well, then how would you like a tour of the Summit? Maybe we can even find some signed pucks and merch." Parker crouches a little until she's level with Liam's wide eyes. Lowering her voice, she adds, "Would you like to see the locker room?"

"Yes," Liam says in a reverent whisper. Then, as though just now remembering he has a mom and probably needs to check with her, he grabs her hand. "Mom, *please*? Can I?"

I already know there's no way she'll say no to that face. Instead, Naomi looks at Parker with wary reluctance. "Are you just doing this so we won't sue the organization?"

Parker laughs. "I mean, we hope you don't sue, but no. We want every child who attends an Appies event to leave with a positive experience. And though your Liam definitely deserves a medal for his cheerful attitude about getting hurt, we want to ensure he has great memories to hold onto."

"Fine." Naomi stumbles a little as Liam throws his arms around her in an exuberant hug. He says *thank you* over and over into her rib cage. "Okay, calm down, dude. I already said yes, we'll go on the tour."

"Actually," Parker says again, turning sly fox eyes my way, "if you'd rather skip the tour, I know our chef is still here and would be happy to whip something up. You and Camden could catch up and eat. We'll meet back up with you later. You can trust me with Liam, I promise. It's been a while, but I had all the proper babysitting certifications back in high school."

Though Naomi clearly knows as well as I do that this is a setup, Parker's genuineness makes it really hard to say no. Especially when combined with Liam's pleading eyes.

As nervous as I am at the idea of being left alone with Naomi right now, I really don't want her to say no.

"I guess that's fine," Naomi says, pointedly not looking at me.

Parker smiles and plucks a business card from her pocket and presses it into Naomi's palm. "That's got my cell number. Text me, and I'll save your number in my phone, then message you when we're done. I'd also be happy to play tour guide to Harvest Hollow anytime you'd like since it sounds like you're new in town. Or if you want to hang out, I'd love that, too. There's way too much testosterone in my day-to-day life."

Naomi's smile is genuine now, a little more relaxed. I wish I had half an ounce of whatever Parker does that enables her to do this—putting people at ease and drawing them out.

"Thanks," Naomi says. "I really appreciate it." She pulls out her phone and texts Parker, who smiles when her phone buzzes.

"Got it. Now, where would you like to start?" Parker asks, steering Liam toward the door.

"The locker room. Definitely. Did you know that locker rooms don't have actual lockers? Each player has a stall where they keep their gear."

"I *did* know that," Parker says. "It's pretty cool, right?"

"So cool."

And then the door closes behind them, leaving me alone with my ex.

CHAPTER 7

Naomi

PART OF ME—A very large, very opinionated part—urges me to grab onto Liam's good arm and announce that I'm joining him and Parker on their Summit tour. I can feign excitement over a locker room that has *stalls*—a term that calls to mind horses or public bathrooms rather than hockey players—instead of lockers. I guess it fits with the idea of calling this very luxe stadium a *barn*.

Anyway, a Summit tour seems like a better, wiser, less terrifying option than spending prolonged time alone with the man currently watching me with an unreadable expression.

Does he even *want* to babysit me?

I haven't been particularly nice to him today, which isn't fair. I definitely regret the punch, and I mostly regret the glares and fighting with him over getting Liam equipment. That was a sweet gesture. But if I'm going to keep my distance, sweet gestures aren't what I need. What I need is a wall. Space. To clutch my anger tighter, even if I'm not so much angry as I am scared.

But holding onto anger is exhausting. Especially when it's undeserved. It just makes me a shrew.

Maybe I need to just relax and use this time to clear the air. Especially since Camden is apparently working with Liam on Saturdays. When my protectiveness bristles again knowing Camden didn't think to at least text to let me know, I tamp the feelings down.

Easy girl, I tell myself.

"So," I say. "Guess you're stuck with me."

"Or you're stuck with me."

His face gives me nothing. It's the Fort Knox of faces, locked up tight. This is one of the things I liked about Camden from the start, though right now, I dislike it *very* much.

I'm a woman who thrives under a good challenge. The best way to ensure my success at something is how loudly people tell me I can't. Or shouldn't. This move to Harvest Hollow being a perfect case in point. Resistance only makes me push harder.

When I met him, Camden felt like a puzzle to crack. A cipher to decode. Making him smile or getting any kind of reaction out of that stoic face felt like being handed a lifetime achievement award.

Now, I feel on edge. Nervous and off-balance. Whatever headway I made in learning to read him has been lost.

After he left Oakley, Camden and I never spoke again. Over. Done. I didn't block his number because I'm not a teenager. I also didn't delete our text thread, which I read and reread in my lowest of lows. But there was zero contact after that.

I have no idea how Camden feels about me now or how he feels—felt?—about the breakup. He might be totally over it now. Maybe he succeeded where I failed in keeping things casual, just the way we talked about. No part of it felt casual to me. But without any clues or signals from him, I can only guess.

Did he shed any tears? Are hockey players even capable of crying? I honestly can't be sure after Liam told me about a player who got a few teeth knocked out and went right back into the game a few minutes later like nothing happened.

For all I know, Camden jumped right back into dating as soon as he left Oakley. He could have a girlfriend right now. If I hadn't drawn a firm boundary at checking his social media after our breakup, maybe I'd know.

Even the thought of him with someone else makes me feel light-headed again.

I don't know Parker, but she seems nice. Genuine. And only a heartless hag would encourage a guy in a relationship to hang out alone with his ex. Maybe I'm grasping at straws, but it's a semi-educated guess to assume Camden isn't in a relationship.

"Hungry?" he asks, and something about his tone makes me feel like he already knows the answer.

"Not really." An understatement. The donuts and coffee have been swirling uncomfortably in my belly for a while now.

Camden nods, then says, "Come on."

I don't ask where or why. I just follow.

He holds the door open, and I try to hold my breath as I

pass by. I remember too well his spicy, woodsy scent. I don't need the influx of memories it would bring. We fall into step in a long, windowless hallway.

When Camden led me inside the building to find Liam earlier, I got the sense I would never be able to find my way out of this place. I was also so emotionally keyed up, I'm not sure my brain could process the most basic of information like simple directions.

Speaking of being keyed up ...

"I'm sorry for punching you," I tell him. "You didn't deserve it."

"I was the messenger. I'm just glad you didn't have a gun."

I jerk back to look at him, and there's a hint of a smile lifting one corner of his mouth.

"Shut up." I nudge him with my shoulder before stepping a safe distance away again. "I wouldn't have shot you." I pause. "Probably."

His laugh is a low chuckle, and I swear the rumble reverberates down to my toes.

"But honestly. I *am* sorry. I've never actually punched anyone. You startled me at my car, and then told me about Liam, and I guess I ... snapped."

"Understandable."

"Is it? I'm not sure punching people makes the list of common reactions to emotional overwhelm."

"You're not what I would call ... common, Naomi."

"Hey," I protest, but Camden's steady brown gaze stops me from saying more.

"It's a compliment," he says.

"So, were you ever going to tell me that you were working with Liam?"

He's quiet for a moment. "I didn't think you'd want to hear from me."

"When it comes to my kid, being kept in the loop trumps all."

"Noted." Another pause. "Then I'm sorry for not letting you know. I guess it was ... cowardly. I also should have asked before buying him gear. I wasn't trying to imply that you couldn't get it yourself. I just saw a need that was easy for me to meet, and I met it."

"I guess I can understand your reasoning," I say.

"Will Liam be in trouble for not telling you?"

I sigh. "I don't know what to do with him. We'll have a conversation. I doubt there will be any kind of punishment. I mean, if I didn't do anything when he signed up for these classes without permission, I suppose I can't do anything about this. I'm just not used to the version of him where he keeps secrets."

Camden looks like he's about to say something in response, but then he clears his throat and asks, "Elevator or stairs?"

"Stairs," I say quickly. Nothing potentially sexy about climbing up or down a commercial stairwell.

But being alone in an elevator with Camden, on the other hand ...

I am not willing to test my resolve. Not when he's being ... I don't know what he's being. Not quite flirty, but then Camden was never a flirt. He's being kind, at the very least. His version of non-flirtatious flirty, at most. And it's doing things to me. Bad things.

Obviously, my feelings never went away, despite the way I wished they would. Or how hard I pretended they had. I *knew* this, but as long as I didn't see Camden, I could believe my lies. At least, a little bit.

Now, there is zero room for self-delusion.

Glancing to my left, at the tall, quiet man whose stubbly jawline has haunted my dreams for months, the nagging thoughts rise up again.

You made a mistake. You got scared, and you ran.

No, I think, trying to smush those thoughts down into a hermetically sealed box I can sink twenty thousand million leagues under the sea, *I did what was necessary to protect Liam. And myself.*

Coward, the voice hisses as I finally manage to cram that box shut, dropping it into a mental Mariana Trench.

Because maybe I was cowardly. (I was.) Maybe I ran scared. (I did.) But then … I called Camden and tried to take it back and *he* said no.

It was basically a two-for-one breakup special.

Camden pushes open the stairwell door, then gives me an assessing look. "You okay?"

"Sure. Why wouldn't I be?"

He stares for a beat, like he's wondering if I believe my own words. "You had a look on your face," he finally says.

"No look. This is just my face." I push past him into the stairwell. Only, this time as I pass, I forget to hold my breath.

And there it is: Camden's warm, familiar scent, releasing a deluge of memories that almost knock the wind out of me.

Laughter. Sand beneath my bare feet and his big, calloused hand wrapped around mine. His lips, warm and confident, making me forget my own name. The firmness of his chest under my cheek as his arms hold me tight.

Safety. Longing. Joy.

Home.

He's wearing a fitted athletic shirt, and I'm surprised he doesn't smell bad. I've heard about the hockey stink (from Liam, of course), but I bet the hockey classes with someone on Liam's level don't require a lot of actual exertion on the part of pro hockey players. In any case, Camden unfortunately smells great.

Needing an immediate escape, I take the steps two at a time, stopping the next floor up, severely winded. I lean against the wall, panting and cursing my lack of cardio. Camden's steps are slow and measured. When he reaches me, still attempting to catch my breath, he pauses.

"What if we're going down?" he asks.

My head whips up, and I know my cheeks are flushed. Either from the sadly minimal amount of exertion or embarrassment. "Are we?"

"Nope." And then a slow smile unfurls on his stupidly handsome face, dragging an unwilling smile from me.

Without thinking, I reach out a hand and shove him. He doesn't budge. "You're the worst."

"Maybe." Another pause. The smile shifts into a smirk. "We've got another two flights up. Need me to carry you the rest of the way?"

"Absolutely not."

But before I can duck or dodge out of the way, Camden scoops me up and tosses me over his shoulder, then starts up the stairs. I consider pounding my fists against his back, but I know it would be the equivalent of a little fish flapping its fins to wave off a shark. Instead, I go boneless and limp, remembering.

Early last summer, we were walking along the beach and I stumbled, turning my ankle. I didn't sprain it or anything, just stumbled a little in a hole some kid probably dug with a plastic shovel.

And just like he did now, Camden picked me up and threw me over his shoulder. I fought him then, and in retalia-

89

tion, he walked us both right into the ocean. Which would have been fine except we were fully clothed.

Actually, that was fine too. In those days, when we were still insisting things were just casual and fun, everything was fine.

"Really?" I ask sarcastically as he starts to climb. "You're choosing the caveman path again?"

"I guess it's just in my nature."

"I *can* climb stairs, you know." Though it's surprisingly comfortable letting him carry me, I shouldn't let myself enjoy it. But it's hard to find anything *not* enjoyable about being this close to him again, feeling the ease with which he carries me and the strength of his arm, banded over the back of my thighs.

"Sure," he says easily. "But you also seemed poised for a cardiac event after just one flight, and we can't have that."

"I'm *fine*."

"You are."

My stomach does a little happy dance at his words, and I threaten it with no more apple cider donuts ever if it doesn't calm down.

Camden reaches the final landing and heads through a doorway, still keeping me over his shoulder.

"We're done with the stairs now. You can put me down," I point out.

He only grunts at this, tightening his grip a little on my thighs. But I've had quite enough up close and personal time with him. He's simply too tempting. I can already feel my resolve, once titanium plated, disintegrating under the pressure of Camden's presence.

I tap him lightly on the back. "Put me down. Please?"

It's impossible to hide the tremble in my voice, and he

sets me down quickly. I step away, hoping to reset my self-control. It only sort of works.

"Where are we?" I ask, glancing around. We're definitely not in any kind of public space. It's dimly lit and would be creepy if I weren't with someone who made me feel so safe.

Which, ironically, makes him completely *unsafe*.

"I know you're not great with stairs, but how are you with heights?" Camden asks.

"Once again, I'm fine with stairs—if I'm not running up them. And I'm good with heights. We're not bungee jumping off the top of the building or something, right?"

He looks amused. "No."

"BASE jumping?"

"Is that something you want to do?"

"Absolutely not."

"Then no. No jumping of any kind. Not even jumping rope."

"Then I'll be fine."

"Good."

Without offering up any other information, Camden turns and walks away, leaving me to scamper behind him. I keep my eyes on the floor, lest they become traitors and decide to wander in the direction of Camden's backside. Which I happen to know provides quite the view.

But looking down means I don't realize Camden has stopped, and I run right into the back of him. I step away quickly, rubbing my nose.

"Ready?" he asks, eyebrows raised.

"For what?"

He doesn't answer but simply gestures for me to go first to wherever it is he's taking me. I get the distinct suspicion he's testing me, so I lift my chin and walk ahead, my steps slowing when I look around.

"Whoa. This is … cool."

We're on a metal catwalk above the arena. Down below, a Zamboni makes lazy circles on the ice. Otherwise, the arena is empty. I guess they don't have a game today. They probably wouldn't if the players are working with kids. I know from the schedule next week there isn't a class—does that mean they have a game?

You don't care about hockey, I remind myself. But I'm finding myself curious for the first time.

Pausing in the middle of the walkway, I lean my elbows on the rail and look down over the ice with its Appies logo and the wide, shiny streaks marking the Zamboni's path. It's really peaceful and more than a little awe-inspiring. I've never been to a hockey game. Looking out over the seats and the banners and the clean sheet of ice, I'm suddenly struck with the desire to go.

This isn't an altogether bad thing, considering the way Liam will force me to go soon. He's already asked no less than a dozen times. I can probably handle seeing Camden play without falling any harder for him, right? That's what I'll tell myself.

Because one of the reasons for our breakup—besides my fear that Liam was getting too attached—was the fact that distance would be too tricky. Now, there's no distance.

But I have no idea if Camden has any lingering feelings for me. He certainly seemed confident in the breakup when I tried to walk it back, which was humiliating.

"Parker showed me this spot," Camden says, jarring me out of my thoughts.

Jealousy instantly curdles in my stomach. I didn't get a vibe between Parker and Camden. But even the idea of another woman platonically sharing something special with Camden is enough to unleash the jealous beast.

"Are you two dating?" I blurt, regretting the question instantly. I can feel heat creeping up my cheeks.

His head rears back. "What? No. She's engaged to one of the guys on the team. And even if not ..." He glances at me, then away.

"This just seems like the kind of thing you'd share with someone special."

I meant Parker telling Camden and realize the implication as soon as the words are out of my mouth. Because Camden just brought *me* here.

I really should just stop talking.

Thankfully, he seems to gloss right over my words. "I think she just brought me up here because ..."

I wait. But Camden runs a hand over his jaw as he stares out over the rows of empty seats.

"Because?" I prompt.

"Nothing. It's just a nice place to be alone."

"You're not alone," I point out, earning me a long, slow perusal of my face.

"No," he says, stepping closer. "I'm not."

I should move away, just like I've been doing all afternoon. I should do a lot of things. Swaying closer to Camden is not one of those things, yet that is what I'm doing now.

"You didn't tell me you were moving here," he says, his voice a rough honey wrapped in accusation.

"I didn't think you'd want to hear from me." He seems unsurprised when I echo his words from earlier.

"I used to pull up your old texts and read them," he confesses. "I would hope for those three little dots to appear."

I don't tell him that I used to read our old messages, too. Right now, it feels too risky to tell him something so true.

"I shouldn't have left."

"You live here; you had to go."

"I didn't have to go then. Or the way I did. I've been living with the regret every day since."

"Me too," I whisper.

His head snaps up at my words. I'm positive, based on the sudden gleam in Camden's eyes, that one tiny sentence cracked the door, and he seems ready to walk right through.

Camden shifts closer, looming over me as I lean back against the rail, my hands gripping it behind my back.

This is a kissing moment. Heat and electricity and anticipation doesn't just hang in the air; it vibrates through it, making my legs shake and the tiny hairs on the back of my neck lift.

If I turn off my brain and its pesky, logical thoughts, I can focus on only what I want. And what I want is nothing more than to let this man, whose gaze is now locked on my mouth, kiss me.

He wants to. I'd have to be stupid not to see it.

Even stupider would be trying to deny that I want it just as badly.

But as impulsive as I may be at my very core, I now come equipped with an emergency brake in the form of needing to do what's right by my kid. Becoming a mom, having a whole other person who owns a chunk of my heart, shifted something in me. I'm better at self-preservation because it now includes Liam-preservation.

The very last thing Liam needs is to get ideas in his head again about Camden—at least, unless it's something serious.

Am I ready for something serious? Is Camden? Would we even work long-term? Does he want to be a dad to my kid?

A lot of the same questions and doubts I had last summer obscure my thoughts like a worry blizzard.

Breaking up with Camden remains the single most emotionally grueling thing I've done.

Yes, including giving birth.

Which might sound extreme considering the circumstances of how Liam came into the world. I was young—only nineteen—and without a partner since Liam's dad exited the picture immediately upon finding out I was pregnant. I had the support of my dad and Jake, but neither of them were super helpful during actual labor and delivery.

So yeah, birth was no picnic. But I also discovered the power of my body and my own strength and resilience. And I got Liam at the end of a labor in which I declared to Jake while holding his shirt collar, *Never again.*

In contrast, there was no prize after my painful breakup with Camden. No silver lining or sense that something better waited ahead. I broke up with him and got ... nothing. No snuggly baby at the end of painful labor, making my heart expand with warmth and love.

Instead, I was left with an invisible and insidious grief paired with the nagging and persistent thought that I screwed up. The breakup with Camden hit me squarely in the emotional and psychological feels. A deeper pain, largely invisible to the people around me. It's surprisingly easy to hide breakup angst, unlike when your water breaks in the middle of Walmart while you're shopping for beef jerky, your number one pregnancy craving.

I don't want to go through that again.

I'm not sure I'd survive it.

Clearing my throat, I slip away from Camden, taking slow steps across the catwalk, trailing one hand along the metal support. I wish my backbone were this solid. Or my understanding of what I really want.

"Don't you have hockey games on Saturdays?"

If Camden is disappointed, I don't hear it in his voice, which is frustratingly even when he says, "Sometimes. Our schedule is weird. The Saturdays we have games are the ones where we don't have classes."

"Makes sense. So, is Liam the worst skater in his group? You can tell me. Honestly."

A long pause. Because I'm now at a safe distance, I turn around. But Camden isn't where I left him. He's been quietly following. Though he's not as close as he was, he's close enough to be a temptation. I swallow and grip the railing a little harder.

Camden runs his fingers through his hair, leaving it mussed. It's longer than it was when he left, curling over the collar of his shirt and hiding the tops of his ears. Maybe this is one of those hockey things—players letting their hair grow out over the season? I'll have to ask Liam later.

"I'm working with Liam one-on-one," Camden says.

"Is that normal?"

He hesitates but only for a moment. "Everyone else is in a group."

"So, you're the only guy working with just one kid, then?"

Camden nods. "Most kids his age are a little further along, so he was with all the little kids. It wouldn't have been very helpful for him."

Processing this takes more than a few seconds and some serious effort to keep my breathing even when it feels like I'm being crushed inside a trash compactor. Because no guy I've ever dated aside from Camden interacted with Liam, I didn't realize a man being kind and generous with my son was my kryptonite.

But oh, it absolutely is.

"He said you didn't come into the building because you didn't want to see me."

This hurts, even though it's true. I didn't think Liam realized why I wouldn't get out of the car at the Summit. I told him I was using my free time to run errands and joked about having Mommy time. I should have known he was too smart to buy my excuses.

"I'm sorry," I tell him. "I ..."

There are so many words clambering to be said, vying for top spot that they logjam, and I say nothing else.

"I get it," Camden says quickly, saving me. "I know it's not easy for me to see you." Camden scrunches up his face, shifting on his feet. "Not hard to see you as in, you're hard to look at. You're not. Hard to look at, that is. Which is the problem."

I'm smiling by the time he finishes tripping over his words. I probably shouldn't smile, given the context of our whole conversation, but I like seeing Camden a little ruffled. Especially knowing I'm the reason he's ruffled. It makes me feel better about being so ruffled myself.

"Don't look at me like that," he says, but now he's smiling. A tiny one, but still.

"Can't help it. You're cute when you're flustered."

He blows out a breath, looking away as color rises in his cheeks. I've never seen Camden blush, and it makes him even more adorable. This is doing absolutely nothing to help curb my enthusiasm for the man.

But I didn't kiss him when I wanted to, so that feels like a giant win. I can at least allow myself to indulge in this tiny moment of flirting.

"Could this be any more awkward?" he asks.

"Yes," I answer honestly. "I feel like we're handling this pretty well, actually."

"I'd love to hear how this could be worse."

I tilt my head. "Oh, you want some horror stories about exes?"

"No." Camden's answer is quick, his voice and eyes suddenly hard. "I don't want to hear about your exes, Naomi."

I don't want to be one of your exes. He doesn't say this, but the words still seem to hang in the air.

Wishful thinking on my part, probably.

"I don't have a lot of exes," I tell him, but this doesn't seem to help. "I mean, I've just gone on dates. I haven't really had relationships, so I don't mean ex in that sense. Just guys I've dated."

"I don't want to think about you with any men. Casually. Not casually. At *all*."

Should the deep possessive grit in his voice bother me? Maybe. Considering the fact that he doesn't have any kind of claim on me. But I really, really like it.

I also don't know how to respond, so I just stand here, staring at him.

Now the pause between us is awkward. I decide to steer us back into safer territory. Not that any territory with Camden is safe. It all seems strewn with dangers like quicksand and sudden lava flows.

"Level with me—what are the odds that Liam will give up on his hockey obsession?" I cross my fingers dramatically, and Camden smirks. "I mean, I'm his biggest fan and supporter, but I am also well aware he isn't, how should I say ... *coordinated*."

"Before today? I might have said the odds were stacked in favor of him quitting."

"You think he's *more* likely to stay now that he's had his arm sliced open?" I gape at him.

"It's less about the injury and more about how he handled himself. You should be proud. He's a really good kid."

I find myself leaning forward, suddenly eager to hear all the details I didn't get earlier because I was too busy being furious and then passing out at the sight of blood. "What makes you feel like he'll stick with hockey after that?"

Camden considers for a moment. I'm biased, but he has a really nice *considering* face. "I'm sure players in every sport feel this way, but hockey really does take a different kind of mindset. When Liam got hurt, he wasn't concerned about his injury. He only wanted to make sure the kid who hurt him wasn't traumatized. Liam smiled at the boy and told him that it's just part of hockey."

Camden pauses, probably trying to figure out what to do with me since I'm actively trying to hold back tears. I cry so much more than I used to, and often for the weirdest, stupidest things.

Though I guess this isn't stupid. It's *awesome*. One of those moments when the pride in my kid feels powerful enough to crack open my chest.

"Liam has a long way to go with skating," Camden says. "But mentally, he's got something you can't teach. Something most kids don't have. So, if he's determined, yeah—I could see him continuing in one of the youth leagues."

I sniff. "That's ... cool. Thanks for telling me."

"Did you not want him to play hockey?" Camden asks.

"I don't know."

He pauses for a long moment, looking like he's trying to work up the courage to say something. "Is it because of me?"

The answer is much more complicated than that, but avoiding Camden and thoughts of Camden is certainly a part of it. "He's just never shown any interest in sports before ..."

You, I think.

"Now," I say. "Before now. I thought he'd try it, realize he's better at academics, and then give up."

"He seems pretty dogged when he knows what he wants." His gaze holds mine steadily. "Or doesn't want. Not unlike his mother."

Before I can even register the compliment, Camden starts to walk away. "We should probably get back downstairs and find Parker."

This time, I don't stop my eyes from wandering.

CHAPTER 8

Camden

WHEN YOU WALK into your house after a game, thinking about the woman who has occupied most of your thoughts for months and nearly *all* of them for days, nothing will obliterate those thoughts faster than finding someone standing in your kitchen in their underwear.

Especially when that person is a sixty-three-year-old man, and his underwear consists of saggy boxers so well-worn the fabric is almost sheer. At least he's wearing a shirt. A white one—*Why do people ever wear white clothing by choice?*—with yellowing armpits and a hole by his shoulder from which back hair sprouts in a little tuft.

"Hey, Mike," I say. "I'm home."

"Cam!" He turns with a smile and surprise in his eyes. Despite his clothing choice, his face is clean shaven, as always, and his silver hair is neatly combed back. He frowns

101

when he sees what I'm wearing. "Did you have a game tonight?"

Back in the day, Mike would never have missed one of my games. But I didn't tell him about tonight—or my three other games since he arrived—because he would have insisted on coming. And while I did worry about him here alone during the games, I would have worried more about him in the Summit.

"Nah," I say, hating the taste of the lie.

We beat the Dingoes three to one tonight, no thanks to me. I'm not a star defenseman, but more of a grinder—a player who won't get a lot of points or a lot of notice because I'm generally doing all the right things, quietly. Until this season, in which I've been noticeable for all the wrong reasons. I wouldn't be shocked if I'm a healthy scratch and sit out for at least one of our upcoming road games. There are guys who would love my spot, and I'm well aware that I'm not fighting hard enough for it. I just can't bring myself to care. My head is in too many other places at the moment.

Including Naomi and Liam but also the man standing in his underwear in my house.

"Good. I would have been there if you had a game," Mike says. "And I would have put something in the oven if I knew you were coming home now."

"Or maybe you would have put on pants?" I suggest mildly.

Looking down at his bare chicken legs, Mike chuckles. "Maybe. Maybe not. Are you hungry? I was making ... something." He blinks at the counter, and I can see him cataloging the same mess I am and trying to come up with a reasonable explanation. "A sandwich?" he suggests.

There *is* bread on the counter. And cheese, though it's shredded, not sliced, and scattered across the counter and floor. He also got out a can of soup, crackers, a head of lettuce and a box of frozen lasagna. I wonder how long it's been defrosting on the counter. Quickly, I glance at the oven, relieved when I see that it's not on.

This is the reason I can't stay away from home long. I have two caregivers: one who's here with Mike on days when I'm at the rink and another for away games. But it's not an ideal setup, and already, the caregiver I hired for away games put in her notice. She'll handle the next road series, but I need to find a replacement after that.

Mike can be by himself, at least for short stretches. For now. Tonight, I got roped into doing some press, possibly as a sort of punishment for my poor performance, and Jordan, the day caregiver, had to leave before I got home.

A few weeks before Naomi and Liam arrived in Harvest Hollow, Mike moved in. We're still very much in the adjustment period as I try to figure out how and *if* this will work. It's been fine, but any time he's left unattended, it's with the distinct feeling of dread that I might come home to find him missing or a smoking pile of rubble instead of my rental house.

Mike isn't my dad, but for years, he's felt like the closest thing to it. After I got drafted by the Youngstown Phantoms at sixteen, I moved seven hours away from home. Billet families, essentially host families, are common for teens who play for developmental youth leagues. I got lucky with the Bells. Mike and his wife, Debbie, were warm and welcoming and had years of experience hosting guys. At first, they were like a second family, and then, after what happened with my parents, they became more like my only family.

Now, I'm a decade older, a good six inches taller, and fifty pounds heavier than I was back then, but Mike often still sees me as that young kid who lived with them. Somehow, this all works in his head. I think because he *needs* it to work in his head.

Human beings are excellent at doing what we need to survive and adapt. From what I've seen, when Mike's understanding doesn't match up with the reality he's confronted with, he bends the truth to accommodate for it. Which is why it's possible for him to talk as though this house is his house and he's still married to Debbie, though they've been divorced for years. Most of the time, he thinks I'm in high school even though I no longer look like I did back then. Mike simply jams the ill-fitting pieces together to craft a reality that makes sense.

I used to fear a career-ending injury more than almost anything. Now that I've seen memory loss up close and personal, this is a more chilling possibility than a physical injury.

Despite the decline in his cognitive function, Mike's mood stays upbeat, same as always. His personality hasn't changed or been dampened. Every so often, when there's a crack in his carefully constructed narrative and he can't find a way to reconcile his memory with reality, he wilts. The best option I've found seems to be playing along and ignoring inconsistencies rather than pointing them out.

"I ... wanted a midnight snack." Mike's eyes land on the oven clock, and he briefly frowns. It's nine thirty-five. We had a late afternoon game today or it *would* be closer to a midnight-snack time. "I mean post-dinner snack," he amends.

"I can make something if you're hungry. Or order something," I add.

I'm only good at cooking a few things: eggs, baked chicken, and hamburgers. Not well, either. But passable.

Honestly, cooking anything feels like too much work right

now after the game, which is why I picked up something on the way home. A fast food grilled chicken sandwich wasn't the ideal post-game meal, but it was enough.

"Actually, I'm not hungry," Mike says, scratching the side of his belly. "I'll just clean up. Don't want to leave this mess for Debbie."

I don't tell him that Debbie is living in Palm Beach with her *new* husband. Or that his second wife divorced Mike a few years ago and couldn't be bothered when she found out he was suffering from an as-yet unspecified form of early-onset dementia.

On the plus side, his leaky memory means he doesn't usually remember the bad parts of his past. Like the way he wrecked his marriage by having an affair, crushing both his wife and his daughter in the process. This is how he ended up with me.

Though I was shocked and disappointed to hear about Mike's affair, it was different for me. The betrayal wasn't personal but a real-life example of realizing your heroes have crumbly clay feet.

"I've got this," I tell him. "You go sit down. Isn't Toronto playing?"

I can hear the low sounds of the game coming from the living room. I'm sure that's what he was probably watching before he wandered in here to make the "midnight" snack he no longer wants. Of all the things that he's unsure about, Mike's love for the Leafs is unwavering. Which is unfortunate for him since the Toronto Maple Leafs have historically struggled in the playoffs.

"I think this is their year," he says. "I've got that feeling."

"We can always hope," I say. With hockey, there's always hope. It's one of the things I love about the sport. Any team can win, any given night.

I've seen comebacks where a team scores three goals in two minutes to win a game. It's why fans should never leave a game early.

I wonder what year Mike thinks it is—that could impact his hope in the Leafs. Time is more fluid than linear for Mike now. He slips between thinking it's one decade and then the next within the same few sentences without even realizing it.

Maybe he'll be right this year. I'd love that for him.

"Will you come watch with me?" Mike asks. "Or do you have plans with friends?"

"I'll be right in," I tell him, loosening my tie. "I need to get out of this suit."

"I'll bet," Mike says with a chuckle as he heads back to the living room.

My stomach twists. With a sigh, I head to my room so I can change before heading back to the kitchen. I actually don't mind cleaning up the mess, as the rote work allows time for me to come down off the post-game high.

Hockey players have a variety of post-game rituals. Some want to extend the high, heading out to party or find company for the night. Years ago, Mike suggested I lift weights after a game. It sounded ridiculous to me, but my trainers confirmed that it can help release the buildup of lactic acid and aid in recovery. After giving it a try, I found that I was less sore the morning after if I spent even twenty minutes in the gym post-game. By the time I'm through lifting and showering, usually the buzz of energy has quieted.

But considering the things I've been grappling with lately, no amount of deadlifts could make a dent. My brain has been spinning out since my conversation with Naomi at the Summit the other day. Honestly, my head hasn't been in the right place for a long time.

Coming home to *this* only adds to the mental load. In short, I'm running on fumes, with no gas station in sight.

As I put away food, my thoughts boomerang back to Naomi and Liam.

I'll admit—having Naomi and Liam move to Harvest Hollow seems like some kind of cosmic sign. It's my opportunity for a second chance. To right the wrong of leaving in the first place. The brief time I spent alone with Naomi above the ice a few days ago only solidified my desire to put things to rights between us. To confess I want a relationship that is the opposite of casual.

And yet ...

I still have the same hesitations and the same fears I did last summer. Liam's earnest face fills my mind. I can't stomach the thought of letting him down a second time. I know what that kind of loss feels like, and I already hurt him when I sent him away from my hotel last summer.

I won't do it again—not to either of them—so I need to be sure before I make any kind of decision.

Sure of what I want. Sure of what I can offer both Naomi and Liam. Sure if I can be the kind of steady person who can commit for the long haul the way my own father didn't.

Not to me, anyway.

I try not to let bitterness rise up again. For years, I've felt okay about my family, but having Mike here has caused a lot of old feelings and memories to resurface. Unpleasant ones, as far as my family goes, tempered by fond memories with Mike. Just having him here makes me happy, even if there's the bittersweetness of *why* he's here.

If anything, Mike himself is a reminder of how fleeting and uncertain life is, how important it is to make use of the time we have. It makes me want to live without the kind of regrets I've been swimming in since this summer.

All this is assuming Naomi would consider a relationship with me again. She didn't want to even come into the Summit—that's how much she wanted to avoid seeing me. Am I stupid to think she's still interested?

But I didn't imagine the electric tension between us on the catwalk. The air between us practically crackling with tension. Her lips parting as my gaze fell there.

Until Naomi, once again, erected a barrier.

Still—all hope isn't lost. Probably?

Mike cheers from the other room, and I wonder what it would be like to navigate a relationship with Naomi while he's living here. Especially when I still don't know how this will look long-term. In hockey, injured players are said to be day-to-day, week-to-week, or month-to-month. I'm not sure where Mike falls. Month-to-month?

Year-to-year?

I try to imagine broaching this conversation with Naomi.

Hey, want to go on a date? You probably need a babysitter for Liam, and I might need to be home early so I can make sure the grown man living with me doesn't forget where he is and wander off. You're welcome to come over any time so long as you don't mind possibly seeing him in his underwear.

It definitely will be complicated.

I have two interviews set up for potential caretakers to stay with Mike during my upcoming string of road games. I really need one or both of them to work out. Having the first caretaker flake on me just a few weeks in, I'd like to have a list of qualified people. Backups upon backups. A few hours alone, like tonight, is fine, but leaving Mike while I'm out of town for days at a time isn't a possibility.

"Are you coming?" Mike calls. "Bring me a beer, would ya?"

On my way into the living room, I grab him one of the

nonalcoholic beers I've started stocking. They taste enough like the real thing that Mike hasn't said anything. I'm not sure if he hasn't noticed or just hasn't questioned it. One more part of his reality he's just rolling with.

"Have you called home lately?" Mike asks casually, sipping his beer as soon as I place it in his hand.

"No."

"You should," he tells me, nodding his head. "I know it's not easy to let your kid go. They miss you."

I don't say anything as I take my seat on the couch, but my hands are shaking. *They miss you.* I wish Mike could remember enough to know how untrue those words are. He definitely wouldn't be bringing up my family if he did.

I realize I'm clenching my fists and slowly release them, taking deep breaths and trying to focus on the game. A fight breaks out behind the net, and it's enough to distract Mike from the subject of my family.

Another thing he doesn't remember: the way my parents had not one but two surprise babies after I left. Twin daughters. Sarah and Elizabeth were premature and required a lot of extra work the first year. I didn't feel jealous or upset when my parents stopped traveling to any of my games. I understood.

But then their weekly calls and texts became sporadic and slowed almost to a stop. When I went home to meet my sisters for the first time, I felt like an outsider. The guest room became the nursery, which meant my room was now the guest room. And because my parents had packed my things and put them in the attic, I *felt* like a guest in it.

And as excited as I was to meet my sisters, it didn't go as expected. I didn't know the first thing about babies, and Sarah and Elizabeth screamed whenever I tried to hold them or feed them. I didn't have the emotional connection with them I expected. I didn't have any connection at all, really. With my parents consumed by feedings and naps and diaper changes, I was sort of left to fend for myself.

It's not that I wanted everything to be all about me. But I no longer felt like I belonged in my own home—or in my family.

So, I left early and went back to Mike and the Bells.

I had a brief rough patch after that where I let this get in my head. I became a bit of a punk on and off the ice. It was Mike who talked sense into me, the way I hoped to do with that kid who picked on Liam.

Whenever I went back home to visit, it felt less and less like home each time. I don't blame my sisters—how could I? —or even my mom and dad. Not really. It felt inevitable, the growing apart. Their world had been completely flipped upside down with unexpected joy. It was more than a new season—it was a new start. One that happened without me.

I could see the guilt on my parents' faces every time they looked at me. So ... I came home less and less. And then I found myself turning down an offer to play for Wisconsin, two hours from home, and saying yes to the University of Maine instead.

The gap between my family and me continued to widen, and it was Mike who flew out to see me play. Mike who checked up on me weekly. My parents and I became blood-related strangers who exchanged awkward holiday and birthday phone calls none of us enjoyed. I'm not sure I'd recognize my sisters if they passed by me on the street.

So being reminded of my family, especially as Mike probably thinks of them in his time-capsule mind, is not what I need tonight.

Is my avoidance healthy? Not particularly. But it's how

I've managed to live through what feels like losing my parents or being lost by them.

We finish the game, which thankfully didn't have much time left. It's a good one for Mike since the Leafs pull out a win. He goes to bed happy and thankfully doesn't ask me tonight where Debbie is. I hate having to pretend his family is still together almost as much as I hate him asking about mine.

Once I hear his deep snores, I hop into bed and check my phone. I haven't so much as looked at it since I walked in the door. Not surprisingly, the Dream Team group chat has been popping. I hesitate, my thumbs hovering over the keyboard.

After my teammates pointed out how closed off I am, I've been looking for an opportunity to change that. Now seems as good a time as any, when I could actually use some advice.

Camden: Hey

Not the most illustrious or creative start, but it's something. And it's immediately met by an avalanche of responses.

Finally, I feel the tension start to leak from my body.

Van: Well well well look who learned how to text
Eli: CAMMIE! LET'S GO!
Felix: Hey, Cam. Everything okay? Because you're actually participating in the group chat.
Logan: Shh! Don't scare him off. Be cool.
Camden: Ha ha
Nathan: Hey
Nathan: Is that cool enough?
Alec: I was sleeping but you're texting so I got up.
Felix: Old man.

Alec: Guilty as charged. So, what's up, Cam?

Van: Are you having some kind of emergency

Eli: IS ANYTHING ON FIRE

Nathan: Why would your brain go straight there?

Alec: Please ignore them both.

Camden: More of an existential crisis.

Van: Is that different than a quarter life crisis

Logan: Shut up Van.

Felix: Respectfully, Van, shut up.

Logan: How can we help?

Wyatt: You guys make it very hard to sleep

I'm grateful Wyatt pops in because it distracts the guys long enough for me to type out perhaps the longest text I've ever written. When I hit send, there are a whole string of texts welcoming Wyatt, who doesn't say much in the group chat since he moved to Boston.

Camden: I have a few things to share. (And no need to insert a crack about me not sharing, Van.) First, the reason I've been rushing home lately is because my old billet dad is living with me. He has early onset dementia and long story short—his family didn't want to care for him. It's been good, but a challenge. Second, I think I want to try again with Naomi. If she'll have me.

Van: *faints in shock*

Eli: WOW. That's WOW DUDE.

Felix: Man. There's a lot to unpack. I'm sorry and also happy for you.

Logan: I'm sorry about your billet dad's condition. Is that the right word to use?

Camden: Thanks. That works, yeah.

Alec: How's your billet dad doing?

Camden: He's in good spirits. He isn't really aware of it, so he just kind of lives in a weird past/present hybrid.

Van: I'm sorry. That's rough

Eli: So rough you got Van to use punctuation

Van: It was a one time thing

Logan: Do you need anything? What can we do?

Camden: I've got a caretaker who stays with him when I'm at practice and home games but need to find another one for our road games. The first one bailed. I have interviews set up, so I've got my fingers crossed.

Van: Not to be rude but can we talk about your woman now

Eli: RUDE

Felix: Reminder: we're adults. Which means we can text using punctuation AND without using all caps. Except occasional all caps for emphasis, as demonstrated in the previous sentence.

Eli: DOUBLE RUDE

Van: Go to bed netminder

Logan: Guys, focus. Camden is talking to us about things.

Alec: Let us know if you need anything with your billet dad.

Nathan: I'd be happy to help.

Eli: SAME

Wyatt: What woman?

Eli: WYATT ENTERS THE GROUP CHAT

Felix: Eli, please stop with the all caps. I'm begging you.

Eli: OK

Van: Maybe if you stopped ignoring our texts you'd know, Oscar

Wyatt: Please don't call me that

Logan: Why? Because you're GROUCHY?

Wyatt: Do you really want me bringing up what the press has said about you in the past, L?

Logan: Touché. No one else call Wyatt Oscar, please.

Wyatt: ANYWAY

Wyatt: I read the texts even if I don't always respond

Wyatt: I don't remember anything about a woman.

Logan: I don't think she made it into the group chat yet.

Van: She was at the Summit the other day

Felix: Can confirm.

Camden: Her name is Naomi. We dated last summer in the off-season. It was supposed to be casual.

Eli: You didn't look at her with casual eyes

Van: WTF are casual eyes

Eli: I just mean Cammie looked at her like it was SERIOUS not casual

Logan: Which is what he just said, genius. Keywords: "supposed to be."

Van: Since no one else is saying it she punched Camden

Nathan: Wow. Guess I should have volunteered at the camp.

Felix: Ignore everyone, Cam. What do you need? Advice? Listening ears? Ideas on grand gestures?

Van: Perhaps witty remarks

Camden: I don't know what I need. Except your attempts at wit, Van. Don't need that.

Eli: Burn

Logan: Take note, Van.

Van: It takes intelligence to understand wit

Felix: GUYS, PLEASE.

Eli: i thought you said no more all caps

Wyatt: Is this the woman who has a kid you told me about?

Eli: Hey, no fair! You talked to Wyatt and not us?

Alec: Maybe because he's not obnoxious.

Wyatt: I may have moved but some people know how to still text me outside the group chat

I start to regret trying to say anything serious in the

group chat when it totally derails into a discussion filled with insults and arguments. It's a game night. Most of these guys probably left the rink and had a handful of beers. Maybe this was a stupid time to try to have a serious conversation.

A separate text pops up. Relieved, I close the group chat.

Logan: Hey, man. Sorry everyone is being so ... everyone. Happy to talk any time. I know a thing or two about second chances.
Camden: I might take you up on that tomorrow. Thanks, man.
Logan: Night.

I briefly consider texting Naomi, but when I open our text thread and see our final messages from just before the breakup, I can't make myself do it.

But when I hear one of Mike's loud snores through the wall, I make a determination that I will talk to her. In person, though, not text. I won't see her until after our next road series, but hopefully she'll come inside to watch Liam now that we've broken the ice. And if not, I'll go out to her car again.

CHAPTER 9

Naomi

THERE'S no reason to hide in my car at the next hockey practice, so I find myself following Liam inside, nervous energy zinging through me. It's been two weeks since the last class because the Appies had an away game last Saturday. Liam told me about it (because of course he did), but I'd already looked at their schedule. Even if I didn't admit that to him.

Why was I checking their schedule? Because I was trying to think of reasons why Camden didn't text or call. For two weeks.

I guess the number of games they played in since I last saw him is a good excuse. (Why are there so many hockey games?) But it's not like he wouldn't have a spare moment in that busy schedule for a simple text.

Not that he said he would. But after our talk on the walkway above the rink, I *thought* he would.

He didn't.

Which is ... fine.

I didn't text him either. Instead, I quietly obsessed. Looking at the Appies schedule and pretty much scouring their entire site. Checking his socials for the first time in months. No sign of a girlfriend, for the record. Only a few random hockey pictures with no captions, which made me a little too satisfied.

I thought about our conversation on the catwalk. And his scent. And the way it felt to have him sling me like a sack of Naomi over his shoulder. I thought about the moment a kiss hung in the air between us, both regretting and applauding my decision to not give in.

I also thought about him buying Liam gear, working with him one-on-one.

I thought about our breakup, what I said to him and then what Camden said afterward to me, all against the backdrop of our conversation at the Summit. I set them all out to examine like some tech genius might do with a dismantled computer. But I'm *not* a tech genius, so I couldn't make sense of things and put them back together. I've just got a messy table full of parts and pieces and no clue how things fit together.

Though I came close to messaging him, I wasn't going to be the first one to crack in what feels like a weird game of silent phone chicken.

Which means that now I'm walking into the Summit feeling all the nerves.

I'm immediately met with hockey parents, and I have a new reason to wish I'd stayed in the car. The hallway outside the rink is crowded with kids and hockey gear and moms who look a lot more put together than I feel.

Most are wearing activewear, like me, but the difference is that theirs are all brand name and clearly worn to look hot. By comparison, my compression pants are neither for activity nor for looks, just comfort, and there's a hole in the right calf. I also didn't realize makeup was required for watching my kid play hockey.

The other thing they all have that I don't? The know-how to put on hockey gear.

"I got it, Mom," Liam says, pushing my hands away.

"But all the other moms are helping their kids," I whisper through gritted teeth.

I don't add that the other parents also seem to know what they're doing with the tape and the weird fabric tubes I'm trying to help Liam secure in place on his legs.

Hockey socks, Liam called them. Which is dumb because they're not socks. More like leg warmers. Except they're made of a thin fabric that will provide no warmth.

Hockey stupid is more like it.

I feel like a massive imposter, clearly the only person who doesn't know what they're doing here. (Or why hockey socks are called hockey socks or hockey pants are actually padded shorts, not pants.) It's like a sign hanging above my head pointing out my hockey ineptitude. Or maybe they're judging me because, for the past two practices, they were all in here helping their kids while my son was totally alone.

"Camden showed me how to do it," Liam says, taking the roll of tape from my hands and wrapping it around the hockey sock. Doesn't look any different than what I was doing. "See?"

I don't, actually. But I nod. "Can I do *anything*?" I ask.

The mom directly to our right is adjusting her daughter's helmet. Granted, the little girl is younger than Liam and needs more help, but I don't feel like I'm doing enough.

When was the last time I felt so out of place? Probably back in middle school. The feeling is rusty yet familiar and wholly unpleasant.

"Just go sit down," Liam says. "I'm fine. Coach Cam and I usually work down at the visitor's end."

I nod like I know which side of the rink that is. "Okay. Well, um, break a leg."

Both the mom and daughter next to us whip their heads my way.

"Mom," Liam hisses.

"Sorry. Wrong activity. That's what you say with theater. Uh, have fun? Skate well? Don't punch anyone in the face? Or *do* punch them?" Liam looks like he's about to melt through the floor. I hold up both hands. "Okay, okay, I'm going."

We're both relieved when I make my way up into the stands. But now I'm faced with finding where Liam wanted me to sit. I thought all the parents were in the hallway, but there are already a lot of seats claimed in here. There seem to be two main groups of parents: hot moms who are here to be seen and men who look like former hockey players, with their beards, athletic builds, and leftover swagger.

Both sets seem to have one thing in common, from the snatches of conversations I catch, and that's a sense that their child *will* be going pro.

Then there's me—mom who didn't even want her kid to play hockey and wants to avoid attention of any kind. Hence the baseball cap, loose-fitting top, and pants with a hole. At the last minute, and after a pointed look from Liam, I traded my bedroom slippers for Birkenstocks with thick socks. By his sigh, this was only a mildly better choice.

"What? I need socks. It's winter," I told him as we pulled out of the driveway.

"So maybe wear closed-toe shoes," Liam said, suddenly sounding more adult than I felt.

Whatever, kid. I don't want to come across like I'm trying to get Camden's attention. Not when I have no idea what he's thinking.

I am here to watch my kid. Period. Full stop. If I can just fly under the radar and avoid attention—

"Naomi!" a familiar voice calls. "Liam and I usually work down here."

So much for that plan.

Camden stands on the other side of the glass, gesturing toward the far end of the rink. It's not easy to hear him with the big echoing space and the barrier, but I heard him loud and clear. So do a number of other parents, both male and female. I'm not imagining the stares now that an actual player just called me by name. *Awesome.*

Camden isn't fully geared up with all the pads Liam has on under the new Appies jersey Parker gave him last week when he hurt his arm. Other than a helmet and a long-sleeve athletic shirt with the Appies logo, Camden has on hockey pants (a.k.a. shorts) and hockey socks (a.k.a. *not* socks). He looks good on skates. His movements are lithe and smooth, natural in a way that makes me think he probably prefers being on skates to walking.

I've seen Camden shirtless on a beach, and that was a good look for him. But this is somehow better. *Much* better.

I force my gaze away, though I've already been staring too long as I make my way toward the far end of the rink with Camden slowly skating backward on the other side of the

120

glass. It's kind of adorable but also makes me something of a spectacle.

I'm now more confused than I was the last two weeks while wondering if he was going to reach out.

"Hey, Naomi!" Camden's teammate with the big smile and messy mop of blond hair zips by, waving a gloved hand. Eli, I think?

I would respond, but he's already gone, dropping orange cones and adjusting long black pads to differentiate areas on the ice. I have to pass by a woman already seated with her phone out. She glares, her spidery lash extensions giving her a more sinister look. I half expect for her to draw a line across her neck or maybe tackle me right here in the stands.

"Excuse me," I say in the politest voice I can muster. She shifts her legs slightly, but it's still a challenge to get by, and I almost faceplant. Based on her little smirk, this was probably her intention.

Women's solidarity is a very real thing. But so is the existence of mean girls at every stage of life.

"You okay?" Camden calls.

"Yep. All good."

Thankfully, no one is sitting down at this end of the ice, and when Camden stops, I plop into one of the seats right by the glass. Kids of all ages start spilling out onto the ice, going to various stations around the rink. I do a double take when I see Liam skating toward us.

He's not *good*, but before he started, I don't think he could stand up on a pair of skates. Now, with a choppy stride, he makes his way over to Camden, pausing to wave at me and almost wiping out in the process. His grin is huge, and I yank out my phone to snap a picture.

He shakes his head, smile disappearing, and if it weren't

for the plexiglass and the general din of dozens of kids now shouting and laughing, I bet I could hear him groaning, *Mom*.

Too bad, kid. A mom's gotta do what a mom's gotta do. In this case, what this mom's got to do is to record some pictures for posterity. Or frames on the wall, if I ever remember to print the photos I take on my phone.

I'm quickly able to forget my self-conscious feelings and the fact that anyone else is in the building. My sole focus is on Liam and Camden. They run through a series of drills focused on basic skating skills like stopping, making turns, and the proper skating stance. It has to be so boring for Camden, who has the equivalent of a double doctorate in all these things. But even without being able to hear their conversation, I can sense his patience with Liam.

Every few minutes, Camden smiles at Liam, gives his shoulder a squeeze, or taps his helmet for a job well done.

Each time, Liam looks so pleased with himself. Then he smiles up at me, checking to make sure I'm watching.

And each time, a tangle of feelings swells in my chest. Mama pride because of my amazing kid doing hard things. Listening. Learning. Falling and getting back up.

But also, my attraction to Camden is growing almost primal. Because I'm not just seeing a man I like for *me*; I'm seeing a man who is really great with my son. I saw glimpses of it this summer, which is one of the things that made me panic.

Being good with Liam doesn't necessarily mean Camden would be a great dad. Or even that he wants to be. But it means *something*. Something really big.

Despite not having a dad in the picture, Liam has always had Jake's steady presence. My dad has been involved, and though he's busy running his pirate-themed bar, he's never too busy for his grandson. More recently, Liam has had

Hunter and Benedict, who married Merritt and Sadie, respectively, and are around a lot. It's like getting two sudden bonus uncles.

But this is different. He's a man giving time to Liam not because he's family or family adjacent. Camden is doing this either because he cares about Liam or ... about me.

Maybe both?

Don't mind me over here, the emotional land mine of a human being, set to explode at the slightest provocation.

Which is why I jump when suddenly, two bodies are climbing into the chairs on either side of me, coming down from the row above.

"Holy Moses!" I grip the armrests.

Parker smiles at me. "Sorry if we scared you."

"It's okay." My heart is still wildly beating in my chest from being startled. I'm not sure if my reaction is so strong because I've been so focused on watching Liam that I pretty much forgot about my surroundings or because I feel suddenly caught because of the thoughts I was thinking about Camden.

"This is Greyson." Parker gestures to the woman on my right. "She just started working for us, handling merch."

Greyson has long blond curls, and her energy matches Parker's. If I put these two in the same room with Eloise, their combined positive energy would blow the roof off a building.

"You can call me Grey if you want, but I'll answer to either."

"Nice to meet you."

Parker leans forward to look at Greyson, pointing toward the rink. "That's Liam, working with Camden. He's Naomi's son."

"That's nice that Camden is giving him one-on-one help,"

Greyson says. "I didn't think he was even signed up to help with this."

"He wasn't," Parker says, shooting me a sly look.

"Really?" I glance back out, where Camden is showing Liam how to stop, sending a spray of ice in the air. Liam tries and falls down, but he gets right back up and tries again.

"Nope. Camden changed his mind when he saw Liam in the group," Parker says. "And I know this because I was helping the first week. Saw it with my own eyes. Some kids were picking on Liam—"

"What?!"

Parker shifts, putting a hand on my knee like she can sense I'm about to jump out of my seat and give some kids—and their parents—a few choice words.

"Camden handled it," Parker says gently. "I guess Liam didn't tell you that either?"

"No. He did not."

I work to steady my breathing. Liam is fine. Right now, he's doing some kind of exercise involving exaggerated steps from side to side. His face is a mask of pure concentration. Cam glances over at me, like he feels the force of my attention. At my expression, he frowns, but then focuses back on Liam, who's asking him a question.

"Sorry. I might have overreacted."

"Don't apologize—you're just worried about your son. He's in good hands here," Parker says. "We don't tolerate that kind of behavior. The one jerky kid was not invited to continue in the program." She looks smug about it.

"Really? What about the other?"

Parker nods toward the ice, where Liam is taking a water break by the benches. Another kid who looks a little older is talking to him. Both are smiling. Camden stands a little way off, watching.

"*That's* the other kid," Parker says. "I think Camden made quite the impression, and now he's been checking in on Liam."

"Aw," Greyson says. "That's really sweet."

"Yeah," I say, swallowing around a sudden massive lump in my throat as I watch Camden watching the boys. "It is."

"I think it's good for Camden, too. He's been down this year."

I know she's not making a pointed or passive aggressive comment, but guilt still squeezes around me.

"He's been especially distracted and distant the past few weeks. Logan mentioned it, and I was getting worried. Camden doesn't seem to realize this, but he has a quiet way of impacting the team. If he's off, they're off too."

Interesting. But I can see it. Last summer, I did the lion's share and a half of talking. Even when he isn't saying things, Camden has a presence about him, a quiet way of making an impact. I could definitely see that having an impact on a team.

Parker turns to me with a smile. "So, with you in the mix, things seem to be looking up."

"Oh, I don't know about that," I say, but Parker only smiles.

"Did you meet my brother yet?" Greyson asks, and I'm glad for the subject change. "The guys call him Van."

"I'm not sure. Maybe?"

"You'd probably remember," says Grey. "It's hard to miss his mouth. His figurative mouth. Not like he has a weird clown mouth or anything. He just says a lot of things that are ill-advised."

I laugh. "Okay, I think I did meet him last week. Was he with Camden while they were stitching up Liam?" I ask Parker.

"Yup," she says. "He's a founding member of the Dream Team."

I raise my eyebrows. "The Dream Team?"

"It was a nickname the core group of guys on the team got in the press. They really leaned into it. Now they have a group chat named after it and everything. They think I don't know they named it that, but sometimes Logan lets me peek. Only when it's not, like, private stuff," Parker adds quickly.

"Is Cam one of the Dream Team?" Somehow, I can't imagine him being part of a group chat.

Overall, this is a kind of culture shock, seeing Camden now in his more natural home environment after knowing only the vacation version of him: Vacation Camden. Not that he seems like two different people, but more like I'm seeing the person he is in different settings.

"Yep. He's not as into the group chat as the other guys," Parker says, which tracks. "Poor Dominik keeps hanging around, hoping for an invite. One of these days, he'll wear them down."

"Is Dominik out there?" I ask.

Parker points toward a guy at the far end, helping a mixed group of guys and a few girls. He has chiseled features, and I can just catch a glimpse of white-blond hair peeking out of his helmet.

"Is he still single?" Grey sounds hopeful.

Parker laughs. "Yes. But he's a little young for you. And do you think your brother would let him get anywhere near you?"

Greyson's look turns mischievous. "What Van doesn't know won't hurt him. Also considering my brother secretly married the coach's daughter, I'm not sure he gets to have an opinion on anything."

Now, there's an interesting tidbit. But I don't get to ask about it because they're still going.

"But Van will still give you his opinion," Parker says. "Just like my brother did about Logan. You have a brother, right, Naomi? I think I heard he's a lawyer?"

I have to wonder what else she's heard. "Yep. And he's stupidly overprotective."

Greyson extends her fist out in front of us. "Stupid brothers club?"

The three of us bump fists. "Stupid brothers club," I agree. But only because it's clear all three of us love our stupid, overprotective brothers.

I wonder what Jake is going to say about me reconnecting with Camden. Even if it's not anything to speak of, I think even having him involved with Liam is something Jake will have Strongly Worded Thoughts about.

I glance back out over the ice where Camden has Liam picking up speed and then balancing on one skate. He's coming our way, wobbling and weaving, his face tight with concentration. Camden skates next to him, clearly encouraging him through the exercise. Liam stops by smacking right into the glass near us. With a big smile, he waves. All three of us wave back. When Liam turns back around, he eats it again.

Parker winces. "He'll get it. Just takes a little while."

"Do either of you skate?" I ask.

"I do," Parker says, which somehow doesn't surprise me at all. "I did figure skating for years because my dad wouldn't let me play hockey."

"I don't skate. I wonder if Dominik would teach me?" Grey says with a sigh. "How young did you say he is?"

"I didn't. But he's nineteen, I think?"

"Hm," Grey says. "I'll round up. Because that only makes

us three years apart, but the idea of dating a teenager sounds really yucky."

"Probably. I can help set that up if you'd like," Parker offers. "Just don't tell Van I helped. I love playing matchmaker."

"You do, don't you?" I give her a look, thinking of the way she scooped up Liam for a Summit tour and left me alone with Camden last week.

She ignores the question. "Hey, want to go out with us this week? Grey and I are planning to have dinner with some of the ladies."

"She means the WAGs," Grey says. "Wives and girlfriends of the players."

Parker rolls her eyes. "Ugh. I hate that term. It's too close to *hags*. Also, it's defining women in terms of men, which I don't like."

"Don't get started with ALL," Greyson says. "None of us like it."

"ALL?" I ask.

"Appies Leading Ladies," Parker says. "I keep trying, but it just won't happen."

"Like fetch?" I ask, and Parker laughs.

"Exactly like fetch."

Grey looks between us. "Fetch like ... a dog?"

"Oh, you sweet, dear baby," Parker says.

"I'm barely younger than you," Grey points out.

"But the gap in your *Mean Girls* knowledge is like a whole chasm between us."

"*Mean Girls* the musical?" Grey asks.

Parker and I both groan, which makes me laugh. "Maybe we'll watch the best—a.k.a. the original—*Mean Girls* after our dinner," Parker says. "For educational purposes. You'll come, Naomi? Please?"

"I'll need to figure out what to do with Liam," I say. Technically, I can leave him alone at home. He's ten. But I haven't done so here yet. Somehow, it feels totally different doing so on Oakley Island. Not like Harvest Hollow is some hotbed of crime or anything. But still.

"I bet Camden would hang out with him," Parker suggests.

She's probably right, but the idea makes my stomach squirm. Not because I don't feel comfortable leaving Liam alone with Camden. Or, at least, not because I don't feel like Liam would be *safe*. More like ... Liam would get ideas. More ideas than the ones already sprouting in his head.

"Text me the details and I'll see if I can make it," I say.

As I watch Camden giving Liam tips on his stance, I'm already stockpiling a list of excuses. Hanging out with Parker and Greyson would be fun. They're easy to talk to, and I can see real friend potential. But I have a feeling hanging out with a bunch of women who are dating or married to hockey players may not be the best thing to help me *not* want to date a hockey player.

And that's what I want, right? To *not* want to date Camden?

Watching him patiently help Liam back to his feet has me questioning my reasons for trying to keep distance between us.

"I know!" Parker says, bouncing in her seat. "We'll come over and do a housewarming party. Everyone can bring something. That way you don't need a babysitter."

"Ooh! That sounds fun," Greyson says. "I love shopping for house stuff! What's your style? What do you need?"

"Um, I don't actually—"

"Just let us know which night is best for you," Parker says, and there is no room for argument in her tone. She and

Greyson stare expectantly at me while on the ice, Liam is throwing his arms around Camden, celebrating some success I missed while trying to come up with a reason I'm busy every night next week or why I'm trying to avoid hanging out with potential new friends.

Camden looks up, and his eyes lock with mine over Liam's head. A tremor moves through me as his gaze sears right to my heart. Liam turns with as big a smile as I've ever seen, Camden's arm still casually draped over my son's shoulders.

I can practically feel the breeze stirring my hair as I wave my white flag. "Tuesday night," I say meekly. "That will work."

"Perfect. Their next game is Monday, so we'll have Tuesday night off," Parker says. "Ooh—do you want to come to the game? I can get you tickets."

"I ... no. Maybe next time." Liam would love it, but I need to have some safe, non-hockey space in my life. Especially since I still don't know what the deal is with Camden, and now this dinner has been foisted upon me. At this point, trying to say no to Parker seems like an exercise in futility.

"I'll text you," Parker says.

"Add her to the group chat," Greyson says.

"I don't have to be an official WAG to get in the group chat?" I ask dryly.

"Eh. It's not a WAG chat." Parker gives me a quick grin, which might be characterized as evil. "And anyway, I don't think you'll be *unofficial* for long. See ya!"

I'm about to argue or maybe demand she tell me why she thinks that when Parker and Greyson dart away. The kids are clearing the ice with Liam somewhere in the crowd of kids in helmets and skates. I scan to find him but get distracted when I see Camden standing on the other side of the glass in front of me. He waves me toward a different exit area of the rink. I don't understand why until I get closer. There's no plexiglass between us now, and I'm able to lean over a railing and talk to him.

"Everything okay?" I ask.

"Liam's fine," he says, clearly reading that my son is my primary concern.

Then he puts his hand over mine on the railing. I go completely still—a rabbit caught in a very tempting snare.

His hand is warm, his fingers curling around my hand in a way that's both comforting and possessive. "I was hoping to talk to you."

"Oh, okay." I sound as breathy as a teenager getting her first phone call from a boy. Then I remember how I stared at my phone for two weeks, watching it *not* light up. "You still have my number. There was plenty of time to talk to me over the last two weeks."

"I was thinking," he says.

I wait.

He swallows, suddenly looking nervous. "Thinking about *you*."

"I also was thinking." I don't clarify that I was thinking about him. Or that in addition to thinking, I was hoping. And … disappointing—which, in this case, is a verb.

"I would really like to have a conversation in person."

My lips twitch. "Like the one we're having now?" I'm not sure why I can't just be easy, but I'm relieved when Camden chuckles.

"Preferably one where we're across a dinner table. Alone."

"Like … a date?"

He nods, and his face is so earnest that I want to climb over this railing and give him a hug. "Yes. Would you like to go on a date with me, Naomi?"

"For the purpose of talking?" I ask.

"At *least* talking."

His eyes flare with a sudden heat that makes my knees feel wobbly. When his thumb grazes the back of my hand, a whisper of a touch, I have to lean more of my weight on the railing to stay upright.

"Okay. Yes."

"I have a game tomorrow and another Monday night. Tuesday I have plans."

"So do I," I tell him, wanting to stay as vague as he is about what those plans are.

"What about a Wednesday lunch?"

"I think that's fine. I can check my calendar and text you. Assuming your phone still works."

"May I text you?"

I raise an eyebrow. "You already bought my kid a whole set of new hockey gear without asking. Which I'm going to pay you back for, by the way. Now you're asking permission to text me?"

"No," Camden says firmly, giving my hand a squeeze. "You're not going to pay me back. Or stop me from doing anything I can for you and Liam. Also, asking to text is more of a formality. I'm *going* to call or text you."

"Is that so?"

He drops my hand, making me immediately ravenous for more of his touch. Producing his phone from somewhere, Camden taps the screen a few times. I feel mine buzz in the pocket on my thigh and slip it out to see he's texted me one word: *Hi.*

When I look up, I'm grinning, but he's frowning down at his phone. "I need to get home." Worry practically radiates off of him, a stark change from his earnest intensity from seconds ago.

132

"Everything okay?" I ask.

He looks like there's something he wants to say, but he only shakes his head. "I'll be in touch."

And then he disappears down the hallway, leaving me torn between being excited about our date and wondering what kind of emergency would make a man who, as far as I know, lives alone, have to rush home.

CHAPTER 10

THE DREAM TEAM

Wyatt: I'm bored

Wyatt: Spill the tea or whatever it is the kids are saying these days

Logan: You must not spend time with any kids because they are definitely not saying that.

Felix: Hey, Wyatt. Hope you're doing well and not freezing your butt or any other important parts off.

Wyatt: So far so good

Wyatt: But it's COLD

Van: Hey Oscar. I keep forgetting ur on this thread

Eli: WYATTTTTTTT!

Eli: Nice hatty the other night.

Wyatt: Thanks. It felt good.

Van: No fair

Van: You didn't score any hat tricks with us

Wyatt: You're doing just fine. Maybe one day you'll grow up and score one yourself, Vanity

Logan: Sound the alarm! We've got a spicy Wyatt tonight.

Camden: Wyatt's spicy? I thought he was just grumpy.

Eli: Why not both?

Nathan: It's late

Van: Ignoring Nathan and speaking of tea, Cole has a girlllllfriend

Felix: Congrats, Cam.

Eli: LETS GOOOOO CAMMIE

Van: Why does no one tell me anything

Dominik: Probably because you tell everyone everything

Eli: Nikki's got a point

Logan: According to my sources, it's not official. Yet.

Eli: Your sources = Parker

Logan: Duh. She could be wrong though and I'd love to be the first to tell her something for once.

Camden: Logan's "source" is correct

Wyatt: So … no girlfriend?

Felix: Is everything okay?

Camden: It's fine. I have a plan.

Van: Reminder—kidnapping is illegal

Alec: Who's kidnapping whom?

Camden: No kidnapping

Alec: Then what are we talking about?

Felix: You know you can scroll back through the chat, right?

Alec: You guys talk too much. It's faster to just ask.

Van: Camden can't lock it down

Felix: I would love to exist in a world where we aren't talking about kidnapping or locking down women.

Logan: Come on, man. You know we respect women.

Felix: Still.

Wyatt: Whatever enlightened term we're going to use, do your plans end with you and Naomi in a relationship?

Camden: That's the goal

Van: Dude. You'd be A DAD.

Eli: Liam's cool

Van: I'm going to start calling you Daddy

Felix: NO ONE IS GOING TO BE CALLED DADDY ON THIS THREAD.

Eli: Whoa

Eli: You got Felix using all caps

Eli: That means he's serious

Camden: I like Liam. I'm not saying I know what I'm doing, but I'm open to it.

Alec: Let me know if you need any tips.

Logan: Hanging out with Juno for a few months makes you the expert now?

Van: Don't forget he's practically raising the twins

Nathan: Truth

Camden: I'll be sure to let you know if I need any tips on babies or barely adults, captain.

Wyatt: Well this has been fun

Van: Is this your way of saying goodbye, Oscar?

Wyatt: Just because I'm far away doesn't mean I don't still know where you live, Van

Van: Oooh a threat

Wyatt: Or who your wife's dad is—come to think of it, Coach said to let him know if I need anything

Eli: LOL

Logan: *grabs popcorn*

Van: I take back all the times I called you Oscar, Wyatt.

Van: Ur not a grouch

Van: Ur REALLY nice

Felix: Selling it a little hard there, Van.

Camden: Heading to bed

Logan: Keep us posted!

Van: And just remember—when in doubt kidnapping might be illegal but it's also effective

Camden: And on that note … GOODNIGHT

CHAPTER 11

Naomi

I WASN'T wrong in my assessment about the futility of resisting Parker. Which is why a few days later, I'm dashing into a barbecue restaurant she recommended, picking up dinner for Liam and a whole smorgasbord of appetizers in preparation for a ladies' night at my house.

Not just any ladies' night, but one with hockey WAGs. According to the informative texts Parker has sent me, this specifically includes a fiancé (Parker), three wives (Amelia, Bailey, and Gracie), a girlfriend (Evie), and a sister (Greyson). Oh, and Evie's bringing a baby, who is not a hockey progeny but apparently has all but been adopted by the recently retired team captain.

Not unlike how all of these ladies seem overeager to adopt *me*. It's messing with my head a little bit. Do they want to include me for me? Or is it because they're hoping

137

Camden and I get back together? And though that seems to be our trajectory, I'm still just as scared as I was when I broke up with him.

The difference now is that I know how much it sucks to be without him.

And with his daily texts—checking in, asking how Liam and I are doing, adding some light flirtations—I'm trying to keep my expectations in check. *Trying* is the operative word.

Failing would be a more apt one.

The teenager at the to-go counter sets my bag of food on the counter with a big smile and a toss of her ponytail. "Here you go!" She is in way too good of a mood for my nervous energy. The only thing shinier than her attitude is her braces. "Order for Fieldstone, all set and ready. Looks like the start of a barbecue-tastic night!"

"Um, yes," I mutter. "Something like that."

I'm handing over my card and trying not to wince at the total when my whole body freezes. Because I happen to spot a familiar head of brown hair across the restaurant. It's like wherever Camden is, my body homes right in on his exact location.

And his exact location happens to be in this very restaurant, just a few short tables away from the to-go counter.

He is not alone.

A pretty blond woman sits across the table from him, smiling widely and fluttering her lashes hard enough to cause gale-force winds. *I have plans Tuesday night,* he'd said. Not once did I consider "plans" to mean what looks to be an intimate dinner.

A riot of emotion careens through me.

Jealousy. Rage. Hurt. Insecurity. Panic. Betrayal. Regret.

All set to impossibly high levels, despite the fact that Cam and I have no official status warranting it. I don't deserve these reactions. I have no right to them—I gave up my rights when I broke up with Camden. But my emotions do not seem to give any credence to logic.

Maybe it's not a date. I'm an adult and shouldn't jump to conclusions just because, from where I stand, it *looks* like a date.

If you break up with a man, you aren't allowed to have these kinds of feelings when he has dinner with a pretty woman, I scold myself.

But a very persistent little voice in my head reminds me of the way Camden looked at me just days ago on the catwalk and the almost-kiss I'm sure I left hanging in the air between us.

I think of the way I've woken up every day since to find an early morning text from him that's been better at perking me up than a pot of coffee.

I think of him patiently helping Liam and the way his eyes met mine over my son's head. The way Camden's hand covered mine on the railing at the Summit after Liam's practice, and the way that touch sent sparks cartwheeling through me.

Not to mention all the wayward thoughts I haven't fully been able to remove from my brain since ... well, summer. These thoughts have taken up residence despite my eviction notice, moving all their boxes and furniture in like a bunch of no-good squatters.

And this is a big problem since Camden really does appear to be on a date.

I jump when the server's cheerful voice yanks my attention away from Camden. "If you'll just turn your attention to the screen, answer a few questions, and add your signature, we'll be all set."

Her cheery mood sets my teeth on edge, and I jab my fingers at the iPad screen while keeping an eye on the table across the room. The woman just reached across the table toward Camden, and I think I might scream.

"Whoa!" the server exclaims. "Thank you! This awesome tip is deserving of a little more cowbell!"

"What now?" I once more jerk my attention away from Camden and his date, wondering what she means by *this awesome tip* as well as *a little more cowbell*. I certainly didn't mean to leave a large tip, and so far, there has been no sight nor sound of cowbell, which is how it should be.

According to my receipt, I tipped fifty percent. My bank account is weeping. I can only hope *cowbell* is some kind of metaphor.

Unfortunately, it is not.

The teenager retrieves an actual cowbell from underneath the counter and starts clanging with wild abandon. She adds a *yeehaw* for emphasis.

I want to grab her wrist to stop her, but would that be considered assault? My brother Jake would probably tell me yes, legally it could be construed as assault. Since I've already punched one person this month, I should really find better ways to manage things.

"Less cowbell," I hiss, as other servers around the restaurant start whooping and clapping. "Please, I beg of you—*less cowbell!*"

The server rings it harder, as though the survival of the human race is dependent on the enthusiasm with which she cowbells.

Why couldn't I have gone to a normal restaurant? But no —I listened to Parker's recommendation, choosing one where accidentally enormous tips are rewarded with the ringing of a cowbell. And coincidentally the exact restaurant where Camden happens to be on what looks like a date.

Camden is now, of course, looking my way with a very

intense expression on his face as we lock eyes. The cowbell is now more of an alarm bell.

Run, Naomi! it seems to say. *Run now!*

It's far too late now that Camden has seen me, but I still snatch the cowbell out of the server's hand, tossing it out the open door as another group of people enters the restaurant.

Thankfully, the cowbell sails over their heads and out into the parking lot. A car alarm blares.

What's next—will my hair spontaneously combust? Is a cartoon anvil going to fall on my head?

"Hey—my cowbell!" the server protests.

"My Lexus," a woman by the door says, glaring.

And for me—without a word, I snatch my bag off the counter and take off.

Not toward the closest door, since that's blocked by a woman whose Lexus I allegedly just nailed with a projectile cowbell, and not toward Camden, who is now standing up, but toward the hallway next to the kitchen. Common sense tells me this will lead to the bathrooms and another exit.

Possibly the alarmed kind of exit, but at this point, if I could, I would run straight through the wall and leave a Naomi-shaped hole in my wake. *Anything* to get out of what is quickly turning into one of the most embarrassing moments of my entire life.

What's a little emergency exit alarm, all things considered?

Thankfully, at the end of the dimly lit hallway is a door with a red exit sign above it. I've almost reached it when an arm curls around my shoulders, pulling me to a halt.

"Naomi, wait."

I do. Partly because Camden's strong arm is banded around my collarbone, making it really hard to keep moving.

141

But also because his voice has more of an effect on me than I care to admit.

I wait for him to loosen his hold, but he doesn't. I don't fight, instead slumping against him in defeat. My back lines up with his chest, and I can feel him breathing heavily.

"What is it, Camden? I need to go."

"Out the emergency exit?"

"I already made a scene. Might as well finish strong."

He sighs, and as he does, his chin drops until it rests on the top of my head. I squeeze my eyes closed.

"Why are you running away from me?" he asks.

"I was running from the cowbell."

"No, you weren't."

"Are you some expert in my motivations now?"

He dips his head, and now his voice is a low growl in my ear. "No, but I intend to learn them—along with everything that makes you tick. I'm still not sure what *really* made you shut things down between us last summer, and I'm scared you'll cut and run again before we can talk things through." He pauses. "Before you give me a chance to win you back."

I blink back tears, grateful that Camden can't see my face. The brush of his lips against my ear and the low timbre of his rumbling whisper combined with the words he said—words that have me trembling from the top of my head to my toes— hit me like a sucker punch.

He wants me back.

My relief is almost as palpable as the same fear that made me escape down this hallway in the first place. Our lunch date tomorrow has been hovering at the very front of my thoughts like a shimmery mirage. I've been hopeful about how it will go, but even Camden's most flirtatious texts have not been firm proof of anything.

I'm still not sure if considering this will be good for Liam, but I shove those thoughts away for now. If Camden wants to start over, to try a relationship not founded on words like *casual* and *temporary*, I will give serious thought to what this means for my son. First things first.

"But you're on a date?" I whisper, hating that I feel so unsure but also hating the mental image I have of the pretty woman across the table from him.

"It's not a date. There's a longer and more complicated story, but this was a job interview."

So much to unpack in that sentence, but I land on one word. *"Was?"*

"She did not get the job. Mostly because I think she wanted this to be a date, not a job interview. And the only person I want to go on a date with is you, Naomi."

For a very long moment, we stand in this dim hallway, me relaxing into his strong embrace, his breath soft on my neck. I can't feel his heartbeat, but I have to wonder if it's going at the same impossibly fast rate as mine. I'm both limp with relief and coiled tight with anticipation.

I forget to even clarify what kind of job that woman was applying for.

"Say something," he begs. "Do you want me to let you walk out of this door? Do you still want to go on our date tomorrow and talk things through?"

"No," I say, slumping against him until he has to wrap his other arm around my waist to keep me upright. "I don't want to walk away from you."

My thoughts and emotions are like a swollen creek overrunning the banks in a wild torrent. I'm drowning, getting sucked under only to pop up again and again, trying to find air.

So I go with my gut, with what makes me feel safest.

"But I'm scared," I say, and I try to pull away from his embrace.

At first, Camden seems like he's going to let me. The arm around my shoulders drops, and he sighs heavily.

But then his hand grips my hip as he spins me so fast I almost drop the bag of food I forgot I was even holding. I drop it willingly when my eyes land on Camden's face, because I need both hands to grab the loose material of his button-down shirt. Holding onto him seems suddenly imperative.

"Don't do it again," Camden says, and his voice takes on a gravelly rasp that hurts when I hear it. "Don't run from me."

"You're the one who left," I tell him, which isn't fair but also happens to be factually true. "You ran too."

"You told me to go," Cam says, and his free hand cups my cheek. His gaze burns into mine. "And I started to think maybe you were smart to send me away. To stop things before they went too far. We both said casual, but it very quickly was not that for me."

"It wasn't for me either," I admit. "But I don't know how to do more. I never have. And with Liam to consider—"

I have to stop. Because I don't know how to finish that sentence.

"We need to talk about Liam. We probably need to talk about a lot of things. But I need to know what you want first."

"I'm scared of what I want." Swallowing, I force myself to keep going. It's hard to do when I keep remembering the devastation I felt after Camden left. "I never want to feel again the way I felt after you left. Even if I was the one to send you away."

"I should never have let you go," Camden says, and his thumb brushes over the apple of my cheek with a tenderness that makes my breath shudder. "I should have fought for you. I was scared, too. I still am."

This big, solid man doesn't seem like he'd be afraid of anything. It feels strangely empowering to know that he's scared of this too. Maybe two scared people together can be brave enough.

"I shouldn't have given up on you and Liam," Camden says. "I should have driven back the way I wanted to. I've thought about this over and over—I even considered leaving mid-season and returning to Oakley. I just ..." His face falls, and his thumb stills on my cheek. "I believed you when you said you wanted me to go."

He looks like there's more he wants to say, but then he presses his lips together, his gaze sweeping over my face.

This is by far the worst and most painful conversation I've ever had. A big part of me still wants to choose avoidance and just run. Another part of me wants to let go of Camden's shirt, which I'm still clutching in both fists, and wrap my arms around him, pulling him close while telling him how sorry I am.

I've been miserable for so many months, convinced that our breakup must not have mattered to him the way it did me. I didn't ever consider that he might be harboring the same fears and the same hurt. Not when he said the breakup was the right choice.

I rejected him only to be rejected right back.

My tears started as soon as our phone call ended, but they didn't really hit their peak until I'd run across the road—almost getting mowed down by tourists driving a golf cart—and onto the beach where I sprinted straight into the ocean in my clothes. The wet, salty slap of waves mixed with my tears. The ocean's roar drowned out my sobs.

I'd never known heartbreak until that moment. Sad songs

always felt a little melodramatic to me. The dark moments in romantic movies always had me rolling my eyes.

Even when my brother was miserable after Eloise left for grad school, I thought he was being a little over the top. Even if Eloise is amazing and totally worth him winning her back.

Finally, standing in waist-deep water and being knocked around, I understood what it felt like to have your chest cracked open and to have all the good things spill out, lost and ruined.

The echo of those feelings now rise in a painful wave. Liam wasn't the main—or at least—the only reason I broke up with Camden.

It was self-preservation, pure and simple. The fear of exactly what happened: I fell in love, and I got really hurt. Even if it was set in motion by my own hand.

"I guess we both weren't quite honest. With each other or with ourselves?"

"That's a good assessment," Camden says. Then he chuckles softly. "I didn't plan to have any part of this conversation in a hallway beside the bathrooms."

His lips curve up in the smallest smile. "Look, you obviously have somewhere to be, and I need to politely tell whatever-her-name-is that she's not getting the job. Or my number."

"Want me to tell her?" I offer.

"I don't think that would be a good idea," Camden says. "Please know this: I don't want to do the lack of communication or miscommunication thing with you anymore. I'm not good at this relationship ... stuff. I don't know what I'm doing or how to do it or even what you want. But we *will* talk about this tomorrow—about *us*. About a future. You. Me. Liam. Some complications in my own life."

146

I suck in a breath, and this draws his gaze to my lips. Almost immediately, he jerks back up to my eyes.

"Are you agreeable to this?"

"That sounds very formal, sir."

Camden narrows his eyes. "Answer the question, Naomi."

"Yes. I agree to your proposal." I realize what I've said when his eyes crinkle with laughter. "Not that kind of proposal! I was just trying to match your weird formal language. Shut up."

He's laughing now, but as I try to wiggle away, he stops. His gaze darkens, and he places both palms flat against the wall on either side of my head. A shiver of delight rolls through me as he leans close.

It feels like we've gone from arguing to digging out emotional turmoil to now ... something very deliciously different.

Camden's eyes narrow as he studies me.

"You look like you need convincing."

"Do I?" I say breathlessly.

"You look like you still have half a mind to run."

"I'm good at running."

"Then I promise to be better at chasing. For now, I'll give you some food for thought."

I don't know what I was expecting—I guess *words*.

Not Camden's mouth to descend on mine: hot, eager, and very, *very* convincing.

Though I've replayed Cam's kisses in moments of weakness more times than I want to admit over the past seven months, experiencing the real thing again almost knocks me off my feet. Mostly because I am no longer aware of my feet. Camden's mouth demands my full attention.

I can barely keep up as his lips move against mine, and he seems to sense my overwhelm, quickly shifting gears and slowing to a pace that's almost excruciating. His hands leave the wall and cup my cheeks, his palms a deliciously rough contrast to the gentleness.

That's the thing with Camden: he is a study in contrast.

So strong yet so gentle.

A quiet man of few words, but when he decides to talk, he has so much to say.

His kisses are demanding, and yet it feels like he is giving me everything.

A sound escapes me, something shamefully revealing, and I can't even bring myself to care. Especially not when Camden chuckles against my mouth, trailing kisses along my jaw until he reaches my ear. His teeth give my earlobe the lightest tug before he whispers, "I've missed your mouth."

I've missed your everything.

I'm glad I don't have enough breath to say the words. If I thought the sound I just made was embarrassing, it would be nothing compared to confessing how I feel.

But it's true.

Kissing Camden is only a confirmation of how much I've missed him. How much better I feel with him. Maybe it's wrong to feel more whole around another person—but that's how I feel. Whole.

I've been on my own for so long. I mean, I've had my family around, and I've had Liam. But I've been functionally and enthusiastically independent for years now, in a way I had to be as a young, single parent.

So, it doesn't seem like a dangerous codependence to admit that Camden makes me feel more *me*. I've conquered independence. And now, maybe it's time to stop making it the goal.

"Naomi?"

"Hm?" My eyes open slowly, like I've just woken from the most luxurious sleep.

Leaving a too-quick kiss on the tip of my nose, Camden steps away and bends down to grab the takeout I'd forgotten all about. "Your food is probably getting cold."

He holds it out, and I want to shove him because after that kiss he wants to talk to me about takeout?

But I do need to go. Parker and everyone else might already be at my house. I don't want to show up late and looking totally kiss-drunk.

"You better call me," I warn, taking the bag of food.

The grin Camden gives me is absolutely gorgeous. "Promise," he says.

And before he can tell me not to, I push right through the emergency exit. The alarm is so loud that I'm almost to my car by the time I hear my phone ringing. Glancing down at the screen while balancing the takeout bag and my keys, I grin.

It's Camden calling.

I can hear the echo of the alarm through the phone as I answer. "Ye-e-e-s-s-s?" I stretch the word into one long syllable, grinning all the while.

"Naomi."

Hearing my name from him, even through the phone line, makes my stomach do a dramatic swan dive. "This is she."

He chuckles. "It's Camden."

"I know."

He clears his throat, and when he speaks again, he sounds adorably nervous. "I wanted to remind you that I need the address for your office so I can pick you up."

"I'll text you." I suddenly remember the nagging questions that have taken a backseat with all of the other big things we've addressed. "By the way, what kind of job interviews are you conducting?"

"Can we talk about it tomorrow?"

"You don't have a Jane Eyre in the attic, do you?"

"From what I remember of Jane Eyre, it was a *Bertha* in the attic. And no—I don't have a wife, girlfriend, or anyone else hidden in my attic."

I'm oddly pleased he knows enough about *Jane Eyre* to correct me. More pleased that he says no.

"I promise, it has nothing to do with any kind of romantic entanglement."

"Okay."

"Naomi?"

I love the way he keeps saying my name. It's as though he takes a little joy in it each time. "Camden."

"I can't wait."

CHAPTER 12

Naomi

"Mom, chill," my son tells me twenty minutes later, his words infused with all the wisdom of his ten years. "It's just a hangout, right? Like you have with Aunt Eloise and Aunt Merritt and Aunt Sadie."

Oh, sweet, innocent Liam. To think that entertaining hockey-related women ranging from never-met to barely-know is anything like having the Markham sisters over.

Not to mention the way my entire nervous system is still trying to reboot after Camden's kisses. I honestly expected Liam to take one look at me and know.

"You're right," I tell him. "I'll try to chill. Careful with the knife."

He's cutting a pan of my s'mores brownies, the only food I really excel at making, and doing a much better job than I would right now. My hands are too shaky. Because despite telling Liam I'll try, zero chill exists in my body right now.

Liam rolls his eyes, then cuts with a much more exaggerated slowness. "It's a butter knife, Mom."

I swear, he's sounding more and more like an almost teenager every day. Still sweet. Goofy. Fun. And, thankfully, a big fan of his mom, but I'm starting to see glimpses of what's ahead. I am ... not enthused.

"Ow!" Liam exclaims, pulling back his hand. I almost leap across the kitchen to grab his hand, so certain I'll see blood that sweat prickles at my hairline and my stomach dips.

Instead, I get a smirky little grin as he wiggles perfectly unmarred fingers. "Kidding. I know how to use a butter knife without cutting myself."

"Too soon, Liam. Too soon."

I tap the skin near his stitched-up arm. It's healing nicely, but it's still nasty, and makes my stomach lurch when I look at it for too long.

"Sorry," he says. His face tells me that he is absolutely not sorry.

"You're pushing your luck, kid."

"I thought you didn't believe in luck, *adult*."

I groan. "Can you just ... maybe not throw my words back at me?"

"What is it Grandpa Ned always says—don't dish it out if you can't take it?"

"That's it!" I grab Liam, and before he can wiggle away, I wrap my arms around him. I swear, he gets a little taller every week. "You're getting a hug."

"Ew. No hugging." He half-heartedly tries to fight me off, but I smile because I can tell he doesn't mean it.

When I release him, he tilts up the pan of brownies for my inspection. "I'm all done."

At least one thing tonight will be excellent. My recipe is foolproof and famous—Oakley Island famous, that is—and Liam has cut them into perfectly even squares. I couldn't have done this well with a ruler.

"Now can I go eat and watch YouTube?"

He says this with all the exhaustion of a boy who's been forced into child labor down in a mine when the only two tasks asked of him were to cut these brownies and to make sure there wasn't pee on his toilet seat. And since I don't trust a ten-year-old boy to have my standards of cleanliness, I even went in after him with cleaning spray.

"Just put the brownies on here and then you can go."

Liam frowns down at the plate I shoved his way. "Did you buy new dishes?"

"No. Fine. Yes. Just a few."

"Do ..." Liam trails off. He's staring at me like I'm an alien. "Do adults get nervous about making friends, too?"

I don't laugh at his question, but only because he's being completely sincere. Apparently one more rite of passage Liam's going through is realizing that adults are people too.

"Yes," I say simply. "Adults tend to feel a whole lot of the same feelings and have the same worries as kids. Only now we get to have *more* worries and bigger ones added to the mix. On the plus side, we've got better coping mechanisms than kids do, and we've got experience, so we know that we'll probably make it through just fine."

I lost him, probably somewhere in the first sentence. But I tried.

With a sigh, I tap the plate. "Brownies here. Then you can go watch YouTube and eat."

Despite his meticulous cutting, Liam carelessly dumps the pan on the plate, snagging a brownie and his to-go container of ribs before darting down the hall. Though I don't usually allow Liam to have the iPad or food in his room —especially the kind of food that requires wet wipes after eating—the ladies will be here any minute and I need some time alone.

It was hard enough walking through the front door and facing Liam, trying not to look like I just made out with Camden in a hallway outside a restaurant bathroom. Not that the location of the kiss matters. I would have struggled with my facial expression if I kissed Camden on a mountaintop or next to a flowing stream or even at the Summit up on the catwalk.

The important part isn't where. It's what. And *who*.

And what next?

The last question is the one that made my voice modulate weirdly when I said hello walking back inside the house. Liam didn't seem to notice, thankfully, but I need to make sure I've got it together before Parker and company arrive.

I was already freaking out about having them over. Because, as I told Liam, it *isn't* easy making friends as an adult. Especially when you're an adult who comes with a ready-made sidekick who happens to be your kid.

At the time Liam was born, all my high school friends were either in college or working while doing the kinds of things nineteen-year-olds do. Partying. Going out. Not worrying about how to care for an infant or how many jobs it takes to afford rent.

This led to a very long, very friendless drought before Eloise crashed into my brother's life and, by extension, mine. Her sisters followed her to Oakley not long after, so it was like I got a ready-made friend group of sorts. Happy birthday to me!

But the women coming over tonight are hockey WAGs, even if Parker doesn't like that term. Wives and girlfriends and fiancés and one sister of the players. Leaving me on the outside as an ex, though as Parker projected, maybe not for long.

I catch myself smiling again, but it's hard not to when I remember the kiss. Or Camden's words. Last summer, we talked very little about our future plans, so his directness today was surprising. But I like it. Feels very adult in a way none of my relationships have been.

I never would have wanted them to be. Though I may never admit this to him, my brother is right about me picking losers.

Until now.

A watch somewhere in the house beeps, telling me I'm almost out of time. I should pop back into my bedroom and freshen up. Or at least consider taking my hair out of its loose braid. Maybe add a coat of mascara. But Parker promised me this would be casual, and I want to take her at her word.

But is casual for a WAG something a little nicer than jeans with holes at the knees?

The doorbell rings, and I rush around, lighting a candle and moving every plate of food at least half an inch on the dining room table. Though I have a tendency toward chaos and disorder, my house is still neat right now. Partly because I did a great purge before leaving Oakley and brought very little. And partly because I haven't done much to make the house feel lived in. Yet.

I ignore the bare walls and rugless hardwoods as I scurry to the front door and throw it open before I can second, third, or fourth guess this evening.

I've hardly opened the door when a small group led by Parker barrel inside with hugs and greetings and plates of food. And gifts. I forgot that Parker suggested a housewarming kind of affair. I definitely would have vetoed it if she mentioned it again.

"Let me do introductions!" Parker says, raising her voice and clapping her hands.

We're all standing around the dining table, whose chairs have been pulled back, allowing access to the table crowded with food. The s'mores brownies, buffalo dip, and various appetizers from the barbecue place have now been joined by cookies, chips and salsa, plus more dips and snacks than we could eat in a week, a few bottles of wine, and some fancy cans of seltzer water.

"You already know Greyson," Parker says. Grey, with a mouth full of brownie already, waves.

"These are amazing," she says, chocolate on her front teeth.

"I cut them!" Liam calls from somewhere much closer than his room.

I sigh. "Might as well come out and do introductions, kid. Since you're eavesdropping."

"I ain't dropping no eaves," Liam says in a terrible British accent as he walks cautiously into the dining room.

"That's from *Lord of the Rings!*" one of the women says excitedly. Her hair is a few shades darker brown than mine and a lot longer, though she has it pulled back in a loose braid like me.

Liam grins. "It's my favorite book and my favorite movie. Well, favorite set of trilogies, if we're being technical."

Personally, I've only watched the movies because Liam made me. While I can recognize their greatness—especially any parts including Aragorn—I fell asleep in all three.

It's not my fault they're so long!

"Mine too," she says, smiling as she looks between Liam and me. "I'm Bailey."

Parker finishes the rest of the introductions, with Liam staying just long enough to make me proud by looking everyone in the eyes as he shakes their hands. Then, he grabs a plate with more goodies and disappears once again to his room.

"He's a good kid," Parker says. "Which means you're doing a good job, mama."

"He is a good kid, but oh man—the mistakes I've made. Am *still* making," I add, thinking about Camden and hoping that this time, I'm not about to make another one.

Turns out, I didn't need to be worried about feeling out of place with this group. Though every woman in this room is gorgeous, they're all unique and no one is snotty. Each woman has a different style, a different personality, and a different take on makeup from full face to fresh faced.

In short, it's the kind of group where the women seem comfortable in their own skins without any of the competitive edge that sometimes comes standard with female friendships. What's more, they genuinely seem to *like* each other.

And they brought housewarming gifts! Nothing over-the-top expensive, but thoughtful and fun gifts. A set of really fun coffee mugs, a print of Harvest Hollow in fall that honestly got me pumped for actually experiencing that season for the first time, two bright turquoise throw pillows that warm up the beige couch that came with the house, and the softest blanket ever that will be perfect for cozying up while bingeing Netflix.

I had to actively work to hide how choked up I was when I thanked them, and they all acted like it was no big deal. Which made it an even bigger deal to me.

Parker, despite not being the oldest of the bunch, definitely steers the ship, but without being bossy or overbearing. Well, not *too* bossy. Her brand of bossy is more like adorably strong persuasion. She naturally exudes the kind of influence people naturally sway toward following.

And if they don't ... she finds a way to make them want to anyway.

Greyson was the newest member of the group until I arrived, and she's also the youngest. Grey's personality is as bright as her hair, and her laugh is infectious. She has two older sisters in addition to her brother, Van, which made me miss Eloise, Sadie, and Merritt. But in a good way.

Then there's Bailey, casual and friendly and getting bonus points for sharing the *Lord of the Rings* moment with Liam. She hardly said a word after that but managed somehow to fully participate in the group. If I needed a good listener, I think she'd be my go-to.

Gracie was the most intimidating to me at first because she seemed the most formal in her black slacks and tailored black blouse. But she apparently came from a performance of the middle school where she teaches orchestra. Five minutes into being on the couch, she'd shaken out her long brown hair and taken off the blouse in favor of the tank top underneath. Two brownies in, and she unbuttoned her pants.

In short, these women seem grounded and comfortable in their own skin and with each other. Oh, and the subject of hockey didn't even come up for the first hour. I don't know if any of these women know about my history with Camden, but no one has mentioned him, either. I'm honestly relieved.

Not that I'm not dying to process what happened earlier, but I also need a minute to process it myself. Plus, not talking about him made me feel like I was being included tonight for me, not just because of him.

• • •

Whatever I imagined a WAG hangout to be—and I'll admit my understanding came straight from social media—this is *not* it. I got sucked into a whole series on WAG playoff jackets, which was fascinating. But it also looked expensive to have custom jackets made every year a team is in the playoffs. I'm also not sure a custom leather jacket is something I could pull off.

The hockey WAGs online all look like they stepped out of a hair commercial and had spent two hours contouring after getting lash extensions and lip fillers. That's a choice, and it's fine if it's the choice women want to make. But I couldn't handle a whole group of women with such uniform perfection, where everyone looked the same.

But this? It feels like I could just be me and who I am is enough.

A few hours in, conversations have split into smaller groups. Liam is in bed, the iPad pried from his sleepy fingers. Gracie headed out a bit ago, and though Parker and Grey keep saying they should go, they've been chatting with Bailey for forty-five minutes.

Me? I'm getting my baby fix. If Evie lets me hold Juno any longer, I might catch a serious case of baby fever.

"Who's the cutest baby in the world, and why is it you?" I coo to Juno, who honestly is the cutest baby in the world.

Liam was adorable because he was *mine*, but he definitely got cuter as he got older. In any photograph from his first year, his face looks sort of smushed and lopsided with a smattering of baby acne, which I didn't know was a thing. I still had breakouts sometimes at nineteen, so we were a matching set. Juno, with her dark hair, perfect skin, and big eyes, could be a baby model.

She and her mom, Evie, arrived late due to a last-minute blowout. From the baby, not Evie's car. This made me chuckle because it still feels like just yesterday I was dealing with poop-up-the-back situations with Liam. It makes me weirdly nostalgic. Not for the actual gross moments (and there were many that first year) but just for when he was my little baby buddy.

Juno gurgles happily, then grabs the end of my nose and gives it a twist. I laugh as Evie manages to pry her baby's surprisingly strong fingers from my nose with an apologetic look.

"Juno! What did we say about noses! Sorry! I can take her back if you want."

"Nope! I mean, unless you want her. We're kind of having a moment here. It feels like Liam was just this small and also like it was a lifetime ago. How is that?"

"I don't know," Evie says. "But it's like babies have a way of bending time. This has been both the longest and the quickest year of my life."

"You said she's eight months now?"

"Yes. And I'm absolutely unprepared for her first birthday. Or for her to start walking."

I saw Juno crawling earlier, and it made me glad I required Liam to keep all his Legos in his room. Juno is fast and puts everything in her mouth. Including my knuckles right now as she uses the same strong grip to drag them toward her open lips.

"Is this okay?" I ask Evie, nodding down at Juno gnawing on me. I can feel teeth, but she's mostly just gumming me lightly. "I don't mind being a chew toy, but I haven't washed this hand since before y'all got here."

Evie shrugs and sinks deeper onto the couch next to me, her eyes fluttering closed. "I had to stop worrying so much about germs. It's impossible. Your hand is probably cleaner than half the things she stuffed in her mouth today before I could stop her." She pauses for a long yawn that makes me yawn too. "We should go. Usually, I have her in bed before now, but I didn't want to miss this."

Evie has the look of a woman who needs a good nap or a full night of sleep. And probably more than anyone else in this room, I get it.

Apparently, Evie's been raising Juno on her own. She also moved alone with Juno to Harvest Hollow a few months back, which makes me feel like we're following parallel paths. Now, though, she has Alec, the newly retired team captain, whom she says is absolutely smitten with Juno.

And, I'd imagine, with Evie too, who is striking with her dark hair offsetting her blue eyes.

I almost work up the nerve to ask how it is dating a hockey player when you have a kid, but it seems a little nosy when we just met. Plus, Alec just retired last month, so she wasn't dating him for long while he was actively playing. He watches Juno now while Evie works, which is honestly pretty awesome.

Younger me would have loved that kind of help, though younger me wouldn't have been open to the relationship part. Just the help with Liam.

I try to stop myself from imagining what our lives might be like with Camden in that way, or if he'd be around at all during the season. It's too soon to go down that particular rabbit hole. One thing at a time.

First, I need to get through our date where we actually talk about things. And maybe do some more kissing—not in a hallway by a bathroom.

The kissing sounds way more fun than the talking. I've never really had a serious relationship.

"Does it get easier?" Evie asks, startling me out of the memory of Camden's lips.

My cheeks feel warm. "What?"

Cracking open her eyes a slit, Evie smiles at Juno. She lost interest in my hand a few minutes ago and is now playing with the necklace I forgot I was wearing. Her eyes are starting to flutter closed as well, and she snuggles into me with a yawn and glassy eyes. I dust off a long-retired mama move and gently bounce her until her eyes are closed, lashes resting on her chubby cheeks.

"Being a mom," Evie says. "Don't get me wrong; it's amazing. But I'm just so tired all the time."

"Yes and no? I mean, this stage was arguably the most taxing for me. Just having this tiny person tethered to you. Adjusting to some new development and stage every few weeks. Panic over everything. Days where you can't manage to eat or take a shower or even pee because there's a tiny person getting a tooth or having an earache. No sleep."

Evie raises a hand without opening her eyes. "Yes. So much all of that."

"When they get older, it's like ..." I trail off, running a hand over Juno's soft hair while I try to find words to sum up so many years with Liam. "You get more breaks and a little more space to breathe. But the worries get bigger, or at least different. You're not as afraid of bookshelves falling on them and more concerned with the kid at school who tells your son he's weird."

Evie's eyes pop open at this, and she sits up so fast I bet she saw stars. "Did someone call Liam weird?"

Her declaration is so strong, Juno whimpers in my arms and the other conversation stops.

"Who called Liam *what?*" Parker looks just as fierce, and even Grey has her eyes narrowed. It's a nice feeling, knowing

162

these women I don't know well are ready to close protective ranks around me and my kid.

I laugh softly, careful of the baby snoozing on my chest. "No one … here. That I know of. But Liam hasn't always fit in very well with kids his age."

"He's very bright," Bailey says with a kind smile. "That can be difficult."

I nod, then glance down at Juno's wispy dark hair that's just starting to curl at the ends. "And it may not have helped with me being on my own. I think I talked to him and treated him too much like he was older. He could carry on a conversation better with an adult than with kids."

"Is that why you were so upset when I mentioned the kid who wasn't nice at hockey?" Parker asks.

"Yeah. I know it's not like he'll never experience mean kids, but I'd like to think we moved past some of the hardest stuff in the past year or so."

"As I said before, I think you're doing great," Parker says. "I may not have my own kids, but I see a lot when I help out with hockey stuff. Trust me, you're raising a good one. Also, hockey will help with the social stuff. I mean, if he stays in. Being part of a team forces it on you, but not in a bad way."

"Do you think Liam will continue with hockey?" Greyson asks. "I mean, after the classes end."

"I don't know. If he wants to, I guess so. Do I need to know what I'm getting into first?"

"Uh," Parker says with a grimace, "maybe it's better to *not* know."

"Liam tends to get fixated on a particular thing, and then it passes, and he moves on. It's been hockey since—"

I stop myself from saying last summer. I don't want to talk about Camden now when I've made it this far without having to discuss what happened between us. Or what's happening now.

"He's been into hockey for a while now," I finish. "So, I'm not sure if he'll stick with it or find a new thing to obsess over in a week."

"Selfishly, I hope he sticks with hockey," Parker says, getting to her feet and stretching with a yawn. This starts a chain reaction, with everyone starting to shift into time-to-go mode. "But even if not, you still have to hang out with us. I mean, if you want."

"Is that even a question?" I ask.

"We can be a lot," she says. "I mean, you didn't even get to meet Amelia or Summer."

"And we also didn't make her answer any questions about Camden, though we all have questions," Grey adds with a wicked grin.

Parker gives her a light shove. "Hey! We agreed not to mention the C-word."

"It's been soooo hard not to," Evie whines, shrugging when I give her an *et tu brute* look.

"You all did great," Parker admonishes. "But for the record, Naomi, he's been so pitiful this year," Parker says, pressing a hand to her chest. "All lovelorn and dramatically sad while completely denying it."

I shouldn't feel happy thinking about Camden being sad, but it does give me a little giddy thrill. I guess it's just nice to know I wasn't the only one miserable since the summer. Especially since I totally thought Camden didn't care as much as I did.

Evie gathers her things, and I hold a still-sleeping Juno while she puts them in the car. The women made quick work of straightening up, and my little house looks as good as it did before they arrived.

I follow them all to the porch, calling soft goodbyes so as not to bother the neighbors. It's after ten on a weekday so I don't want to tick anyone off.

Parker turns and walks back up to the top step. "One more thing. I really wanted this night to be about you, which is why I told everyone not to bring up Camden. But I will say that his game has suffered this year." She reaches out and pats my shoulder. "So, the faster you can make that man happy, the better his game will be. For what it's worth, I highly suggest kissing."

I'm sure my face looks guilty, but she doesn't seem to notice and bounds down the steps, only turning back at her car to call, "The guys are on the road later this week, but Sunday, we have a home game. You and Liam are coming. Bye!"

And then, leaving no room for argument, she slams her car door and takes off like the perfect picture of innocence.

CHAPTER 13

Camden

WAS it a mistake not to give Naomi a heads up about the extra guest on our date? Probably.

Is it still considered a date when you have a chaperone? Probably ... not.

But, as Noami's laughter rings out over the story Mike's recounting about something stupid I did when I was sixteen, I'm not exactly sorry either.

"Since he lost a bet he never should have made in the first place, his teammates got to pick a task." Mike has always been a good storyteller, and Naomi is hanging on every word.

When I picked her up at her office, she burst out of the door with a big smile, then paused at the sight of Mike standing next to me. It was only a tiny pause, though, and after introducing Mike, explaining that I'd lived with Mike's family as a teenager, she just rolled with it. And by that, I mean she spent the car ride all the way through our meals at this bistro that Felix recommended goading Mike into telling her as many embarrassing stories as possible.

There are way more than I remember, and Mike's memory is sharp when it comes to this period of time. He's been more than willing to share. Comparatively, I was a pretty good kid. But when you're playing youth hockey, there's always some kind of trouble. I guess a little dose of humiliation is what I deserve for springing this on Naomi.

So far, Mike seems to be keeping the past in the past. I'm not sure when *now* is for him, but he's telling the stories like they are distant memories, not like I'm currently the teenager who recently lost a bet with his teammates.

Naomi's eyes, sparkling with mirth, fix on me. "You're telling me this guy, the one who uses as few words as possible as *often* as possible, did Lady Gaga karaoke—complete with choreography?"

Mike grins. "Yup."

"Can he even sing?"

"Absolutely not."

As she turns to me, she grins. It takes work not to let my gaze fall to her lips or my thoughts to go back to our kiss last night.

I swallow. "How about dancing, Cam?"

The nickname slips out, and she doesn't seem to notice. I do. And it reminds me of last summer and the way she stopped using my whole name by the second week we were hanging out. I wonder if she was aware back then? It makes light, warm and golden, flood through my chest.

I want to reach for her, but so far, I've kept my hands to myself. It just seems wiser, at least for now. I didn't tell Mike this was a date per se, only that I wanted him to meet someone. His eyes lit up knowingly when he saw Naomi, but nothing else has been said. Somehow, I feel like taking Naomi's hand across the table might curse how well this has gone.

Trying to navigate this situation isn't easy. My thinking was that having Naomi meet Mike would make more sense than just an explanation. I've never been great with words anyway.

Naomi leans forward, and the movement reminds me that she's still waiting on my answer. I got lost in her lips and then in my thoughts.

"I'm terrible at dancing," I say. "And it took me hours to learn the steps."

"But he fully committed," Mike says, sounding as proud as if he's talking about a game-winning goal. "Outfit and all."

Naomi cackles. "*Outfit?* Tell me you have photo evidence."

"Of course." Mike already has his phone out.

I'm sure he did have pictures at one point. But as he starts swiping through his photos, his forehead creases in a frown.

"Huh. I can't seem to find them. I must have ..."

He trails off, and I tense, realizing perhaps too late that scrolling through his phone might mean crashing directly into a confusing reality. It's the first stumble he's had during our lunch, but it's subtle enough Naomi hasn't noticed.

Mike's frown deepens, and his voice drops to a whisper. "I don't ..."

She notices now. Concern paints her features as she reaches over to touch Mike's shoulder gently. He jumps and drops his phone on the table. I catch a glimpse of his screen, still lit up where it landed. It shows a lot of pictures of Mike at the lake with some people I don't know. He doesn't seem to recognize them either.

"It's okay," Naomi tells him. "You can show me the pictures another time."

"Mike—" I start.

"Right," he says. "Maybe I'll find them later." A smile appears, smoothing out the worry lines from his face, though I can see the effort it takes for him to override the moment of confusion. "I probably have one printed out somewhere."

He clicks off his phone and turns it facedown, abandoning the hunt for pictures as well as any sense of momentary confusion he had.

Naomi looks between us, too observant to have missed the brief tension, even though it's clear she doesn't understand it.

Thankfully, Jordan appears by the table then, just as he and I talked about earlier.

"Hey," he says, running a hand over his dark ponytail. "I hope I'm on time."

Mike smiles, clearly recognizing the man who's been spending most days with him but then seems to fumble for his name or any context. With his long hair, hemp necklaces, and patchy goatee, Jordan has the crunchy hippie thing going on. It threw me off the first time I met him, but his warmth, confidence, and his way of handling Mike with ease earned my confidence quickly.

"Good to see you … again," Mike says, still searching through a mental database and coming up short.

I step in. "Naomi, this is Jordan. He's my personal assistant and acts as Mike's personal chauffeur."

This is the story Jordan suggested to explain his presence to Mike. "A hockey player could use an assistant," he'd said with a shrug. "Easy."

It's worked so far, though every so often when Mike

thinks I'm back in high school, he assumes Jordan is an unlikely looking teammate.

"Nice to meet you." Jordan holds out a hand to Naomi, who shakes it, offering him a friendly smile. "I'm here to grab Mike."

Naomi glances at me, eyes narrowing a little. I give her a little nod that I hope communicates, *Hang on and I'll explain everything.*

"I *can* drive, you know," Mike tells her. "My car just ... isn't here."

And it's true; he *can* drive. Technically. Up until he moved here, he was driving, and the thought terrifies me. His car actually is here, but I'm currently paying for long-term storage.

Mike's driving is actually how his family found out he needed help. Mike left home, then forgot where he was going and where he lived. Eventually, he ran out of gas and the police found him on the side of the road, overheated, a little dehydrated, and totally beside himself. They found his daughter's contact info in his phone, and Lisa called because she thought I'd want to know. I'm sure she didn't expect my offer to take him in.

Anyway, the whole incident started the process that led to him being here. Without a license. Or access to his car.

I keep my car keys hidden at Jordan's recommendation.

"But Jordan loves your company," I tell Mike.

"I do," Jordan says easily. "Are you ready to head out? I thought you and I might stop for a malt on the way home."

Chocolate malts have always been one of Mike's favorite things. I didn't even know what they were before living with him, and I don't particularly like the taste. But for him, they make an easy bribe.

He pats his belly. "I'd love a malt. But how will you get home?" he asks me with a frown.

Naomi takes a sip of water, watching me carefully over the rim of her glass.

"We'll be fine. Don't worry about me."

"Will you give him a ride home?" He glances earnestly at Naomi. "He's not supposed to drive our cars. Insurance purposes—you know how those companies are."

"Um," Naomi says, still looking at me.

Jordan jumps in to save us. "They'll be fine," he tells Mike. "And I bet they'll enjoy their privacy." He gives me a roguish look then elbows Mike, who chuckles. "If you know what I mean."

I'm not a man who blushes, but I can feel the heat traveling up the back of my neck. This was not part of the plan Jordan and I discussed earlier. But then, when we're both playing roles, playing along is part of the game.

I heave a good-natured sigh and roll my eyes.

"Don't do anything I wouldn't do," Mike says with a smirk, and I have a brief and terrible flashback of him saying those exact words the one and only time I had a girl over to their house back in the day. "And remember your curfew, young man."

I give him the only correct response in this case, which is a polite "Yes, sir."

To her credit, Naomi sits quietly through the exchange, not looking embarrassed or even confused—just like she has a million questions she'll lob at me as soon as Jordan and Mike are out of earshot.

"Hope to see you again soon, sweetheart." Mike winks at Naomi. "And I'll dig up that photo of Camden for you. In fact, I'm pretty sure there's a video of the whole thing somewhere."

"No," I groan dramatically, though if such a thing does exist, I'm sure he won't be able to find it.

"Yes! Please. It was great to meet you."

"Normally, I might try to tell you you're too good for him," Mike tells her, then cuts his eyes to me. "But he's a pretty decent kid. No singing voice and zero rhythm, but otherwise, decent."

A swell of emotion rises, and my gaze falls to my hands in my lap. Mike's approval hits me in a visceral way, a warm wave that buoys me at first before I'm dragged under by unwelcome thoughts of my own father. Who probably doesn't know or remember my lack of singing or dancing ability.

Who might suspect I'm a decent guy but not have any actual data points to be sure.

I'm vaguely aware of Naomi standing to give Mike a hug. By the time she turns and hugs a surprised Jordan, I've mostly shuttered up the thoughts of my family.

Jordan is a hugger. He squeezes Naomi back tightly, giving me a wicked smile over her shoulder, as if he knows I don't like seeing him touch her. It's probably written very clearly on my face. So, why hide it?

I glare at him.

"I'm sure I'll see you again sometime soon," Naomi tells Mike. "How long will you be in town?"

Confusion flashes quickly across Mike's face, and he glances between Jordan and me. "I think ..."

"A while," Jordan answers quickly. "Ready for that malt?" Jordan gives Mike's shoulder a squeeze and starts to move toward the front of the bistro.

"Absolutely." Mike's expression smooths out and he smiles once more at Naomi. "You're welcome at our place anytime. But"—now he turns to me— "remember the house rules. No girls in the bedroom. Especially pretty ones."

Jordan laughs. "You'll have to remind me of the other house rules," he says. "I think I forgot a few."

"Will do. Important to keep these young guys in line. Speaking of which—and this is the last thing before we go— can you convince Camden to let me cut his hair?" he asks Naomi.

I swear, they are *never* going to leave this restaurant. This extended conversation is making me twitchy. I'm starting to think this was a really terrible idea in the first place.

Naomi tilts her head a little, giving the top of my head a once-over. I want to squirm under her attention but force myself to be still.

"I kind of like the messy look," she says. "But maybe a trim wouldn't hurt."

"I do a great job," Mike says.

"He does," I agree. During the time I lived with him, he was the only person who touched my hair with scissors. I still think he does better than anyone else I've found, no matter how much I pay now for a cut. "Can we talk about this later?"

"You could use one too," Mike tells Jordan, who looks aghast and touches his ponytail protectively.

"Locks of Love would be able to make a beautiful wig," I tell him, payback for the extended hug with Naomi.

"It would," Naomi agrees, giving Jordan a little smirk.

He presses a hand to his chest in mock horror. "You two deserve each other. Let's go, Mike. And if you so much as mention my hair again, I'm not stopping for that malt."

As the two of them walk away, laughing and talking, Naomi's sharp gaze lands on me, somehow at once both inquisitive and accusatory. But before she can ask one of what I'm sure are many questions in her mind, our waiter stops by, asking if we want dessert.

I order a cappuccino and Naomi does the same but also adds a chocolate raspberry cheesecake. The waiter clears our plates, and as soon as he's out of earshot, Naomi leans forward, steepling her fingers together. She doesn't ask a question. She just waits, which is almost worse.

Clearing my throat, I wipe my hands on the khaki pants Mike insisted I wear when he saw me in jeans. "Can't wear jeans for a date," he'd said.

"Did I say it was a date?" I asked.

"No, but your nerves did." He was right. Though I wish I'd gone with jeans. I don't get the feeling Naomi cares about my pants.

Right now, for instance, she's more concerned with the very confusing scenario I just dropped her into.

"You met Mike." Not a great way to start, and Naomi seems to agree, giving me the smallest of eye rolls.

"I did meet him. And Jordan. Your ... assistant?"

"Not quite." I take a sip of my water while Naomi waits. "He's actually a caregiver I hired who helps out with Mike when I'm not home. You might have noticed a few times, but Mike has early-onset dementia. He's not aware anything's wrong—at least most of the time. But his short-term memory is very affected, and he kind of bounces back and forth between the present and the past."

Understanding passes over her face, then something a little sadder. "So, you just ... play along?"

"Basically. He's able to make some sense of things, even if he's mixing up the present and the past in the same conversation. When he runs into a wall, like things that he can't make sense of or remember—"

"Like the photos on his phone?" she asks.

"Exactly. He gets agitated. The doctor said it's fine to just go along with most things, unless it comes down to a safety issue. Most of the time, he thinks I'm back in high school, living with his family."

"Ah. This is the complication you had at home," she says, and I appreciate her putting the pieces together from our conversation at the Summit.

"Yes."

"He's not just visiting, is he?" she asks.

I shake my head slowly. "He moved in with me a little over a month ago."

"He doesn't have any family?"

"Mike had an affair a few years after I left," I say bluntly. "Debbie divorced him and remarried. I'm not sure his daughter, Lisa, ever forgave him. She was in college while I was living with them, so we weren't close, but once she found out about Mike's condition, she called to let me know. I don't think she expected me to want him to come live with me. But when she said she was planning to put him in a home, I just couldn't live with that."

"The woman you were interviewing was another caretaker?"

I grimace. "So she said. I've switched services and think I have a few good options lined up. Jordan handles the day-to-day, but I need a few other people for away games."

Naomi is quiet, and I can't tell if she's quiet because she disapproves of my choice or because she pities Mike. I just have no idea. Lisa made it clear she doesn't think this is a good idea long-term. And maybe she's right.

The waiter returns then with our cappuccinos and Naomi's cheesecake. As soon as he's gone, Naomi reaches across the table, clutching my hand. I go still.

Her touch makes me realize how tense I've become. As

she brushes her thumb over the back of my hand, tension lifts from my body, a fog burned off by her brightness.

"Mike was right about you, Cam. You are a very decent guy."

My throat works, but I can't swallow or manage words to answer, so I just nod.

Naomi drops my hand and pops a bite of cheesecake into her mouth with a smile. I'm distracted by the tiny smudge of chocolate in the corner of her mouth as she says, "Too bad about the dancing and singing or you might just be the total package."

———

After I answer more of Naomi's questions about Mike and we finally leave the bistro, I manage to redeem the date that really wasn't a date.

Or, rather, the weather redeems it for me.

"It's snowing," Naomi says, halting on the sidewalk. She tips her face up to the soft gray sky, closing her eyes as fat snowflakes drift around her, caching in her hair and lashes.

She smiles, eyes still closed, then just the tip of her tongue peeks out, catching a few flakes.

"Guess you don't see too much of this," I say, shamelessly watching her mouth until she opens her eyes and I meet her gaze.

"No, we don't. This is ..." She shakes her head. "I was going to say magical, but I'm not that cheesy."

But it is kind of magical. Especially seeing the way the flakes land in her hair and on her shoulders, tiny white flecks that almost immediately melt and disappear.

"Maybe the occasion warrants it," I tell her.

When she smiles up at me, her eyes are soft. "Maybe it does."

I reach into my coat pocket, hesitating for a moment when my fingers brush soft fabric. I'm as nervous as I've ever been around a woman to pull out the scarf I've kept hidden through this whole lunch, unsure when the right time would be.

"I got you something," I say, sounding every bit as awkward as I feel. Pushing through, or perhaps pushing aside, the feeling, I step closer to Naomi and drape it around her shoulders, lifting her hair as I secure it around her neck. My fingertips brush the soft skin of her throat, and I hear a catch in Naomi's breath. Not quite, but almost a gasp.

I'm aware of her eyes on me as I knot the scarf under her chin, methodic and slow. Wanting a reason to be this close, knowing I probably don't need a reason at all.

"I don't know your favorite color," I say, still avoiding her gaze. I am typically a quiet guy. Quiet—but not shy like I feel now. "This one had a lot of colors. Bright, happy, fun. They made me think of you."

"Camden," she whispers.

Finally, my hands still grasping the fringed edges of the scarf like they're all that's keeping me on my feet, I meet her gaze.

"Thank you," she says. "This is really, really nice."

"It wasn't expensive." I'm not sure why I feel the need to point this out. I immediately backpedal. "I could have gotten a nicer one. I just liked these colors."

"I don't need an expensive scarf, Camden. You thinking of me, saying colors remind you of me, it's—"

She presses her lips together, and for a moment, I have the sickening suspicion I'm about to make her cry. But resolve takes over her features and she reaches up, grabbing my hands with hers.

"I love it. Thank you." She pauses. "And my favorite color is turquoise. More on the blue side than green."

I nod, like I know what the hell that means. I intend to learn it. Later.

Because right now, I need to kiss her.

So, I do, leaning forward and brushing my lips over hers, even though I told myself before this date I wouldn't.

Naomi makes a tiny sound, a hum that sounds like pure contentment, and then she wraps her arms around me, tugging me closer, like the inches between us were just too far. My heartbeat riots in my chest as her mouth moves against mine with an intensity clearly assuring me that I wasn't the only one who replayed last night's kiss in my head.

Or maybe all of our past kisses for all the months we've been apart.

This wasn't how I intended to do things. Not kissing her last night in the hallway or right here on the sidewalk when we still haven't talked about how we feel or what we want. I planned to do things right this time with her. No pretending like I think we both did last summer—saying it was casual while something much deeper was growing underneath.

Now that the door has been opened, though, I can't go back to not kissing her. Not feeling the way her lips move under mine, somehow both pliant and firm, an agreeable fighter. As if to illustrate this very thing, she pulls back just slightly and nips at my bottom lip.

I chuckle, the sound low and sandpaper rough. "I wasn't going to kiss you again. Not when we haven't talked about this, about us."

Naomi's lips graze the corner of my mouth. "Well, that

just seems cruel and unusual. I vote we keep kissing on the table." A pause. A kiss. "Kissing on the table sounds fun."

I groan, remembering late nights of leaving Naomi at the doorstep of the little cottage on Oakley, returning to my hotel feeling kiss-drugged and effervescent.

She's been teasing me with her light kisses, and I turn the tables now, letting go of her scarf to cup her cheeks, tilting her mouth up to mine. I don't get very far though because the door to the bistro suddenly opens behind us, reminding me there is a bistro at all—and we're making out right in front of the door.

Curling an arm around Naomi's shoulders, I move us away from the door, putting our backs to the people who just came outside. Honestly, the interruption is for the best.

Being a hockey player isn't like being an A-list celebrity or even a famous football or basketball player. There won't be paparazzi hiding in bushes or using telephoto lenses to see into our windows or yards. But the Appies are all over social media, and we're an institution here in Harvest Hollow. It wouldn't be unheard of for some random person to snap a photo or a video and post it online somewhere.

I really haven't had to worry about this, but I've had a very boring life off the ice. Somehow, I have a feeling kissing a woman on a sidewalk in the middle of the day might invite more attention than I want.

"I have to get back to work," Naomi says with a sigh that brushes across my cheek, warmth mixing with the cold of the snowflakes that are falling harder now.

"I want to take things slow," I say, tracing the line of her jaw with a fingertip, "but this isn't quite what I had in mind. We spent half of our time with Mike telling terrible stories about me, and the rest talking about him." I shake my head. "I'm sorry."

"Don't be sorry. I'm glad he came, and I'm glad you told me. It's really amazing what you're doing for him."

I want to argue that anyone would, but I also know that's not true. In some ways, being abandoned by my family made me the exact kind of person who couldn't leave Mike in a home somewhere. I won't leave him.

"You have a Mike, and I have a Liam." She shrugs. "If we're going to have an actual relationship, we have to figure out what that means."

She's right, but I still regret not taking her on a proper date alone. Or is that just the part of me that's still drawn to her mouth like it's a task I've started and now need to finish.

"I have to tell you something maybe I should have told you before."

"That sounds ... dire. Okay. Tell me."

"Liam came to see me on Oakley. After you broke up with me."

She stiffens. "He did?"

"He wanted me to stay. He was crying and—" I have to pause and clear my throat. "I think I realized why you broke up with me. For him. It didn't make sense until I saw his face."

"So, when I called you and apologized, it was because of Liam you left."

Her voice is flat, and I can't tell if she's angry or maybe just processing the information.

"Yes. I probably should have told you but—"

"Not probably, Cam. You should have." Her voice is firm, but not angry. "Like you should have texted me to say you were working with him during hockey classes. When it comes to Liam, there can't be secrets or things you don't tell me."

"I'm sorry." I cup her cheek. "You're right; I shouldn't have kept this from you. I … didn't think of it like that."

When she smiles, relief is a balm washing over me. "I appreciate you looking out for Liam. And for me."

"So, this isn't a dealbreaker?"

"No. I'm not going anywhere, Camden," she promises.

But as I gaze into her stormy blue eyes, the tiniest flicker of something flashes there and then is gone. It looked an awful lot like hesitation, almost like she's trying to convince herself but isn't quite certain yet.

This tiny, possibly imagined emotion I see plants a tiny seed of concern.

I may not have known her favorite color until moments ago, but what I *do* know and what I can see in her is a woman who still runs when she's scared. And if I'm being completely honest with myself, I only recognize it because running away is my tendency as well.

CHAPTER 14

Naomi

"MOM, we're going to be late," Liam says. He's nervously pacing by the front door, every so often opening and closing it, letting cold air gush in.

The snow didn't stick and was barely more than a magical flurry enhancing a romantic moment. But it's still cold. The downside of this old house is how drafty it is. Some of the rooms heat better than others, and it's really making me miss the beach. Even in winter, the winds don't feel punishing like this.

Without snow to make things pretty and fun, freezing weather just seems cruel.

"Close the door!"

He does. With a sigh.

"And we can't be late because we're already going early," I

grumble, fussing with my purse. I can't remember if there is a bag policy at the Summit.

Do I need to worry about a bag policy if we're not going through normal security?

Parker, as promised—or threatened, made plans for us to attend the Appies game. "I have something special planned," she'd said over the phone, and I could hear the smile in her voice. I might have made the decision right then and there to bow out of this "special plan" if she hadn't added, "Mostly, this is something special for Liam. But I think you'll enjoy it too."

I am a person who doesn't like surprises. This might seem at odds with my whole restless energy thing, but it's more about being out of control. When other people surprise me, I can't prepare, mentally or otherwise. As opposed to when I decide to impulsively choose a new direction, which allows me to be the captain of my own ship—a ship headed toward new, adventurous waters of some kind.

Parker's surprise has me feeling extra layers of nerves when I already had enough of them. I'm not sure if it's because things with Camden are still kind of up in the air, or maybe just because I'm still struggling a little to switch my brain into seeing hockey as not bad or at least neutral when I've carried a chip on my shoulder about it since last summer. Some of it might be the residual fear of not fitting in, despite the dinner with Parker and friends this week that I genuinely enjoyed.

It's just a lot at once, and that's not even considering what Parker's secret is.

But she said the magic words: *something special for Liam.*

So, we're going to the Summit a few hours before the game starts—*puck drop*, Liam keeps correcting me—and doing I don't know what. I'm not even sure if I'm wearing the right thing. According to my social media WAG search, getting ready for a game involves a lot of work to look super hot.

Look—I have no problem getting dressed up. I like dresses and shoes and clothes that make me feel cute. I don't have an issue wearing makeup. Though I don't quite take it to the level that some of the women in the Get Ready With Me videos do. I almost choked when I stumbled upon the five pumps of foundation tutorial. FIVE PUMPS! My pores clogged just watching a woman spread that much foundation over *even her eyebrows*.

No, thanks.

I don't expect that kind of effort—not based on the vibe I picked up from the women who came over earlier in the week. Parker said there was not a dress code and they all wore whatever they felt like. For some, that's jeans and a jersey, while people who like dressing up do.

"Don't worry about it," she told me. "Promise. Just wear what you want and come early to the gated area of the parking lot. Security will have your name. It will be so fun."

Liam's the lucky one. As he shoots me another exasperated look, his hand on the doorknob, I wish it were as easy as just throwing on an Appies jersey like the one Parker gave him over a pair of jeans and sneakers. Even if I wanted to go that route, I don't have any Appies gear. So, I'm in a sweater that's close enough to the turquoise of the Appies' logo, dark jeans that fit me like a glove, and knee-high boots.

"Finally," Liam says as I pull on my coat and the new scarf Camden gave me. I've taken to wearing it daily, leaving it on even when I remove my coat.

I love it. It's beautiful and so soft. I always thought scarves looked itchy, but this one feels like a caress on my neck. Also, it still smells like Camden. I'm sure that will fade soon, and then I'll have to decide if it's too creepy to ask him to, like, sleep with it in his bed for a few nights to regain his scent.

Okay, it's definitely kind of creepy.

I'll probably do it anyway.

"Can't you go any faster?" Liam grumbles more than once on the way to the Summit. It's only a ten-minute drive, but he's so anxious and excited about the game it's making him grumpy.

When he gets like this, the best option is just to leave him alone and let him work through it, so I continue driving the speed limit while not pointing out how we're still earlier than Parker even asked. I also don't tell him she has some kind of surprise. If I told him Parker has something planned, he'd run through possible scenarios, then maybe be disappointed in whatever it is.

I'm glad I made this decision when some Appies staff person I don't know greets us once security lets us in the back door. The guy has the eagerness and fresh face that screams intern, and he babbles about hockey things with Liam while leading us to a nice room with a whole table of food and a bartender in front of a table of drinks.

"This is the family suite," the intern tells us. "Though families don't usually arrive this early."

I wonder if by families he means the WAGs. Or maybe parents and siblings who happen to be in town for a game?

"Thanks," I tell him. Liam is already checking out the food for things he can eat while watching one of the televisions. It's streaming what I guess is footage from past games.

"That's from last year's Calder Cup Championship," the intern tells me without explaining what that means. "Parker said she'd meet you here in just a little while. Please, help yourself and just relax."

Liam has a plate piled high with nachos while I go with a

beer to help me relax. My nerves are shot with Liam's pressure to leave on time combined with a nervous energy I didn't expect to have about this game.

It's not me caring whether Camden's team wins or loses so much as getting to see this side of him fully: the hockey player in his natural habitat.

What if this makes it feel like things with Camden won't work? What if I don't like his natural habitat? Or who he really is inside of it?

"Mom, this is so cool," Liam says with a mouthful of chips. He, obviously, is not having the mini freakout I am about this as he settles into one of the leather couches to watch the screens.

I'm glad when Parker finally enters the room, bouncing up and down on her toes and fiddling with the zipper of a black cross-body bag. She has on black pants, black sneakers, and a gray polo shirt with the Appies logo. Her excitement is palpably contagious, and my nerves shift slightly into something more like anticipation than anxiety.

"I have something so cool planned," Parker says, grabbing Liam by the hand after hugging me hello with rib-crushing force. "Did you get enough to eat?"

"Definitely. Thank you. Are there usually more people?" The room is still empty aside from Liam and me and two servers who looked very bored.

"Having a family suite is new. Before last year, most of the guys were single, and very few have family nearby. It seemed silly to have something like this without people to enjoy it." She glances at her phone and then waves us toward the door. "They'll probably get here in the next thirty minutes or so. But there's also food up in the box, so some just eat up there. You're welcome to watch from up there or from the seats I got you. Bailey will be sitting with you as well."

That makes me feel a little better. Bailey has a calming presence, and I think I'd feel more comfortable in normal seats than a suite for family when things with Cam and me are still so new. It will also be good to have another adult there. Liam is great company, but he's my company a *lot*. Bailey will be good balance.

Parker leads us down a hallway that looks like every other hallway I've seen in this building. I'm not sure how anyone can navigate the Summit without getting lost.

"All of this is so cool," Liam says.

Parker beams at Liam, then at me. I didn't know she had a whole other gear of excitement.

"I know, right? How's your arm, by the way?" she asks Liam.

"Good. I got the sutures out two weeks ago. See?"

He pulls up the sleeve of his jersey to show off the neat line of his scar. I'm only bothered by blood and open wounds usually, but the scar calls to mind the panic I felt that day knowing he got hurt. I also haven't completely been able to get rid of the mental image of the blood. I look away, studying some of the framed team photos on the wall.

"Looks great," Parker says. "Glad it didn't keep you from continuing in classes."

"I was sad we didn't have class yesterday," he says.

"I know, and I'm sorry," Parker says. "This is our first time trying to do a series of classes with the players helping. It hasn't been easy. Their schedules are so busy, I'm not sure we can do it again."

"Maybe in the off-season?" Liam says hopefully.

"Maybe." Parker nudges his shoulder. "But by then, you might have moved beyond that kind of class."

"You think?"

Before responding, Parker glances at me as though

looking for approval to broach the subject of moving beyond what he's doing now. Liam has only had three classes because of the Appies' schedule, but his hockey talk hasn't slowed down at all. In fact, he convinced me to buy him rollerblades so he could play street hockey with some guys in our neighborhood when the streets are dry. He has three classes left over the next five weeks, and I don't anticipate this slowing down.

I give Parker a quick nod, feeling a little like I'm sealing my doom, but also minding a little less than I would have a few weeks ago. I'm not sure if it's because there's no reason —and actually no possibility—to avoid the topic of hockey now that Camden and I are ... whatever we are. It might also be Parker's influence, which is hard to ignore.

"Are you thinking about signing up for the youth league later this spring?" she asks.

"I'd like to."

Now Liam is the one looking at me with a question in his eyes. Though he's definitely been talking about signing up for the rookie program with Appies Youth Hockey, I have so far remained noncommittal. I raise my eyebrows and my shoulders, giving him a noncommittal we'll see. Which is more than I've given him before, and as such, he seems to be taking it as an absolute answer.

But then his face dims a little. "I'm probably not ready yet."

"Nonsense. We've got kids who sign up for the rookie program who haven't even been to classes like the ones you're doing. And they definitely aren't getting to work one-on-one with a player like Camden. You've got an advantage. Plus, at the last class, I could see a real improvement from your first week. You're doing great."

I hope Parker means the things she's saying about Liam's

ability to fit into the rookie program at his level (see: my whole opinion about setting up expectations), but she strikes me as a very genuine person. And it does make me proud to hear her encouraging words to Liam. Even if I am starting to feel like hockey is about to consume my life like some kind of giant, ravenous bird.

Bass thumps through the walls from the arena, a heartbeat of anticipation. A line of cars had already been entering the other side of the parking lot when we pulled through the security gate, and even in these hallways where we pass only an occasional other staff person, the excitement almost crackles in the air.

As I trail behind the two of them, wondering if I should be leaving a trail of cracker crumbs from the emergency stash in my purse so I can find my way back out, they discuss the youth hockey league. I swear, I can actively hear the credit card within my purse weeping.

I guess at least we have gear now, though I meant what I said to Camden and want to pay him back somehow. I haven't had the guts to look up all the things he bought and how much they cost yet. But I will.

"I didn't tell your mom why we're here early," Parker says, stopping in front of a door. "But I think you're going to love this."

She pauses dramatically, and my stomach tightens a little with nerves. I'm sure whatever it is will be good, but I cannot take the anticipation any longer.

"How would you," Parker starts, taking a breath and a dramatic pause that has me feeling murdery, "like to read out the starting lineup in the locker room before the game?"

From the hockey knowledge I've gleaned from Liam, I think a starting lineup is basically five guys. Well—five guys plus a goalie. So, Liam gets to read a list of six names. I'm not sure what I was expecting as Parker's surprise, but this honestly feels a bit underwhelming.

Not to Liam though.

His eyes go wide, and his mouth drops open. He glances at me, and I widen my eyes right back, hoping to fake match his energy.

"Seriously?" he asks Parker in an awed whisper.

She nods and then pulls a folded paper out of her cross-body bag. "Yep."

Liam takes the paper like he's holding some kind of delicate, breakable thing, and gingerly unfolds it.

"You can keep that too," she says. "I bet we could get the guys to sign it."

My son looks like he might expire from the excitement of this, and he shocks us both by throwing his arms around Parker.

"Thankyouthankyouthankyou," he says in a rush. "This is —wow. Oh my gosh. *Bruh.*"

I don't even roll my eyes at his use of the word *bruh,* which I keep trying to ban from his vocabulary—unsuccessfully.

Parker laughs as Liam releases her. His full focus moves to the page in his hand, which he reads over and over like he's memorizing it.

"I'm glad you're excited," she tells him. "Your energy will help pump up the guys. Come on, let's go."

I don't have time to react or freak out before Parker leads us through a few more doors and past a security guard to the locker room. Or dressing room, as I remember Liam saying it could also be called. Parker knocks, opens the door an inch, then calls out a warning through the crack.

"Please warn me if you're not decent! Women and child about to enter!"

"Are we ever decent?" one of the guys calls, immediately followed by laughter and several voices saying to come in. Parker throws open the door all the way, and then we step inside the Appies' locker room.

I remember from Parker and Liam talking that the locker room doesn't actually have lockers, but I'm still surprised by the bright, open space. The floor is some kind of rubber matting with an Appies logo in the very center of the room. A padded bench runs around three of the four walls, with wooden built-in shelving units meant for the gear and nameplates above each guy's head. It looks like a large, expensive mudroom.

Stalls, Liam said when he was about to take his tour with Parker a few weeks ago. The term fits more now that I'm seeing everything. This is not the idea I had in my head of a room with metal lockers, cheap wooden benches screwed to a cheap tile floor, and a cloud of spray deodorant hanging in the air, barely covering the smell of old socks and body odor.

I realize only in this moment that in my head, I was picturing my junior high locker room where we had to change for gym class.

Not even close.

This room looks expensive, as I guess a professional sports team's locker room should be. I've heard rumors of hockey gear smelling horrendously foul, but at least right now, the only thing I smell is the scent of very masculine deodorant or body wash. There's a definite vibe in here, a heady anticipation almost like fire, bright and fierce, licking the air and fed by these powerful-looking men preparing for battle.

A few of the guys I've met smile at Liam and me, but others are clearly in serious game-day mode as they gear up. There are a lot more unfamiliar faces, including other Appies staff buzzing around, some in polos like Parker and a few men in full suits. Coaches, I'd guess. All in all, there are way more people than I would have anticipated in this room.

Immediately, I feel out of place, what with all the testosterone, and the sense of something larger I'm very much not a part of.

Needing an emotional anchor of sorts, my gaze finds Camden. Not surprisingly, he looks great. His hair is damp, like he just worked out or showered, curling a little at the back of his neck and over the tops of his ears. His dark-gray athletic shirt clings to his torso and arms. Over it, he has on his shoulder pads, which, like most of the hockey gear I feel like has been poorly named, covers his chest as much as his shoulders.

When I was helping Liam get ready the one time, I told him the shoulder pads reminded me of a superhero costume. I think it's the shape of the chest part, which falls right where a logo would, like Superman's S. Liam only rolled his eyes and groan-whispered, *Mom, stop.*

Camden's skates are on but unlaced, and he's wearing his hockey pants (again: shorts) while currently taping up his hockey socks (louder for those in the back: *not* socks). He has a sort of swagger about him right now, even while seated. It's in the confident set of his shoulders, the smirky little smile he gives me, like he knows I'm checking him out and ready to hand out a high approval rating.

Another version of Camden that's new to me: Game Day Camden.

It's a very good look on him.

"Hey, guys!" Parker claps her hands and raises her voice, though a lot of the guys looked up as soon as she came in.

Logan, notably. The way he gazes at her is somewhere between really adorable—he's clearly such a simp for her—

and also slightly uncomfortable … for the same reason. The raw, unabashed adoration in his dark eyes feels almost too personal to be visible for everyone to see.

Logan does not seem to care in the slightest.

Parker puts an arm around Liam, who is clearly about to perish from sheer excitement. "I've got someone special with me today. Some of you have already met Liam."

"Yo, Liam!" Eli is sitting close enough to reach out for a fist bump.

A few of the other guys call out greetings, and Camden stands, taking a few steps over in his skates to shake Liam's hand.

Why this just about does me in, I can't say. But I find my throat suddenly tight with emotion as I watch them.

"Liam."

"Coach Cam." Liam stands straighter now, and I can see him giving Camden a good grip with the handshake. He gets an approving nod from Cam.

Before he goes back to his seat, Camden passes me by, his hand gliding down my arm before he gives my fingertips a quick squeeze. My cheeks feel hot, and I'm suddenly zinging with nerves.

Someone whistles, and Cam grabs a ball of discarded tape from the bench and pegs it their way. Not surprisingly, the target is Van, Greyson's brother, and I almost laugh, remembering her comment about his mouth.

When the laughter subsides, Parker continues in a brisk, business-like tone. "Liam is halfway through our new youth class and doing great. I thought it would be fitting to have him read the lineup today."

There is a chorus of clapping and cheers, and Parker urges Liam to step forward into the room. I don't miss the tiny tremble in his hands clutching the paper with the lineup on it, and I'm grateful when Parker, who I'm learning is always a few steps ahead, presses a tissue into my hands.

"Just in case," she whispers with a smile.

Liam clears his throat, then starts to read in the loudest, most grown-up voice I've ever heard him use. I do my best to be surreptitious as I wipe my eyes.

"And for your starting lineup tonight, we have ..." He pauses, looking down at the list. I'm sure he has them memorized already. Glancing down is just to be sure he doesn't make a mistake due to his nerves. "Number seventeen, Barnes."

I startle when all the guys chant, "Hey!" and clap their hands in unison. Barnes is on the nameplate above Logan, so I'm guessing they use last names or nicknames for lineups.

"Number thirty-seven, Vanity."

Van flexes as everyone claps.

"Number twenty-one, the Kid."

"Hey!" *Clap*.

"He only wishes he was twenty-one!" Van adds, and a few guys laugh.

The Kid must refer to Dominik—the one Greyson was talking about that Parker said was very young. Up close and with no helmet on, he does look young. Liam's voice gains confidence with each name and so does the warm pride bubbling up in my chest.

"Number twenty-three, Sanders."

"Hey!" *Clap*.

"Number eleven." Liam pauses. "Cole. A.k.a. Coach Cam."

This *hey* is a little louder and longer than the others, and so is the clapping that follows.

Camden grins at this, and Eli gives him a friendly shove. I

feel like my stupid heart swelled up and will require some serious renovations if it wants to stay in my chest.

"And between the pipes, Felix Jamison."

"Hey!" This is followed by a whole round of clapping and cheers.

When it subsides, Parker steps forward next to Liam again, but before she can speak, Liam says, "Let's have a beaut of a game tonight, boys!"

More cheering. More guys getting up to fist bump or high five Liam. More of me sniffing and trying not to visibly cry. I don't really care about sports, though I guess I need to at least consider starting to care about this one. I'm not sure why I'm so in my feels about this, other than Liam caring so much and seeing the way Camden and his teammates are being with him.

"You okay there?"

Camden is standing next to me, and I really have to crane my neck to look at him. I'm not sure of his actual height, maybe somewhere around six feet or just over, but with him in skates, I feel Lilliputian.

"Me? I'm totally fine."

"Mm-hm," he says, clearly not believing me but willing to let it go. "I got you something for tonight."

"I want to tell you to stop getting me things."

He raises an eyebrow. "But?"

"But … I kind of like being pampered by you," I confess.

He chuckles. "Good. Because I have no plans to stop. Here."

From somewhere behind him, Camden produces a jersey I didn't notice him holding. He shakes it out and turns it so I see his last name—which I now know—and number on the back.

"You don't have to wear it," he says. "What you've got on looks ... really nice."

I grab the jersey and immediately tug it over my head. It's a little too big, but I like the way it hangs down over my hips. It would probably look really good with leggings under it. Or a shorter skirt and boots.

"How does it look?" I ask, turning so he can see the back. When I glance over my shoulder at him, his smile is pure male pride.

"Like it belongs on you," he says. "A perfect fit."

And it's funny because after my concerns about today and how it might be to see Camden in his element and have the full hockey experience, so far, it feels as fitting as wearing Camden's jersey.

CHAPTER 15

Naomi

I HAD no idea there were so many whistles in hockey. Or at least, for so many boring things. I would maybe have expected whistles for players punching each other in the face but have to admit I'm a little disappointed.

I mean, I wouldn't feel good about Camden fighting. Probably. I shouldn't feel good about it—both for the sake of his face and also for the example it might set for Liam. But hockey fights are different than street fights. This is what I'm telling myself. I'd be able to say this with more confidence if I actually got to see a fight.

Camden isn't on the ice right now, which makes it a good time for questions, which Liam and Bailey, sitting on my other side, have happily answered through most of the first period. The other WAGs—I'm with Parker and want to come up with a new name—are up in a special family area, and we'll go up there during intermission.

But I suspect the three of us will end up back down here, closer to the action. Even if there's free food.

I wasn't sure how it would be at a loud event like this with someone as quiet as Bailey. She seems to actually thrive in the noise and chaos, and I find that I like her even more than I did the first time we met.

She has an inherent sweetness to her, which, on someone else, might be an annoying characteristic. With Bailey, it's not.

She isn't cloyingly sweet or fake sweet. Just genuinely kind.

Then again, when some guy on the other team knocked Eli down earlier, she did yell some things that might have gotten her arrested if she were yelling those words anywhere but a hockey game.

While the guys were out doing warm-ups, Bailey told me a little about her relationship with Eli. She fell for him totally not knowing who he was and not knowing the first thing about hockey. I asked how it works with the travel and schedule and Eli being semi-famous.

"At times, really hard," she told me, biting into the chocolate bar Eli slipped me in the locker room and asked me to deliver. "But also, completely worth it. You find a way to make the hard things tolerable, the not-so-great parts manageable, and the rough patches navigable. Because the person you love makes all those difficult things forgettable."

Simple words, spoken with a raw honesty that squeezed between my ribs and lodged right in my heart like an arrow.

"Now what?" I groan, as the refs blow the whistles again, just when two Appies were chasing a puck down toward the other team's goal.

"That's an icing call," Liam explains as the play stops for like the fourth time in as many minutes. "Did you see how the ref has his arm up? That tells you it's icing."

"What even *is* icing?"

Liam patiently explains the rule, which keeps defensive players from just whacking the puck out of their zone and all the way to the other end of the ice over and over. Apparently, one of the Appies just did that to clear the puck. Though there's no score on the board yet, it's been very back and forth.

"But why *can't* they just hit it all the way down? And they did that over and over again just a minute ago without any whistles."

"That was during a power play," Liam explains. "If you're down a man and on the penalty kill, you can ice it all you want."

Bailey leans closer so I can hear her soft voice over the din in the sold-out arena. "They put the rule in place to stop teams from doing it over and over to protect a lead. It would be really annoying to watch."

I guess I can see that. What I *can't* see most of the time is the puck. It moves so fast that by the time I locate it, I lose it again. Liam told me to watch the players' bodies rather than looking directly for the puck, but I still get lost.

Except when Camden is on the ice. And because he's on what Liam explained is the top defensive pairing, he's out there a lot. Then, I don't really give a rip where the puck is—Camden has my full focus. His job involves a lot of knocking guys into the boards and trying to get pucks out of the defensive zone—without icing.

Once I got over thinking he was going to get hurt every time he slammed into someone, I started to enjoy watching him.

It was one thing to see Cam on ice with Liam during the class, where slow and steady is the name of the game.

Tonight, I've seen Camden's explosive power and speed that has honestly left me awed. Like, this quiet man, this secretly funny man, this patient man—he's holding all *this* inside him all the time?

All the buzz about hockey romances—okay, fine. I get it now.

As Camden hops over the bench and takes position on the ice for a face-off (look at me with the hockey terms!), I lean forward, my hands clenched. We're only a few rows back from the glass, in great seats that Parker arranged for us, but if I could, I'd have my face pressed up against the glass.

The ref drops the puck, and Eli knocks it back to Camden, and Bailey claps beside me. It gives me a little baby buzz to realize that guy out there—the one who just cut to a stop behind his net and switched directions to make a pass is *mine*.

Mine-ish.

We've danced around the topic of labeling our relationship this week, with Camden keeping up a party line of saying he wants to be serious but slow.

My personality hears *slow* and wants to jam my foot on the gas, but Camden's schedule will definitely help in this department. He left the morning after our lunch for a few road games. Other than a few video calls we had in addition to our now-daily texts, I didn't get to see him until last night —and only for a few minutes.

You up? he'd messaged me at close to midnight.

Duh, I responded. *I've been waiting to hear you landed safely.*

For some trips, I guess the team takes a charter bus, but this time, they flew to the West Coast for a series against a team in Bakersfield.

Knock knock, he'd texted next, and by the time I realized why, he was actually knocking softly at my front door.

I threw myself into his arms and barely felt the cold as he pressed me up against the front of the house and kissed me until I could hardly breathe.

Then he put me down and stepped back. "Go inside before your toes fall off," he'd ordered in just the kind of tone I both love and want to disobey.

I crossed my arms and stood my ground. "You're not coming in?"

"Nope. Just needed to see you."

When I tried to protest, he only grinned, backing away to his car while repeating, "Serious and slow."

When I got back inside and put on socks to warm my feet up, I composed a long text making an argument for why slow and steady wouldn't actually win the race and therefore he should consider another catch phrase.

He'd texted back four words: *Something to think about.*

Then three more: *Serious and slow.*

Serious and slow. Serious—and slow. His new mantra, his chorus line, and the bane of my current existence. At least ... the slow part. I have *no* problem with serious.

In truth, it's probably a wise choice to go slow. This is my first real adult relationship. I can't pretend to know what I'm doing or how this works. And though Liam loves Camden and vice versa, it's not enough. If things progressed to the level of a marriage type commitment, Camden has to be okay not just being a husband, but an instant dad.

He'd see Liam at his worst, when he's being bratty or difficult. Admittedly, this isn't often. Liam's a stellar kid. But maybe such a big change would make him bratty and difficult?

No—I doubt it. Not with how much Liam loves and looks

up to Camden. It would be an adjustment, but Liam would be absolutely *thrilled*.

Which brings up a whole other issue making slow a good choice—What if it doesn't work out?

Like last summer, I'd be dealing with my own heartbreak plus my kid's. Only much worse, because things are already more intense than they were. I guess that's how it works when you restart a relationship: you aren't starting over exactly, but spring-boarding from where you left off.

Also, Cam wouldn't be signing up just for the Liam of right now. I've lived through a whole host of developmental changes. One of the biggest is still to come: the teen years. Who knows how he'll behave when puberty hits Liam full force.

Sticking with me for the long haul is like shacking up to someone holding a grenade. There's a chance it might not go off, but you won't know until it does!

Has Camden even considered that? Do I need to warn him of all the worst-case scenarios that come with me like a bag of party *un*favors?

If those reasons weren't enough, Camden has Mike, and that's a whole other complication I'm not sure about. Mike is great, and it's amazing what Cam is doing for him, but even from our brief conversation over lunch and the few we've had this week, I can't help but wonder if he's in over his head.

And is Mike a package deal for Camden like Liam is for me? Again, this is looking maybe too far ahead, but it's definitely something to consider.

Begrudgingly, I think serious and slow is the right choice. Even if I don't *like* it.

"Yeah!" Liam and Bailey jump up along with most of the arena as a very loud horn sounds. I guess we scored.

I'm a few seconds behind everyone else getting to my feet but waste no time screaming because Camden is out there, part of a group hug involving all the Appies on the ice.

"Did Camden score?" I ask Liam, shouting to be heard over the horn that won't stop blaring.

"No. Eli got the goal, but Camden got a point," Liam says.

"I ... don't understand."

"Eli scored the goal. But Camden gets a point for an assist."

Just when I think I am starting to understand hockey, something new confuses me again. "But there's only one point on the scoreboard. Not two."

"The points are just hockey stats. Players get a point for a goal and a point for an assist. I'll show you later. We can look up Camden's stats." Liam grins, clearly thrilled that I finally care (at least a little) about his obsession.

"Go Cole!" Liam shouts, his hands cupped around his mouth.

The announcers mostly use the players' last names or a nickname, so since the game started, Liam dropped Coach Cam in favor of Cole.

I think it's funny I didn't *know* Camden's last name until today. We had no need to be so formal on the island last summer, and Cam's social media handle is simply Camden_CO11.

The celebratory hugging has broken up, and the guys on the ice skate by the short wall, tapping gloves with their teammates on the bench. The horn finally stops blaring, but the fans are still on their feet. An upbeat 90s rock ballad blasts over the speakers while the big screens above us show the goal again in slow motion.

Camden passed to someone whose number I couldn't see, and that guy passed it to Eli, who was planted in front of the goal and barely tipped it in. When they show it at regular speed, I can't even see the puck.

How in the world do goalies ever stop them? It makes no sense to me, even if I've watched Felix make multiple saves tonight.

Wearing thirty pounds of pads, apparently, which was one of the facts I learned from Liam on the drive here and still remember for whatever reason.

All in all, I'm more impressed—and slightly confused—by hockey than ever before. And as far as how it's impacted my view of Camden ... well, let's just say I'm a fan.

As he takes his spot on the bench, I don't miss the way he scans our section. Though he's all the way across the ice, I know when he's found me because his gaze stops. He doesn't smile, but he inclines his head the smallest bit, kind of a less bro-y chin lift. Grinning, I wave wildly because I just don't care if I look silly.

Seeing me wave, Liam glances over at the bench, then he starts waving too. Camden's smile grows, though he appears to be trying to hide it behind a water bottle. We're being kind of ridiculous, but I can't bring myself to care.

Bailey leans over, a knowing smile on her face. "It's pretty great, isn't it?"

It is. And it might be the hockey high talking, but for once, when it comes to a man in my life, letting loose seems like the best option of all.

———

During the break between periods—intermission, Liam corrected when I referred to it as halftime—Bailey, Liam, and

I head up to the box Parker told me about. It's similar to the family suite downstairs with food and drinks and comfy seating with several screens. Unlike the suite, which is somewhere in the bowels of the building, this box is high with a great view of the ice. It also has a decent number of people I don't know milling around.

I hoped for a few familiar faces, but I haven't seen Parker since the locker room, and she told me Grey is working. We probably won't see her tonight—at least until after the game when we're all going to Felix's. I'd rather not go with my kid in tow, but since I haven't figured out a babysitter, it's take him or not go at all. Parker assured me it won't be some wild party and they'd be happy to have us both. I'm also reluctant to keep Liam up so late on a school night, but this game had a five o'clock start time, so it won't be *that* bad. Probably.

Liam immediately gravitates toward the food again, making me wonder if he's about to hit another growth spurt. I should eat, but my nervous stomach says otherwise.

"There they are," Bailey says, linking her arm through mine. "Come on and I'll introduce you."

Gracie is talking to two other women who wave as they see us crossing the room. All three are dressed up, wearing skirts with nicer tops, not jerseys and jeans like Bailey and me. But I notice each wears something with a number on it that I assume belongs to their guy.

The woman with dark hair in a sleek ponytail has on a gold necklace with a delicate number twenty-three hanging down over her black scoop neck blouse. Gracie wears a charm bracelet with a variety of hockey and other related things. The biggest charm is a thirty-one inlaid with what looks like tiny sparkling diamonds. When the woman with soft, honey-blond waves turns, I realize she's wearing a fitted short-sleeved shirt with a thirty-seven across the front.

"Naomi, this is Summer and Amelia. They're married to Nathan and Van, respectively."

"Apologies. I know it might be hard to keep us all straight," Summer says.

It is, but meeting the women a few at a time has helped. If I had met them all at once, I'd never remember their names and couldn't say which guy they're with unless I have a program in hand to know whose numbers they're wearing.

"I'm glad y'all decided to grace us with your presence," Amelia teases.

But it's playful, and Bailey rolls her eyes good-naturedly. "You know I like watching the game from actual seats. Though I do like the free food and drinks. Speaking of which ... want something?" she asks me.

I glance over, where Liam balances two hot dogs and some cookies on a plate while swigging a giant plastic cup of soda.

"Maybe in a minute. Thanks."

I realize as soon as she leaves that I should have gone with her because I'm now feeling like the new girl on the first day of school. Not sure if I'm wearing the right clothes. I hate giving into that kind of insecurity, so I remind myself that everyone has been great to me and shove down the stupid feelings.

"Let's," Summer says, nodding to a seating area that just opened up.

I end up on a couch between Gracie and Amelia with Summer taking a chair next to us. We can still hear the buzz of the arena from the open balcony and the televisions play quietly, but overall, the noise is a bit muted, which is a relief. The couch is definitely preferable to the seats downstairs.

"You look ready to be convinced you should stay up here with us in the fancy seats," Summer says.

"And the free food," Bailey says, sitting down with a plate that's mostly sugary things.

"And away from all the fans." Amelia gives a dramatic little shiver.

"Do fans give any of you a hard time?" I ask.

I'm sure the women are publicly linked with the guys through photographs or articles, but I'd be surprised if they would be recognizable in a crowd.

Or maybe I'm just not in the hockey bubble to understand how obsessive the fans get.

"Not me," Gracie says. "I just prefer a little space from the chaos down there. I get less nervous for Felix up here. I'm not sure why."

"My dad's the coach," Amelia says, taking a sip of her white wine. "Every so often I get recognized and people want to talk to me or tell me what my dad is doing right. Or wrong." She smirks. "And if anyone happens to know who my husband is, I might get an earful. Especially from the other team's fans for whatever Van might have said or done on the ice. He's always the most hated player by other teams."

She says it proudly, which surprises me. I don't think I'd handle that kind of negative attention well. I might end up fighting someone if they made a comment about Camden.

"Don't worry," Bailey says. "We mostly go unnoticed and unrecognized. If you don't want attention, you can absolutely avoid it."

Amelia laughs, but it's not unkind. "I think we're still traumatizing her. Do we need a subject change? Because I have to assume you're the reason Camden is finally playing well tonight. We'll really be in trouble with my dad *and* the guys if we scare you off."

"I'm fine," I tell her. "Honestly, it's probably good to know this kind of thing before …"

I trail off, not wanting to say *before I get fully invested.*

I'm already invested in Camden—even after he left and I didn't *want* to care about him—I did. But now, until there's some kind of official title on the table, I'm saving an escape hatch for myself.

Just in case.

In case I don't love this hockey life or this version of Camden. Though so far, in this admittedly small sample size of experience, I'm loving it.

Or even in case I don't turn out to be the kind of person who can handle a long-term committed relationship. I have no idea what will happen if my restlessness starts to buzz again and Camden becomes the collateral damage with my need for change.

Or in case this relationship seems like a bad choice for Liam for any reason at all.

My eyes find my son across the room, parked in a chair in front of a flat screen, watching replays as he shovels cookies into his mouth. He's been on whatever cloud is above Cloud 9 since he got to read the lineup. This might just be the best night of his life. I'm happy for that, and I'm happy he's glued to the screens.

I don't really want him to be involved in this conversation. For all his hockey knowledge, what it's like to be in a relationship with a player isn't something he has stats on. Or that I want him thinking about.

"Actually, can I ask some nosy questions about being with a guy who does *this* for a living?" I jerk my thumb toward the screen Liam's watching, where a goal is being replayed in slow motion.

"Nosy questions are my favorite kind," says Amelia with

the kind of sly grin that makes me feel certain she's the perfect counterpart for Van and his smart mouth.

"Happy to answer what I can," Summer says. "I'm a pretty open book."

"I like the way you worded that," Gracie tells me. "Because a good starting point is to remember hockey is their *job*. Identity gets tied up in there too, but ultimately, it is their career. A different one than, say, an office job, but still. It is but it isn't who they *are*."

I see her point, but also how different this would be as a job, and also how identity would get tangled up in hockey, maybe more than other, typical jobs.

"The pay isn't bad," Amelia says with a smirk. "On the very shallowest of sides, that's a perk."

"I thought minor league players didn't make much," I say, feeling slightly awkward mentioning money. But I did google this, and the base salary for an AHL player was somewhere around fifty thousand dollars a year. Which sounded incredibly low for how much time this takes and also the amount of success these guys seem to have.

"Not all AHL players make great money," Summer says. "But it depends on their contracts—many of these guys have a contract with the NHL affiliate. Plus, the Appies are incredibly popular because of social media. I handle a lot of their contracts with brands, and they do well."

"I'm not interested in Camden for the money," I say quickly. "And not having tons of money wouldn't be a deal-breaker. We've definitely scraped by for a lot of years."

"Me too," Bailey says. "And you don't need to defend yourself about the money. Honestly, it does make some things easier—like my vet school—but we can tell you're not just with Camden for that."

"Best thing about dating a hockey player?"

Gracie smiles at this. "The best thing? It has nothing to do with hockey. The best thing is just who the guys are."

"Agreed," Summer says.

"I like that they come ready-made with friends." Amelia smiles. "Without being too cheesy—their friendships and the ones we get."

"The worst part," Gracie says, "assuming you were going to ask about that too, is the uncertainty. We've had a good run with the guys mostly staying put. But they won't forever. Or even for long. Logan definitely will be called up soon. It's a matter of time."

"And cap space," Summer adds.

I don't know what that means, but Liam has mentioned salary caps before, so I can assume it has something to do with however that works.

"We lost Wyatt to Boston before this season started. Camden was close with him, I think," Gracie says.

"It doesn't happen as much in the AHL as the NHL, but sometimes the moves happen really quickly," Summer says. "Right before a game or in the middle of the game. The player might need to be on a plane that afternoon, leaving the wife or girlfriend to pack up their life and join him ... or do long distance."

Long distance isn't something I want to do—it's one of the things I kept telling myself last summer when I was trying to keep my feelings for Camden in check. If it weren't for Liam, I could thrive under uncertainty. I'm sure my restlessness would love the idea of a new city. Travel and a fresh start.

But I'm not a single woman in her twenties. I'm a single *mother* in her twenties. Though I just made a multi-state move in the middle of the school year that's working just fine, it wouldn't be fair to Liam to keep doing that.

"Some of the guys have been here for years," Bailey says, clearly reading the internal freakout I'm having on my face. "There are career AHL players who spend years on one team."

"Like Felix," Gracie says. "He turned away offers to go elsewhere. He wants to stay."

"And Alec," Summer says. "Before he retired, he was here forever. What else do you want to know?"

Of course, now my brain blanks with what other questions I might ask. I happen to glance down at the rink and my eye catches on two women seated behind the bench. I remember seeing them hold up posters with their phone numbers when the guys sat down for warm-ups. My brain circles back to what Amelia said about the fans.

"Is it weird being with a guy while knowing there are probably dozens of women who have no shame about sliding into their DMs?"

"Dozens is a low estimate," Amelia says with a laugh, and it makes my stomach twist.

"I hate it," Bailey confesses, looking at me apologetically. "And though I trust Eli, he's so sweet and friendly, those qualities can make it harder when it comes to someone who's pushy or manipulative."

"You know Eli says no and draws lines when he needs to," Gracie says kindly, reaching over to touch Bailey's arm.

"I do know," Bailey says. "Sometimes ... I still worry or feel insecure. That's on me, but it does come with the territory."

"It's definitely one of the worst parts," Gracie agrees. "The public nature of what they do and the way people feel a sense of ownership. Or like because they follow them on social media or know their stats or watch interviews that they *know* them."

"Ugh—social media," Amelia says. "I do hate that. I can't go on my own feed without seeing edits of my husband."

"Edits?" I ask.

"Fans put together video clips or photo montages to music," Amelia explains. "Often with a caption like, 'Possibly the One' or 'NGL—I'd have his babies tomorrow.'"

"Ew. People really do that?"

"Yes," they all say in unison.

Gracie wrinkles her nose. "And those are pretty tame examples."

"I actually like the edits of Nathan," Summer says, laughing. "Because I don't want to do the work of making them, but I like looking at Nathan. It's like they're giving me a little gift. And if they're too creepy or weird with the captions or song choice, I just report them for copyright infringement since they don't have permission to use most of the clips they use."

Amelia cackles. "Summer! Are you serious?"

Summer shrugs, looking unapologetic. "Sometimes I'm petty. I won't apologize for it."

"Can I report videos, too?" Bailey asks.

"Yup. And if that doesn't work, I can also send a legal takedown notice. Half the time, they're using videos the Appies own."

"I love having a lawyer friend," Amelia says with a laugh. "I wish I had a cool skill to contribute. Gracie can play amazing music, and Bailey can spay or neuter our pets."

"Don't sell yourself short! You could write our life stories," Bailey says. "And I can't spay or neuter pets until I'm done with vet school." She makes a face. "Also, saying I can just spay and neuter animals sounds really weird. How about … I can help people find the perfect dog to adopt?"

"I want to adopt a dog!"

Liam appears behind me, and I almost jump out of my skin. I'm just grateful he wasn't here when we were talking about edits.

But maybe this is actually worse.

"Can we?" he asks, borderline begging.

"We can't have a dog right now," I tell him. For like the hundredth time.

Look—I like dogs. All animals, really. But dogs require a stability we haven't had, what with me switching jobs and moving from Oakley to Savannah then back to Oakley, mostly staying in apartments where we—let's be honest, I— would be responsible for walking the dog all the time without having a yard. Liam is responsible. But would he do most of the dog-related things? Probably not. Because he's responsible *for a ten-year-old*.

"But now we're in a house," he argues now. "There's a fenced yard and everything."

"A house we *rent*. I'm sure the rental agreement says no pets."

"Did you even look at the rental agreement?"

I signed it. Did I read it? Unlikely. But I definitely will *now*.

Before I can answer, Liam turns his full charm on Bailey. "Can you help us find a dog to adopt?"

Bailey glances between us. Liam, with his adorable, pleading eyes. Me with desperate ones saying *Don't you dare*.

"Um," she says.

Just then the announcer welcomes the Appies back to the ice and the crowd cheers.

I stand up. "We better get back to our seats! Time for the second half."

I know very well it's a period, not a half, and that there are three of them in a hockey game.

But I'm hoping to distract Liam from any talk of dogs, and it works because he corrects me and then talks about the breakdown of a hockey game all the way back down to our seats.

CHAPTER 16

Camden

THE HOUR after our game almost kills me. It's interminably slow.

Coach doesn't keep us long, since his notes can basically be summed up by him telling us we played well, and that we can't take our foot off the gas through the stretch leading to the playoffs.

Yeah, yeah. Got it. Play good hockey. Repeat.

I expected a little more of a speech after our decisive five-one win, since Coach loves a good win and gets a little wordy. Tonight, I didn't mind the brevity.

But then Larry Jensen appears like a mustachioed specter in the locker room, wanting to give us an owner's speech, which is basically a whole lot of grandstanding about how *we* are doing. Last time I looked, the man wasn't on the ice. Or at a practice. I'm not sure what he does, other than overbook us for all kinds of appearances and activities designed to exhaust us and line his bank account.

Coach barely holds back his eye rolls, and when the two of them disappear into Coach's office, I'm reminded of the tense meeting they had the first day I found Liam in class.

I'd forgotten all about the yelling and haven't thought once about the potential shift in the organization it might signify. But the tightness in Coach's mouth before he shuts the door makes me feel more certain something bad is happening literally behind those closed doors.

Before I can escape to the showers, I'm forced into doing post-game interviews, which I've avoided for the past few months. Partly because I've played so poorly no one wanted to talk to me, and partly because the only person worse at interviews than I am is Nathan.

I'm not a grouch like he is, glaring at the press like they're personally violating his space and privacy, but I'm not eloquent. Alec was always good at giving good sound bites— saying things that sounded smart, showing off his hockey IQ. Van is good for the kind of funny quotes that go viral on social media. And then there's me.

I give the quintessential dumb hockey player interview people make fun of online. *Yeah, we uh, just tried to control the puck, uh, get it in deep and, uh, put it in the back of the net. Yeah.*

My *yeahs* and *uhs* are out in full force, and I can tell the correspondents are not getting what they want from me because they look bored.

Good. Maybe they won't ask me to do interviews ever again.

I take the fastest shower possible to wash off the sweat and the stink of the game. I give myself a little extra scrub for good measure. Per the usual, I ignore most of the conversations in the room as I button up my dress shirt. My wet hair drips down my back, and I think about Mike saying I need a haircut. Maybe he's right.

The past few months, I've been rushing home to Mike. But there's very little worry now that I've got a team of three home caregivers who split the time. Jordan, who remains my favorite, is there now. I'd like to get both of them out to a game sometime, maybe with Liam and Naomi. But for now, I've set up an app on the TVs at home so they can watch.

Good game! Jordan texted. *Mike says to be home by curfew, but I say stay out as late as you want.*

So, it's not worrying about Mike that has me disengaged with the guys and rushing to get ready. Tonight, I'm in my head and not paying attention in the room because I know Naomi and Liam are waiting for me, and every moment I'm in here, not out there, feels endless.

Someone smacks me on the arm with a damp towel. Van. I wish he hadn't stripped the towel off his body to hit me with it, but ... it's Van. "Finally, Cole! You showed up."

I frown. "What? I've been here the whole time."

"No, I mean, your head was back in the game."

"Cammie's back, baby!" Eli crows.

I ignore the other guys agreeing, but they're right. I *was* back on the ice, figuratively speaking.

And it felt really good. Great, actually. I'd forgotten the whole-body satisfaction of a game played hard. I'm sore but my muscles are singing and adrenaline soaked.

But it wasn't so much that my head was in the game. My head was with Naomi and Liam, sitting a few rows back near the center line. I may not have looked up every time I was near, but I was constantly aware of them. Aware of how my actions on the ice might look to them. I wanted to make a good showing, to make them proud.

If I was effective on the ice, it's because I needed to prove something to them both. Even if I already know they're two people who wouldn't see me differently if I'd played as badly as I have all season.

I wanted to be better. For them. And maybe, a little, for myself.

For the kid who wanted to look up and see his mom and dad in the stands. Maybe, just once, his sisters. The teenage boy who was almost a man but still felt like a kid. A kid who very much wanted his family to show up. To care. To make the bare minimum of effort.

There was Mike, and it helped to be wanted by *someone*, but I wanted to be wanted by my *parents*. Seeing how quickly they gave up on me made all my previous memories feel tainted somehow. Like, could the happy, normal family I remembered be real if they could just move on without me— like I'd never been part of them at all?

I couldn't grasp that. Still can't.

I'm usually better now about gatekeeping these thoughts at games, but tonight, having Naomi and Liam here stirred up the memories and the sense of longing that used to drive me.

For a few years after my sisters were born, as it started to sink in that my family had changed, the hurt morphed into an anger that drove me. The emotions I couldn't process became my fuel. I became a better hockey player because of it, but also a bit of a goon. Late hits, dirty hits, any hits. I chased the pain and used the physical roughness as a way to work out my feelings.

Only, it didn't work. And it was Mike who finally called me out on it.

My first year of college, he came to one of my games where we won, but I had two minor penalties and then got thrown out with two minutes left for back-checking their star

218

center into the boards. Coach wasn't happy with me, but I didn't think it was a huge deal. We won. I led the team in hits and had two blocks. So what if I also got kicked out?

Afterward, Mike took me to a diner where they served breakfast all day. I scarfed down eggs and bacon while Mike sipped a malt.

I didn't notice how quiet he was—probably because I was running on a post-game high—until he said, "You're playing against ghosts, Cam."

I almost choked on my eggs. Immediately defensive because I knew he was right, I started to argue. But when he shook his head, I noticed he had tears in his eyes. That shut me up.

"You're playing against ghosts, which means you can't win. You will always lose," he told me. "Every time. The only way to win is to stop playing against them. Let the ghosts go."

I didn't want to listen. I didn't want to recognize the truth. In fact, after Mike dropped me off, I met up with my teammates and drank myself into oblivion.

But I woke up the next day with a pounding headache and an unignorable clarity: I didn't want to fight the ghosts.

That one talk changed not only how I played hockey but how I lived. I still felt—and feel—hurt and rejected and confused. But I didn't let those feelings be my fuel. I stopped fighting the ghosts.

And I never got to tell Mike that because soon after is when everyone found out about his affair. His life imploded, and it felt like the wrong time to thank him. We sort of drifted apart then. Nothing like what happened with my parents. We still talked, but he came to fewer games, and we didn't have any more heart-to-hearts.

He was, I suspect, ashamed of his actions. And I was still

just a kid, probably too focused on my own self to know what to say.

Anyway, tonight was the first time in years I thought about my parents not being here. But instead of those wounds reopening and being any kind of motivation for my play, I simply recognized the hurt and let it go.

Naomi and Liam being in the stands, being there for me was like a balm, soothing over those past scars.

I know this is probably too much weight to place on them. I'm moving too fast, wanting too much.

But it doesn't seem possible to staunch the flow of my feelings. So, I just … gave in.

I didn't even know what the score was for most of the game. I just knew I needed to win every battle along the boards, clear the zone, and hit anyone who had the puck. Each shift on the ice was about doing the work. For them.

The by-product, I guess, is that my teammates are thrilled. *Yay.*

"You're coming over, right?" Felix asks.

Though a handful of the guys have already cleared out, our goalie still hasn't showered. After a game, he sits in front of his stall for at least thirty minutes, stripped down to his bare chest up top but still wearing his goalie pants and pads. He's never said why or what he's thinking about when he sits there, but I suspect he's trying to replay every shot on goal and his response.

Goalies are weird.

"I'll be there," I tell him. If I ever get out of this locker room. I've changed back into my game-day suit, which I probably will change out of as soon as we get to Felix's. But I was in such a rush earlier, I left my other change of clothes in my car.

I don't really mind wearing a suit in front of Naomi. She's

only ever seen me in beach clothes, hockey gear, and casual clothes.

"Are you bringing Naomi and Liam?" Eli clasps his hands together like he's begging. "Please say yes. We need to thank them and see what we can do about getting them to every game so you play that well."

"We promise not to embarrass you too much." Van smirks.

"The rest of us promise that," Logan says. "Van absolutely will embarrass you every chance he gets."

"Consider it a test," Van says with a shrug, finally pulling on some pants. "If she sticks around afterward, she's worth it."

"She's totally worth it. Did you see this guy lay out their pretty-boy rookie?" Tucker asks. "It was glorious, man."

"Yeah, you can't jeopardize that," Dumbo says, and Tucker gives him a high five. "Maintain the status quo."

Dominik rolls his eyes and says something in Russian. Tucker looks down at his phone, then cackles.

"Dude, you shouldn't say stuff like that about his ears. Or his mother." When Dominik looks at him, confused, Tucker holds up his phone. "I got a translator so I could figure out if you were actually insulting us or not. Spoiler alert, everyone: he absolutely *is* insulting us. Dumbo, he said your big ears come from a mother who—"

Tucker gets cut off when Dominik tackles him, grabbing for the phone. Dumbo piles on top, and I step around them all, straightening my tie and ignoring the scuffle.

"Looking sharp," Van says with an approving look. "Good way to lock that down."

I roll my eyes and walk on by and pause by Felix. "Need me to bring anything?"

Finally done with his post-game ritual, he stands,

221

stretches with a groan, and starts to remove the rest of his pads. He grins. "Nope. As long as you bring the woman and kid who reminded you how to play hockey, I don't care if you come in your underwear. Though the suit does look nice."

As I push my way through the door, I give his bare shoulder a shove, then have to listen to his laughter as I make my way down the hall to find Liam and Naomi.

———

The look on Naomi's face makes wearing the suit worth it. When I walked into the family suite, she dropped her phone but didn't even seem to notice. Her eyes went hazy, and she bit her lip in a way that made me really have to hold back. Because a few other people are still in the family suite. Including Liam.

He definitely did *not* care about the suit and practically knocked me over when he threw himself at me in an unexpected hug. This isn't the first time he's hugged me, but this hits different somehow. I swallow, hugging him back as I meet Naomi's gaze over the top of his head.

She still looks a little dazed, and the smile she gives me promises a better greeting later. When we're alone.

If we're alone. Going to this party with Liam in tow won't exactly afford us any privacy. And with Mike at my place and Liam at hers, I guess that's the way it's going to be.

Better get used to existing in a state of wanting what I can't have.

He releases me quickly and starts babbling about the game, his whole face alight with excitement.

"The way you laid that guy out at the end was awesome! And two apples—clutch."

"Apples?" Naomi asks.

"Assists," Liam and I say at the same time. He laughs, and Naomi looks between us, smiling as she shakes her head.

"No chance he's getting over hockey," she says as I bend down to pick up her phone. "Not now."

"I was never getting over it," Liam says. "Get used to it, Mom. Are we really going to Felix's house?"

"Are you more excited to hang out with Felix than me?" I tease.

"No way. But ... he's really tall."

"And I'm not?"

Liam scrunches up his face. "I mean, you're six-one. He's six-five."

"I'm not sure you're one to talk, bud," Naomi tells him.

"I'm just saying. Cole—I mean, Coach Cam—is hockey *average*."

"Hockey *average*? That's it. Hold this." I hand Naomi back her phone, making sure my fingertips brush over her palm a little longer than necessary. Then I toss Liam over my shoulder, balancing him against the weight of my bag, and march out of the family suite. "Someone needs to be thrown in the ice bath."

I don't *actually* throw Liam in the ice bath. But I do walk him down there and threaten it, holding him over the water while he squeals.

Then we make our way out in the cold to the parking lot where I finally set Liam down at the car. "Oh, I brought you something," I tell him, pulling a puck out of my bag. "It's the game winning goal. Logan signed it for you."

Liam goes still, staring at me with wide eyes. "Seriously? He didn't want to keep it?"

"Nah. He's already got enough pucks."

I don't look at Naomi, but from my peripheral vision, I can see her pressing a hand to her chest. Tentatively, Liam holds out his palm and I drop the puck into it. He turns it over, running his finger over Logan's messy scrawl in silver Sharpie.

"He wrote my name," Liam says.

"I told him it was for you." This earns me another hug, this one tighter and longer.

Finally, I allow my gaze to find Naomi. She still has one hand pressed to her chest, the other wrapped around her waist, like she's giving herself a hug. She looks somehow both happy and sad at the same time.

"Come here," I tell her, opening one arm. And then I'm hugging them both, one tucked under each arm.

There's no moon, so the only light comes from a very unromantic streetlight, but as we stand in the parking lot surrounded by equally unromantic chain link fencing and the sound of highway traffic, it feels like the kind of special moment that's going to shift my entire world.

Or ... like it already has.

CHAPTER 17

Naomi

I ALMOST BACK OUT of going to Felix's. The long day, the excitement of the game, and the emotional moment in the parking lot after Cam gave Liam the puck—it was a *lot*. I feel like a wrung-out cloth, twisted up in the feels. And Liam is probably more ready to crash than I am.

But I didn't want to leave Camden. To the point that when he offers to drive us, I don't argue or try to figure out the logistics for later. I just say yes.

I turn on the seat warmers, snuggling down into the soft leather seat of Camden's SUV while Liam starts rattling off facts about pucks.

"Did you know they freeze pucks before a game?"

I answer because I'm sure Camden is already aware. "I did *not* know that. Is there some kind of puck cooler?"

"There's usually a puck freezer in or near the penalty box.

Keeping them cold helps reduce the bounce. A puck that comes bouncing erratically at the goalie is called a knuckle puck. Usually, if the linesmen notice a puck behaving erratically, they'll grab a new one."

I yawn. "I guess they use a few pucks per game, huh?"

"On average, it's between thirty and forty," Liam says.

"Really?" I don't know why this fact surprises me or why I look to Camden for confirmation when I know Liam has extensively researched all this.

Camden nods.

"Sounds expensive."

"Usually between six to eight hundred per game," Liam says. "That's nothing compared to the cost of broken sticks."

He continues, talking as much to himself as to us, it seems, and I lean a little closer to Camden. "Did I tell you yet that you had a great game?"

His lips twitch into an almost smile. A tease of a smile that feels like a challenge to earn more. "You might have said so in your texts, but you haven't said it to my face."

I started sending texts to Camden midway through the first period, after the assist. Then, I couldn't stop texting, even though I knew he probably wouldn't see them until after the game.

Naomi: You got a point!
Naomi: That sounds weird to me since you didn't score the goal, but Liam says you get points for assisting.
Naomi: OH MY GOSH YOU JUST SENT A GUY INTO THE BENCH
Naomi: Does it make me bloodthirsty if I really liked it?
Naomi: They should have called that stupid hit on you. How was that legal? Is your face okay?

226

Naomi: (Is it ironic that I'm asking you this after I punched you in the face a few weeks ago?)

Naomi: Sorry for punching you, by the way. I probably already said it, but it bears repeating.

Naomi: Question—are all of your teeth real? Asking for a friend.

Naomi: Liam says to tell you "nice deke"—whatever that means

Naomi: YOU WON! Loved every minute of it. Especially the minutes you were on the ice.

"So, you did get my texts," I tease. "You never responded."

"I never look at my phone until after the game."

"It's after the game," I point out.

We're pulling up to a red light, and Camden turns to me, his face all hard lines and soft lips in the glow of the streetlight. "My only focus was getting to you as fast as possible."

He stares just a little too long, and someone taps the horn behind us to let us know the light turned green. With a last glance at my lips, Camden turns back to the road.

A moment later, he reaches across and takes my hand.

My eyes fly open, immediately looking toward Liam. He's not looking up here, still obsessing over the signed puck he's turning over and over in his hands. I think the console between our seats is blocking our hands from view, but Camden reads my hesitation and starts to pull away.

I grab his hand before he can, linking our fingers for the rest of the ride.

So far, we haven't said anything to Liam. What would I even say? *Hey, bud—Camden and I are dating, though we haven't officially given it a title yet. We're kissing every chance we get, and I think it's serious, but there's still a chance that things won't work out*

227

for a second time, so don't get your hopes up. I don't want you to get crushed again.

It seems better to keep things just friendly in front of Liam—for now.

Which makes the hand holding just out of Liam's sight feel like a fun little secret until we reach Felix's and I let go.

I'm grateful that the gathering is more that—a gathering —than a party. Felix's apartment, first of all, is gorgeous. It's a repurposed loft with high ceilings showing ductwork and beams with an open concept floor plan. The industrial touches are offset by comfortable seating areas and bright artwork. Quiet music plays from speakers I don't see, and I realize it's classical versions of pop songs. There are only about two dozen people here, standing or sitting in various small groups around the loft. Parker waves, and I get a head nod from Summer, who's sitting in Nathan's lap.

Gracie greets us near the door and gives me a hug even though I saw her hours ago. "I'm so glad you came! Good to see you again, Liam. I've got some snacks in the kitchen if you're hungry."

I can't imagine that he is after what he's already eaten today, but Liam immediately scurries off, the outline of the puck visible in his back pocket. As I watch him inspect the food and start piling a plate high, I realize I'm going to need to rework my grocery budget if he keeps this up.

"I brought wine," Camden says, handing Gracie a bottle he must have picked up earlier in the day.

"I brought nothing," I say, and Gracie laughs as she takes the bottle from Cam.

"Wow—this is a good one. Thanks! I think this counts for you both."

"This place is beautiful. Who did the decorating—you or Felix?"

"Mostly Felix, but now a little bit of both," she says. "The library is the one space that I didn't touch. It was already perfect."

She points to an area off the loft with tall bookshelves and a leather sofa clearly defining the space.

"Liam will undoubtedly end up there later. Once he clears out your food. I'm sorry in advance."

"Don't be. We have plenty." A timer goes off, and Gracie glances toward the kitchen. "Make yourselves at home. If you need somewhere to put your coats, there's a guest bedroom back there."

She gestures toward the back area of the loft as she walks away, leaving Camden and me standing just inside the door. I suddenly feel shy.

"Shall we drop off our coats?" I ask. "Because I really want to snoop."

He chuckles and tucks both of our coats under one arm. "Then let's go, little spy."

"I'm not a spy! *Snoop* isn't really the right word. I just like their place and want to look around."

"Is this the kind of place you want to live?"

I think about the question before answering. My gut wants to say yes because this place is honestly amazing. But it's not quite me. I think of the little green craftsman where Liam and I are staying. And even though I love the style of the house and the updates, I'm not sure it would be a forever kind of home either.

When I really consider what feels like home and where I'd want to be long term, my mind goes straight to Oakley Island.

Living in a city like Harvest Hollow, with its historic and adorable downtown, all encircled by a ring of gentle mountains, has been great. I even enjoyed the brief snowfall we had and love the idea of experiencing four full seasons.

I like it here. I like my house. I like this loft.

But home for me is the sea breeze and the cry of gulls. It's seagrass waving in the dunes and sand under my bare feet. A house with a view of the ocean. Air that tastes of salt and makes my hair wild.

I hesitate, but there's no reason not to be honest. If Camden and I don't have matching priorities or ideas of what the future holds, it's better to know it now.

"I can't imagine a life where I don't end up back on Oakley Island," I confess, nerves making my chest feel tight.

Camden doesn't look surprised. "It suits you," he says. "You look like you were born for the beach."

"Where did you grow up?" I ask.

He stiffens. "Wisconsin."

I wait, hoping for him to say something about where he grew up or if he ever thinks about going back. Anything at all about his past or maybe where he sees himself settling down.

Could I just ask him? Absolutely.

But something about his expression and the way he reacted to my question has me hesitating. Logan and Parker interrupt anyway, so I make a little mental note: *talking about his past equals sensitive topic; pry later and pry gently.*

"Did you have fun at the game?" Parker asks me, her eyes bright. Her arm is hooked around Logan's waist like she's not going to let him out of her direct proximity.

And he looks like he has no plans to go anywhere as he asks Camden something about the game.

"Loved it," I tell her. "Seriously. So much fun."

"Yay! Hockey is the best. Anytime you want tickets, let me know. I've got you."

"Are you sure?"

230

"Absolutely. Camden gets two free tickets per game anyway," she says, then lowers her voice, "but he probably doesn't even know how to access them since he hasn't ever had anyone come to a game."

Camden and Logan are laughing about something that happened on the ice earlier, so they're definitely not listening.

It makes me wonder about his family, especially after the way he reacted to my simple question about where he grew up. Though I'm honestly relieved he's never brought another girlfriend to see him play.

Someone calls for Parker, and she and Logan wander off.

Camden raises an eyebrow. "Shall we get rid of our coats then get some food? I'm starving."

We make our way back toward the back of the loft, pausing for brief hellos, and I scan the room to locate Liam. As I predicted, he's in the library area. His plate of snacks has been discarded on a coffee table while he peruses the shelves.

"I never liked to read," Camden confesses, his gaze cutting to the floor. "School was always a struggle. If I'm being honest, Liam intimidates me a little. He's so smart."

I lean into Camden. "He intimidates me too. He's definitely smarter than me and more academically inclined than I ever was. His ability to retain facts amazes me."

It's funny—we managed to sidestep these kinds of conversations last summer. Talking about Liam and reading isn't exactly deep, intimate conversation or anything, but I feel like the things we talked about while we were on Oakley were barely surface level.

We were trying *so* hard to stay casual, even though it didn't work, that we skipped out on the most basic of basics. Still—I got to know Camden the man. Not a list of his likes and dislikes or a plotted-out history but who he is at his core. How he treats others. What makes him smile on a sunny day.

The way he cherishes the people who matter to him.

We've got some catching up to do on the basics we skipped. Clearly. Though some normal topics, like Camden's childhood for example, might be complicated.

We reach the back of the loft, where there's a little alcove. The bathroom door is open in front of us, and Evie is just coming out of a room to the right. She holds a finger to her lips as she pulls the door closed.

"Hey!" she says, giving me a quick hug.

"Don't tell me my new favorite baby is asleep in there," I groan.

"Finally," Evie says, patting a baby monitor I didn't notice, which is clipped on the waistband of her jeans. "But if she doesn't stay asleep, I'll happily let you hold her for a while."

Someone drops a glass out in the main area, and a chorus of *boos* erupts.

"Party foul!" someone shouts. Sounds like Van.

"That's not going to wake Juno up?" Camden asks in a low voice.

"Thankfully, she's gotten used to sleeping through noise. Once she's out, she's out. If you're looking for the bedroom for your coats, it's the one behind you."

She heads back to the main part of the loft, and I follow Camden toward the open door. But the moment we're out of sight, tucked into the small area outside the bedrooms, his mouth is on mine.

I'm not sure I could describe in words the absolute relief it is to finally kiss him after not being able to touch him the way I'd like to since we first got to the Summit. But we're still barely out of view, so I tug him by the shirt toward the open bedroom door.

Camden tosses our coats toward the bed behind us, and then both of his hands are on my waist. His kisses shift from desperate and hungry to languid, like my mouth is a dessert he wants to savor.

Unfortunately, it feels too weird to make out with Camden in someone else's bedroom, even if it's a guest room. After a quick moment of dizzying kisses, I pull back. He seems to feel the same way and doesn't protest, though the heated look in his eyes tells me he'd love nothing more than a private space.

He bends, his forehead on mine, our breath mingling. "Hi," I say.

Camden kisses the tip of my nose, something that should feel cute and funny, but instead makes my blood feel like it's about to ignite. "Hey, there."

"You played a great game tonight."

He grins, and it's so cocky that I find myself laughing. "So you said."

"Well, it bears repeating. Though I probably wouldn't know the difference between great and mediocre playing." I tilt my head, pretending to give it serious thought. "Maybe you were actually terrible and I just thought you were good because it was my first hockey game."

Camden makes a low rumbling sound, almost a growl. "You were right the first time. I played a great game."

"Humble much?" I ask with a laugh.

"Usually, yes." In an instant, his gaze goes from teasing and playful to intense. "But I've played terribly for months now."

I remember Parker saying something about that before.

"I'm sorry. That really sucks. I'm glad you had a good night, though."

But Camden's expression doesn't change. If anything, it intensifies. He slides his hands from my waist to my hips, gripping me almost like he needs me to stand.

"You don't understand," he says. "I've played badly since this summer. Since I left *you*."

"Oh," I say, my voice a little breathy.

"It meant a lot to me that you and Liam came tonight." He starts to say something else but then glances away.

I can see him working to swallow, his throat bobbing. Lifting my hands from where I've been clutching the lapels of his suit, I place my palms on his stubbled cheeks. His brown eyes meet mine again.

"You don't always have to come," he says quickly. "I don't want you to feel pressured or anything. But I want you to know that it meant something to have you there. Both of you."

Again, I sense something he wants to say but is holding back. I want to ask, to drag whatever it is out of him to sate my curiosity. But if he's struggling with whatever he wants to tell me, maybe he's not ready.

And if we continue on his slow and serious track, we've got lots of time.

Unless he gets traded in the middle of a game, I think, the conversation I had with the women earlier coming back to haunt me in the worst kind of way. *Or unless I get restless, not about a place or a job but about a person—about Camden.*

I shake off those worries and lift up on my toes to press a quick kiss to his lips. "I would like to come to as many games as I can," I tell him. "And I know Liam would be thrilled. I mean, if we can get tickets."

"Parker was right—tickets aren't a problem. You really want to come?"

"Yeah. Maybe we could bring Mike sometime? With Jordan," I add quickly. "Just in case. I don't really know what to do if Mike has an issue."

"You'd want to do that?" he asks, and I'm not sure why he's acting like going to a hockey game is some massive inconvenience.

"It's no big deal," I tell him.

He kisses me once, deeply but quickly and then steps back. "It is a big deal," he says, and his smile looks a little sad. "You have no idea how big of a deal it is."

CHAPTER 18

Camden

NAOMI and I have basically regressed back into living like teenagers. At least, that's how it feels. Stolen moments interrupted too soon. Never enough time.

And a whole lot of kissing in cars.

"Mmm," Naomi says. The word vibrates my lips, which are on her throat.

"Do that again," I whisper.

"I will, if *you* do *that* again," she says.

When I kiss her again in the same spot, she repeats the sound. I'm not even sure she did it because I asked so much as because I've found a sensitive spot. I capture the taste and feel of her sound again with my mouth.

I can sense bright light through my closed eyes, and Naomi pulls away as a car turns onto her street. We're in the front seat of my SUV, parked in her driveway, fully in view.

My windows are tinted, but not nearly enough to provide actual cover.

Dropping my head back against my headrest, I groan. "This is ridiculous. I feel like I'm sixteen again."

"Is this what you were doing at sixteen, Camden?" Naomi's voice sounds amused, but when I tilt my head to look at her, I see a spark of something else too.

Jealousy?

"You're giving me way too much credit. I didn't have nearly this much game at sixteen. I also had a ton of acne. A lovely by-product of playing hockey."

"Is that a thing? Hockey acne?"

"It can be. Think about it: normal hormones plus gear that fits around your face combined with sweat. It's like a bacteria factory."

"Ew!" Naomi grabs the door handle. "You have just effectively killed the vibe. Goodnight!"

Before she can escape, I reach across, taking her hand off the door and linking our fingers. Leaning closer, I brush my lips against the shell of her ear, keeping my voice low. "Are you *sure* I killed the mood?"

Naomi sighs. "Not totally sure. We should probably test it."

We do. Long enough to fog up the car windows a bit, which only makes me feel more like a teenager—one with less acne and more game than I had back then, of course.

Every chance we get, Naomi and I are together. The problem is—there aren't many chances. It's late February, and we're in a constant churn of games. Having Naomi and Liam at all my home games has given me a renewed love of being on the ice. And whether I'm just noticing because I'm dialed in or something else has shifted in our team dynamics, we're all playing better than we ever have. I feel more connected, as though being with Naomi has allowed me to open up with my teammates, too.

But off the ice, it's a constant stream of events. Workouts and recovery with the trainers, charity work, community appearances, interviews, social media days. I haven't missed the mounting tension between Coach and the owner about all the added work. A few of the guys' agents have pushed back about contractual obligations, but so far, we haven't seen any signs of cutting back.

I did hear rumors that some reps from the AHL were here —lawyers and the VP of hockey operations. Hopefully, they'll help Larry get back on track so we can have a more reasonable schedule.

If that weren't enough, I have Mike, and Naomi has Liam.

Despite having people I trust at home to watch over him, it isn't the same as someone who cares for him. I feel guilty every time I choose to be somewhere other than home with him. And though he's doing fine, I wouldn't say he's *thriving*. Jordan tells me Mike is just bored and needs purpose. But I'm not sure what to do about that, and it's not exactly under the purview of the caretakers making sure he doesn't wander off or accidentally leave the oven on.

Naomi and I have managed a few dates here and there, but it's not easy. Our relationship is mostly built on a foundation of text messages and stolen kisses. It's nowhere near enough.

I keep telling myself that things will be different in the off-season, but I'm honestly not sure that's true. I'll still have Mike. Naomi will still have her job, and I haven't asked what her plan is yet for Liam.

The reality of our situation is: it's complicated.

What lessens the complication for me, though, is the very sure and also terrifying sense I have that Naomi is it for me.

She's worth staying up late to text even if I'm dragging in the mornings. She's worth sneaking kisses in a car because she still isn't ready for Liam to know about us yet. I'm starting to long for a future where busy days won't matter because we'll share the same house, the same bed, and the same last name.

Naomi pulls away suddenly as a light goes on in the front window of her house. I see movement behind the curtains, the vague shape of a boy walking toward the kitchen.

"He's going to see my car if he looks out the window," I tell her, amused at the way she's peeking over the dashboard.

"He knows you're here, and I'm with you, but I don't want him to see us *kissing*."

When the light turns out a moment later, she relaxes again, but a thread of disquiet weaves through me. I slide my fingers over the steering wheel, tightening and then loosening my grip. Naomi hasn't mentioned telling Liam about us yet, and I'm not quite sure I understand why.

I think of last summer and the way Liam's face crumpled before he rode away on his bike.

Maybe I do understand.

"I should probably go in," Naomi says, but the tone of her voice and the way she leans across the center console is saying something else.

"And I should probably go home."

"Probably."

"Probably."

"Prob—"

I cut off her next word with another kiss, not even attempting to hold back any of the longing I'm feeling. Or even the frustration at knowing our time is almost up.

Naomi breaks off with no warning. "Wait, wait, wait. Hang on. I need a moment."

She presses a hand to her throat, eyes darting around the car until her gaze lands heavily on me.

"What are we doing here?" she demands.

"I thought it was clear what we're doing." I smile and lean over to place a kiss on the corner of her mouth, willing it to lift in a smile. She doesn't.

Instead, she huffs and crosses her arms over her chest, leaning back against her car door. "Yeah, I know we're kissing, Cam."

Even in the dim light coming from a streetlamp outside, Naomi is so beautiful. It's the fire in her eyes, her strength and resolve and the independence I'm chipping away at little by little as I carve out space in her life. She amazes me—who she is. How she's taken care of herself and Liam for so long.

I want to give her rest. To be the one who shoulders some of the responsibility she's carrying. Not because she can't do it on her own, but because she deserves a little pampering. She deserves support and someone to take care of her for a change.

I want that someone to be me.

And I need to tell her.

I shake my head and drag my gaze from her kiss-swollen lips to her eyes. "I wasn't talking about kissing." I cup her cheeks in my palms and lean closer. "You want to know what we're doing here? I thought it was obvious—I'm in love with you."

The words slip out, but I'm not sorry. Even if I hadn't meant to say them at a moment like this. Why not, I guess? These are the kinds of moments we have together. And the words are true. I *do* love her. I think when realization dawned on me, it had already been true for a while.

She blinks rapidly, her face slack with shock.

And then she launches herself across the console and into

my lap. The car horn blares before her mouth finds mine, and my seat is pushed too far up to pull her off the steering wheel and stop the noise.

Scrambling and desperate, she dives back across the car, elbowing me in the process. She hits her head as she ducks down below the dashboard, watching the house.

I'm torn between amusement and something a little edgier. Not annoyance, exactly. Betrayal feels a little too strong, but something more in that direction.

Stupid, I tell myself. *You blurt out something like that and you expect her to have some perfect reaction?*

I don't expect a perfect reaction. But I do expect something more than silence. It's the first time I've ever said those words to a woman.

Honestly, I can't remember the last time I told *anyone* I loved them.

For a moment, sheer panic envelops me at the gravity of my confession. I wonder if it was a mistake to tell her so soon. Have I even officially asked her to be my girlfriend?

I wanted to go slow, to do things right, but somewhere along the way, my feelings swept me up and carried me along in their current. I assumed we were on the same page without checking to be sure.

Should I have waited longer to tell Naomi I love her?

Or even just officially asked her to be what I stupidly assumed she was: mine?

I'm opening my mouth to see if there's a way to fix what feels like an epic blunder, when Naomi reaches across the car, grabbing my hand.

Her eyes are bright as she says, "I think it's time we tell Liam about us."

It's not the words I want to hear most, but close enough.

CHAPTER 19

Naomi

I CAN'T BELIEVE I'm doing this. For years, I've held firm. This was one boundary I said I wouldn't cross. No matter what.

Does it make me weak that I've caved? Am I still the same strong, independent woman after finally cracking under the immense pressure to say yes?

I just don't know.

But I feel like this moment somehow marks a complete shift ... in something.

"Are you sure about this?" Camden asks.

"I've never been less sure of anything. Is it that obvious?"

"You look like you're about to throw up."

I appreciate Camden's presence beside me, steady and warm to contrast the pit of swirling emotions in my stomach and the icy cold air outside. Though I do *not* appreciate the amusement in his voice.

Does he not understand the gravity of this moment? Or the full extent of my panic over this?

"This isn't funny," I tell him.

"It isn't," he says, but his tone makes it sound almost like a question.

I elbow him in the ribs but then link my arm through his before stuffing my hand back in my coat pocket. It's freezing out here, with what will hopefully be the last cold snap. Early March should be the start of spring in my book. The oppressive gray clouds promising imminent weather do *not* agree.

Which only makes me long for the beach, further questioning the wisdom of the decision I just made since it's the kind of decision you make when you're putting down roots.

Liam's delighted laughter rings out, his smile as wide as I've ever seen it, and I think, *Okay—maybe this won't be so bad. Maybe I'm not making a mistake. I don't need to panic or overthink or freak out.*

Then the black and white dog Liam's been playing with, the two of them rolling around in the backyard like they're both overgrown puppies, sprints directly at me, lip curled up and teeth bared.

I screech and duck behind Camden, who is not even bothering to hide his booming laughter. At least he's blocking the dog from reaching me. He makes a very good shield.

Bailey, out of breath from sprinting across the yard, tugs at my arm. I peek up from where I have my head buried in Camden's back.

"It's okay!" she says. "That's how Panda smiles."

"Smiles? You're telling me *that* was a smile?!"

"Some dogs smile like that when they're happy or excited."

"No. Dogs do not smile."

"Panda does," Eli says.

He's got the decency to hold in his laughter, unlike Camden, who's still chuckling—while rubbing the black and white dog's belly. The dog who has its tongue out and looks incredibly happy. Not terrifying like it did moments ago.

I guess Bailey and Eli would know, since they've been fostering Panda for a month or so. They would never put Liam in harm's way, either.

"Mom." Liam steps up on my other side. "Please just try petting him. He's so nice."

"He ran at me like he was going to bite my face off."

"Yeah, really scary puppy," Camden says as he finds a ticklish spot on Panda's belly and the dog starts kicking its back leg. Singular. Did I mention in addition to apparently smiling, Panda only has three legs? "Aren't you a mean old doggy?" he continues in baby talk. "Do you want to bite Naomi's face off?"

I pinch Camden's ribs. "You are the worst."

When I look at Liam again, he's got those pleading eyes. The ones I don't usually have the strength to say no to. The ones he used on me just last week after contacting our landlord to get a copy of the leasing agreement so he could read it. Turns out we *can* have a dog. Yay.

Despite me being upset that Liam went behind my back to talk to the landlord, which feels not so dissimilar to signing up for hockey without permission, he wore me down about the dog.

Well—it was a concerted effort. Liam, Bailey, Eli, and even Camden got in on this. Because it is a full-blown conspiracy now.

"Come on, Mom," Liam says. "Just give him a chance.

You handled Steve, remember? You can't be scared of a dog who smiles at you."

"I still don't believe that was a smile."

"His tail was wagging," Liam says.

"Who's Steve?" Camden's voice suddenly sounds sharp, clearly assuming Steve is a person.

Which is way more likely than the actual story.

"Oh, no one important," I say loftily, and suddenly, Camden twists his head to look at me with a murderous expression.

"Steve is a pelican," Liam says.

Camden looks relieved. But then, as though remembering my comment playing into his mood, he narrows his eyes at me. It's a promise of playful retribution, and I cannot wait for him to exact it.

While Liam starts to explain that Steve thought the bed and breakfast on Oakley was his home and kept finding his way inside, I take a breath and crouch down.

I use Camden as a shield, keeping one arm wrapped around his legs as I peek around his knees at Panda. I've never met a dog I didn't like.

But anyone who saw a dog running at them with a curled lip and bared teeth would be hiding behind a giant hockey player, too.

As if reading my hesitation, Panda waits, one blue and one brown eye fixed on my face. I can't decide if the two different eye colors are beautiful or creepy. The longer we share prolonged eye contact, the more I lean toward beautiful.

I do wonder why, of all the dogs in the shelter where Bailey used to work and all the dogs being fostered who need homes, she brought over this one for Liam.

I tentatively hold out a hand. "Hey, Panda. Are you a nice

245

boy? Or are you just fooling everyone and you really want to eat my face?"

Just as tentatively, Panda leans forward and sniffs my fingers. Why I wait with bated breath, like this dog's judgment of me matters, I'm not sure. But I *do* feel like this dog's approval rating of me somehow matters more than my feelings about him. I'm also very aware that everyone is watching.

If this dog doesn't like me, does it say something about my character?

Panda pulls back and for a second I feel like I've just been voted off the island in *Survivor*.

Then, as though knowing I'm still slightly freaked out, the dog inches forward on his belly until he rests his soft muzzle in my palm. Then he looks up at me with plaintive eyes that, other than their different colors, look *exactly* like Liam's when he's pleading for something.

Like, for example, a dog.

"Oh, you are *good*," I tell Panda. "But I'm onto you. A master manipulator, that's what you are."

Panda blinks at me as though to say, *Yeah? But can you say no to me?*

As it turns out, I can't.

Twenty minutes later, I've said an official yes, and once the paperwork is submitted, Liam and I are now the owners of a dog with two different colored eyes, only three legs, and a toothy smile that might scare off an intruder.

"How did he lose the leg?" I ask Bailey.

She and I are sitting inside the house now, watching Liam, Eli, and Camden play with Panda as snow begins to fall. They've tossed tennis balls, thrown a frisbee, and played tug-of-war with a knotted rope Bailey brought. Panda loves it all, running faster than I'd expect given the lack of a leg.

"He was found by the side of the road after being hit by a car. At least, we assume that's what happened. The leg was too badly mangled to save," she says.

"I can't believe anyone would hit a dog and just drive off," I say.

"I know. And he wasn't microchipped or wearing a collar, though he seems to have been loved. He's well-trained and very smart. Most border collies are, and that's what he looks like."

"Doesn't seem to slow him down much," I note as Panda manages to outrun Liam and Eli, who are both trying to take the rope from his mouth.

"No, he adapted really well. He's a pretty special dog. That's why I thought of him when you asked about a dog for Liam. He's smart, protective but not aggressive, playful, and very loyal. He'll be Liam's new best friend."

"You can stop trying to talk him up," I tell her. "I've already said yes. There's no way I could separate those two now."

Liam pretended to faint, and Panda is now sitting on his chest, licking his face with great enthusiasm. Camden looks up, his eyes meeting mine through the window, his smile huge and his eyes bright.

Just when I think it's time for those fluttery, new relationship feelings to stop, they ramp up and explode into something totally different.

I'm not experiencing butterflies or some kind of delicate flower of a feeling for Camden. He is two paddles of a defibrillator pressed directly to my chest. I have lost my ability to breathe—and possibly stand up.

"How did Liam take it?" Bailey asks, sipping her hot cocoa. In addition to the dog, she brought a basket with various kinds of hot chocolate and even some fluffy home-made marshmallows purchased from some bakery in town.

Basically, she's my new best friend. It was precarious with the whole dog thing, but after watching Liam play with Panda for the last half hour, she keeps her status.

"You mean me telling him about Camden and me?"

Bailey smiles and gives me the tiniest of eye rolls, barely registering on the scale. "Yes. Your hard launch, as the kids would say."

"Gah. Kids these days," I say lightly. Then, to stall, I take a sip of hot cocoa and lick the whipped cream off my lip.

It's been a few weeks of letting Camden invade my life. We see each other every chance we get—which is never as often as I'd like. I go to all his home games, upping what Liam calls my hockey literacy. I watched him work with Liam in the final few hockey classes and a few times when Cam got extra ice time for the two of them.

Once—and only once—they convinced me to try skating. I'm pretty sure one of my butt cheeks is permanently bruised from how many times I fell on it.

We've been texting late into the night, every night. Sometimes we even talk on the phone, though we're equally opposed to using the phone as an actual *phone*. We've gone on occasional dates while Liam is hanging out with his new friends and once while Parker and Logan offered to have him over while we went out.

Oh, yeah, and Camden said he loved me.

I'll admit—it was unexpected.

Especially when he still won't really talk about his family. I haven't pushed, because when someone doesn't mention their mom or dad or siblings, they are actually saying a lot. Am I dying to know? Yes. But I'm forcing myself to wait on his time, his terms.

Despite the clear understanding that Camden and I have been in a relationship, there was never a discussion. No actual words laying out the terms. We were acting on an unspoken commitment.

Which made me kind of feral, just waiting.

And with such a conversation not even appearing as a mirage shimmering on the horizon, I never expected his confessed I love you.

When I recovered from my utter shock, I almost proposed to him right then and there. *Vegas wedding, here we come!*

But I wisely refrained since jumping from I love you to wedding bells might be a little fast.

I didn't say anything, actually.

In trying to kiss him, I made his car horn honk, then tried to hide in case Liam looked out the window. It was while ducking down behind the dashboard that I realized how ridiculous I was being.

In short, I pretty much ruined Camden's proclamation of love. Or, at least, the mood surrounding his declaration.

With the moment ruined, I opted not to tell him I love him too—yet. I need to redeem myself, so I've been looking for the right time. He hasn't said it again, so I feel like he understands.

At least, I hope that's why.

Eloise—who was absolutely thrilled and full of *I knew its* and *I told you sos*—said I'm being stupid and should tell him as soon as possible so he's not left hanging. Part of me thinks she's right, but Camden didn't seem bothered. I don't think he was saying it so that I would say it back. And I really want it to be a *moment*.

"I'll tell him when the time is right," I told her.

Not when I'm falling all over Camden's car and hiding from my kid. And not just because I promise someone I'll do it. It will be at the perfect time, and I trust myself to know when that is.

I *did* decide it was the right time to tell Liam. Finally. Which we did this morning before Bailey and Eli arrived with Panda.

My thinking, which I shared with Bailey earlier this week, was that if Liam wasn't happy about Camden and me dating —kind of unfathomable, but you never know—then Bailey and Eli would arrive with a dog and make it all better.

Does this make Panda a bribery dog?

Technically, no, because in the end, Liam was thrilled to find out Camden and I are dating. Actually, he was more unsurprised than anything.

"Did you think I didn't know you were together?" he asked, looking at us both with confusion.

"Uh," Camden said, looking my way.

"How did you know?" I asked, earning a very pre-teen look from my son.

"Mom," Liam said with a hint of exasperation, "you guys are *so* obvious."

So, that was that. No bribe dog needed.

But I don't regret Panda. He makes Liam too happy, which makes me happy. I'll just have to get used to the "smile."

"Liam was totally already onto us," I tell Bailey now. "So, it was a little anticlimactic for all the worrying I did."

"Were you really worried? Liam seems to love Camden."

"He absolutely does. I think after last summer, I just thought he might be scared," I say.

"Scared that it wouldn't work out again?"

"Yeah."

She's quiet for a moment. Outside, the snow starts coming down harder. Panda zooms all over the yard, trying to eat snowflakes. This apparently is a contagious infection, because now Camden, Liam, and Eli are doing the same. I could charge money for admission to my backyard right now, and it would sell out faster than Taylor Swift's Eras tour.

"Are *you* scared that it won't work out again?"

Bailey is good at sucker-punch questions. This one makes me go very still. Like, if I don't move, maybe the monster of doubt won't see me and will just keep on walking by.

But I'm not fooling anyone—myself or Bailey.

"I'm terrified," I admit.

She reaches over and gives my arm a quick squeeze. "It's okay to be scared. And you don't have to, but if you want to talk about it, I've been there. I mean, obviously, our situations aren't exactly the same. But I can speak to what it's like to be in a relationship with a hockey player. And I was definitely terrified before Eli and I got married. But I just did it scared." She smiles at her husband, who is shaking his floppy blond hair out the same way Panda is shaking his fur. "Best decision I've ever made."

I grab one of the oversized marshmallows off the table and pop it in my mouth. It's melty and delicious. I should ask her where she got these and stock up.

I should also stop being a big chicken and talk to her.

Before I can re- or over-think it, I blurt out, "I'm scared of marrying someone with the whole hockey player thing. I'm scared of how fast I've fallen. And I'm scared of myself." I take a breath.

"Of yourself?" Bailey asks.

"I'm not good at committing to things. I get bored and restless." I swallow, and it takes effort. "I'm so scared I'll want to run, and it will break both our hearts. Liam's too."

Bailey, ever the good listener, tilts her head and thinks for a few seconds. When she smiles, it's soft.

"I know I don't know you very well," she says, "but from

what I've seen, I don't think you have reason to be scared about that."

"No? To be fair, you haven't seen me cut ties and jump ship."

She shakes her head. "Maybe you get bored and restless with *things*, but you, Naomi, strike me as someone who is very good at committing to *people*."

It's a big statement, one that hits me right in the feels. I need to process. I might be processing it for a while.

"What about the other stuff?"

Her smile takes on a mischievous edge. "You're talking to someone who married a hockey player within a few weeks. And I couldn't be happier. So ... I'm not going to talk you out of a hockey player or moving fast."

I laugh. "Touché."

The guys come in then, and I'm glad this house has a laundry room at the back to collect the wet boots and coats.

I'm also glad it takes them a moment to take off their wet things and dry Panda with a towel because I need to blink back my unexpected tears.

Because Bailey is right. I am good at committing to people. I decided to commit to Liam when he was still the size of a grape or whatever fruit the app compared him to the week I found out I was pregnant. I'm committed to my whole family back in Oakley. Not just Dad and Jake, but the whole extended not-blood-related family I've found with Eloise, her sisters, and their significant others.

I might have left them in the geographical sense, but my heart is very much still with the people I love back home.

After Bailey's assessment, I'm seeing my fear as it really is—not huge, as it seemed to me, but a tiny little thing that simply casts a big shadow. With the bright light cast by her true words, the looming shadow is gone.

The fear is real and it's still there, but I see it in its true proportion now. I remember Bailey's earlier words about marrying Eli.

I can do this, too, I think. *I can just do it scared.*

"What'd we miss?" Eli says, coming into the room with a wide grin and eyes only for Bailey.

"Nothing," she says, giving me a wink.

But it feels like our little conversation and this whole morning of telling Liam about us and getting a long-term commitment kind of pet was a very, very big *something.*

CHAPTER 20

Camden

I'M NOT sure why I'm nervous when Naomi and Liam arrive at my house with Panda in tow. Mike finally convinced Naomi to let him cut Liam's hair—and mine—the night before I leave on a weeklong road trip. Jordan still refuses even a trim but said he wanted to be here to watch the show. I think he even brought popcorn.

Despite all the time we've spent together, she's never been to my place and Liam hasn't met Mike or Jordan. I wrap an arm around Naomi as soon as she's through the door, pressing my lips to her cheek. Jordan's grin is big enough to be picked up from outer space.

I ignore him. "Hey," I tell Naomi quietly. "I'm glad you're here."

"I finally get to see your house!"

"It's not really very ... me."

"I can see that," Naomi says, sounding amused.

Her house is also a rental, but it already bursts with life and personality in the short time she's lived there. Meanwhile, I've somehow managed to live here almost two years without changing anything. It came furnished with very model home-esque pieces and framed art prints and stock photos. Clean, functional, and it could belong to anyone.

This feels deeply embarrassing as Naomi's curious eyes drink in every nondescript detail visible from the front hall. I want to defend myself, but what would I say? Telling her I'm never home only emphasizes how impossibly busy my schedule is. It would sound even worse if I tell her it's because I never settle down anywhere.

This is the third team I've played for since college. Harvest Hollow and the Appies have felt the most like home of anywhere I've been, but I never assumed I'd stay.

Suddenly, I remember the certainty in Naomi's voice as she said she wanted to end up back on Oakley Island at some point. I've never felt that passionate about living anywhere, and I think it shows.

Oh, hey—maybe it's not time for an existential crisis in my entryway.

"You know, I'd be happy to help," Naomi says. "I'm no decorator, but it's fun to make a house look more like the person who lives there."

"It's just a rental," I say, and then want to take those words back at the quick flash of hurt flashing over her face.

I don't know if it's because she's also in a rental and I've somehow insulted her, or if it's because I made it sound like I don't have long-term plans to stick around.

Whatever bothered her about my words, now she's hugging Jordan and introducing him to Liam while I stand off to the side in the crowded entryway.

"Come on in," Mike says, ushering them further inside like this is his house.

"Yes," Jordan echoes with a smirk. "Make yourselves right at home. And who is this handsome and hairy gentleman?"

"This is Panda," Liam says. "Panda, sit."

I'm impressed by the way the dog immediately flops back on his haunches next to Liam. Panda practically vibrates with energy, waiting for a command.

"Okay," Liam says. "Good boy. Go say hi."

Immediately, the dog lunges forward with his version of a smile, shoving his head toward Jordan and then Mike for scratches.

"What am I, chopped liver?" I ask after a moment, raising my eyebrows at the dog. In the past week, I've spent more than my fair share of time throwing balls for Panda in Naomi's backyard and finding his favorite spots to be scratched.

Now that Liam knows about us—or now that we know Liam already knew about us—there's less making out in cars and more kissing on the couch after Liam's in bed. It also means more time with the dog, who has grown on us all.

Panda might come to me last, but I swear his butt wiggles just a little harder for me when he wags his tail. I never had a dog growing up, and my schedule now wouldn't have allowed it. I'm glad I get to vicariously because there's something so solid and comforting about Panda. He'll be good for Liam.

As he presses his head into my hand, demanding more scratches, I think he'll be good for me, too. Especially tonight with the off-kilter way I'm feeling.

"Debbie made dinner. So, let's eat, and then I've got everything set up in the kitchen for haircuts," Mike says, still playing host.

I can see Naomi bending to whisper something to Liam, probably explaining who Debbie is. She told Liam about Mike's condition, and he seems to be taking it in stride.

Jordan was actually the one who made dinner. We've discovered his love of cooking—especially if I'm the one footing the bill for ingredients. I even bought a fancy set of pans and knives after hearing him talk about them. It makes him very happy, and it makes Mike and me very happy as well, since we're beneficiaries of his newfound culinary interest.

"As long as you don't quit on me to become a chef," I told him, and he only laughed, which didn't reassure me. I'm not sure how I'd do this without Jordan.

How would this work if Naomi and I got married? The thought has crossed my mind before, but never with the urgency it does now. Hearing the voices bouncing off the walls in the kitchen, watching as everyone loads up their plates and sits around the table, I'm getting a very real glimpse at what this might look like. It's ... a little weird.

There's Jordan, with his hemp necklaces and earthy patchouli smell, cracking jokes and now cooking for us while keeping Mike stabilized.

Mike, who might be existing in any decade at any given time. Jovial but in and out of touch with reality as the rest of us do improv to whatever he says.

Naomi, with her wit and quick comebacks.

Liam, with his litany of facts and passion for so many things.

And now, Panda, with his incessant need for scratches, nudging his head into my lap under the table.

Weird, yes. But the house is no longer devoid of personality. It's not about having artwork on the walls or whatever else might make this look like a home, but having the people bring life into it.

Under the table, Naomi's hand finds mine, giving me a quick squeeze. She smiles, and it grows as a wet dog nose snuffles right into our palms.

———

If I had known that the familiar feel of scissors snipping at my hair and the buzz of a razor on my neck would hurtle me back in time, I would never have agreed to let Mike cut my hair.

Especially not with Naomi, Liam, and Jordan here, watching while I try to pretend nothing is wrong. The mild headache that began during dinner has morphed into a pounding in my skull as I fight off memories.

Hopefully, I'm keeping the feelings off my face. Eyes closed, I have my fists clenched beneath the black plastic drape Mike placed over me. He and Jordan went shopping earlier in the week with my credit card to get supplies. I wonder what happened to Mike's old set, the one he refused to replace even though the razor's cord was held on by duct tape, a total fire hazard.

Snip.

"Are you going to cut my hair that short?" Liam asks.

"I'll cut it only as short as you want it. Or," Mike amends, "how short your *mom* wants it."

"Good call," Naomi says, and even with my eyes closed, I can picture her tilting her head to examine Liam. "Let's see ... I'm thinking maybe a mohawk? Or a sideways mullet."

"What's a sideways mullet?" Mike asks.

"Shaved along the top and long on the sides. I'm not sure

258

that's the official name, but I think it would look good on you, kid. Really bring out your eyes."

Mike laughs, pausing at his trimming, and Liam groans. I almost smile. But then there's another metallic snip of the scissors, and I tense again.

It's strange—I'm able to think back on my time living with the Bells fondly. They went above and beyond what my teammates talked about their billet families doing for them. Especially that second year, they really became more of a family. I had good teammates and friends. I played well enough to impress the scouts.

And yet something about having Mike cut my hair is throwing me back to the worst parts of that time. The parts I have locked away in my mind and refuse to think about. Right now, though, I'm not remembering so much as viscerally experiencing a whole host of emotions I've shoved down for years.

Mike's fingers gently tugging my hair ... rejection from my parents as their weekly calls trickled to a stop.

The silver snip of the scissors ... the sense of abandonment as all my teammates took pictures with their families at the end of our second season and I stood alone in a suit I had to borrow from Mike.

The razor buzzing at the back of my neck ... the bitterness and anger burning hot through me as I shifted into a self-destructive spiral.

Mike, waiting up for me one night when I came stumbling in after drinking beers some college girl had bought for us. The disapproval on his face and the kind but firm words that were the start of my turnaround.

Panda whines softly as he settles next to me.

I'd like to reassure him, to tell him it's okay, but I think that's what he's trying to say to me.

Drawing in one steady breath after another, I clench and unclench my hands. Why now? Why does all of this need to bubble up tonight?

I thought I had dealt with this—or at least shoved it all far enough down that it couldn't reach back up again like a hand sticking up from a grave.

Maybe when it comes to hurt inflicted by family, you can't do either of those things: get over it or bury it.

One thing I haven't tried, something that comes to me now, when I'd least like to think about it, is reaching out. Taking a step to mend things.

Mike sets the clippers down and goes back to trim the hair around my ears. I almost tell him just to grab the clippers and shave the whole thing so it will be done. I'm almost willing to do it myself.

Snip.

Naomi's laughter at something Jordan said pulls me back into the moment, and I'm grateful.

Opening my eyes, I zero in on her. She's seated at the kitchen island, knees pulled to her chest, bare feet hanging off the edge of the stool. Her smile changes when she catches me looking.

It softens, and for a moment, I can breathe again.

Then Mike says, "Your dad called me this week. Said he couldn't reach you."

I go very, very still.

So does everyone in the room except Mike, who switches to my other ear.

"Are you planning to keep ignoring him?"

I don't answer. I can't look at anyone's faces, afraid of what I might see there.

"Avoiding them won't fix anything," he continues, his

voice gently reproachful. "I think you should consider going home for spring break instead of—"

I stand swiftly. The scissors nick the top of my ear, but I ignore the sting of pain as I rip off the drape.

"All done. Looks good." My inflection sounds dangerously manic.

"You didn't even see it," Liam says, a tremulous question in his voice.

"I'm fine—I mean, it's fine."

Mike blinks at me, the scissors still in his hand. His frown tells me he knows something is off, but not what. I can almost see his brain scanning, trying to follow the threads, plucked loose by his condition.

"Your ear," Naomi says quietly, and I realize she's standing in front of me.

She lifts a paper towel toward the side of my head, but I grab it from her hands and press it to my ear myself. "I'm fine."

"If you say so," she says, and I can't stand the hurt in her voice.

"Hey, Mike," Jordan says, hopping down from his stool and shaking his hair out of its ponytail, loose and long around his shoulders. "How about giving me a fresh look?"

Jordan is being my shield, offering up hair he doesn't want cut as a way to pull Mike into a tangible moment. As a way to defuse whatever bomb is about to go off in my chest.

I don't feel like I deserve his kindness.

"You know," Mike says, "normally I'd say yes. But to be honest, it suits you. Liam—you ready? Hop up here, kid."

Liam, still clearly trying to figure out what just happened, does as Mike says and climbs onto the stool I just vacated. Mike picks up the drape I left on the floor, shaking off the hair.

"What'll it be? Just a trim or something a little more dramatic?" Mike asks. "Naomi? What do you think?"

It's still startling how Mike can shift from thinking I'm in high school one minute to remembering Naomi, a woman he's only met a few times. He did forget her name earlier, but only Jordan and I caught it. Once, I caught him frowning at Liam, as though trying to place him. There's no rhyme or reason for how it works.

I step past Naomi and start down the hall leading to the bedrooms. The paper towel comes away from my ear red. Maybe the cut is a little worse than I realized.

"Do whatever Liam wants," Naomi says, and I hear Liam's cheer over Mike's chuckle.

I duck into the hall bathroom. It's the one Mike uses, and though Jordan must have come in and cleaned off the countertops, the room smells of English Leather—the same scent Mike has been using for years.

Gripping the edge of the counter, I lean forward until my forehead touches the cool surface of the mirror.

It's all too much, and I'm buckling under the weight.

Back in Wisconsin, tree branches would break off during a winter storm. Ice would make them rigid, and when strong winds blew in, they were unable to bend and would simply snap.

That's me—frozen, inflexible, breaking from the slightest breeze.

"Camden?" Naomi knocks softly on the door.

I don't answer, but I guess I didn't lock the door because she comes inside and closes it behind her. We lock eyes in the mirror, and I'm not sure what she sees in my face, but she steps up behind me, wrapping her arms around my waist and pressing her cheek to my back.

For a moment, I'm stiff, waiting for her to ask what's wrong or try to make me talk about it.

She doesn't. She just holds me. And holds me.

"I ..."

"You don't need to say anything," Naomi says after a moment. "Not until you're ready. And only if you want to. But I'm here either way."

This is more comforting than anything else she could say.

Unless ... she told me she loved me. Because I've been waiting for her to say it. Waiting for her to reassure me she feels the same. Maybe her actions are already telling me, already showing me.

But now, with the sour feeling swirling in my gut, my head still pounding, and the memories of my family invading my thoughts, I could really just use the words.

She doesn't say them.

It's not about her, I remind myself, relishing in the warmth of her body against my back. *I don't need her words.*

What I do probably need is to deal with my hurt over my family or it will just keep festering under there, popping up at the most inopportune moments. *Avoiding them won't fix anything*, Mike said tonight, an echo of an exact conversation we had years ago.

And he's right.

But now that it's been years of doing exactly that, I'm not sure how to go about fixing any of it. Or fixing myself.

"I'm sorry," I whisper, and Naomi's arms tighten around me. I let go of the sink and turn so I can wrap my arms around her in a real hug.

"Please don't apologize. I just want you to be okay. Are you okay?"

"Not really," I admit. "But I'll work on it."

CHAPTER 21

FHL

Parker: HELLO AND WELCOME TO THE NEW AND IMPROVED GROUP CHAT!!!

Amelia: Hi, y'all.

Bailey: Hey!!!!

Evie: Hi! And Juno says hi.

Gracie: Give that baby a kiss from me, please.

Bailey: Me too!

Evie: Done.

Summer: Parker—you know this is the same group chat, right?

Parker: Okay, it's not NEW.

Greyson: So what's the improvement?

Amelia: IS there an improvement?

Parker: I renamed it! I finally came up with a name.

Amelia: FHL? I can think of a few not very Parker-like options for that.

Parker: MILLS, STOP RUINING MY THING.

Amelia: Sorry.

Naomi: Are you sure I should be in the group chat?

Greyson: Don't be ridiculous.

Amelia: ABSOLUTELY.

Gracie: You are an FHL, whatever that is.

Summer: Parker, cut the suspense. We know you like a big, dramatic reveal, but just tell us.

Parker: Y'all are no fun. FHL stands for First Hockey Ladies.

Bailey: I like it.

Amelia: You like everything.

Bailey: Maybe. But I also DO like it.

Summer: I also like it but …

Amelia: Oh, no. Here comes a Summer but.

Summer: Wouldn't First Ladies of Hockey sound better?

Parker: But the abbreviation wouldn't be as good. FHL is like NHL and AHL. Get it?

Summer: Okay. I concede your point. FHL it is!

Gracie: Agreed.

Evie: SO much better than WAG.

Amelia: Here's how I feel about WAG: [barf emoji]

Naomi: If I get a vote, I like it.

Bailey: Of course you get a vote!

Evie: You totally get a vote. And I'm not just saying that because you held Juno so I could eat the first night we met.

Naomi: I'll hold her anytime!

Amelia: No more talk like you don't belong, okay?

Parker: Speaking of belonging, I may need to borrow your dog.

Summer: Nice non sequitur.

Naomi: Sure. What do you need with my scary smiling dog?

Parker: The team needs a dog. Stupid Larry Jenson won't approve an official one. He didn't say anything about BORROWING a dog.

Amelia: Nice. My dad will love it.

Naomi: There might be an issue with that.

Parker: What kind of issue?

Bailey: I'm not sure if this is what Naomi means, but we don't know how Panda is with crowds. Or ice.

Parker: Maybe you can bring him to the Summit on a practice day and see? Would that help, Naomi?

Naomi: Probably, but my issue is more about ... Camden.

Naomi: I know I'm being paranoid, but he won't answer my calls or texts.

Greyson: Back up—did you have a fight?

Summer: How long has it been? Could he be sick?

Parker: How can we help? (And I'm not just asking because of Panda.)

Amelia: Suuuure

Parker: I'M SERIOUS.

Gracie: If you don't want to talk about it, you don't have to. But I'm here if you need anything.

Evie: Me too. Anytime!

Amelia: But we're all nosy, so you should tell us and tell us now.

Naomi: So, the other night, he got really upset about something to do with his family, I think. He won't talk about his childhood or his parents. I don't need details, but does anyone know anything about his family?

Greyson: Nope.

Summer: I don't.

Parker: Not a thing.

Naomi: I've known it's a touchy subject. But he kind of ... freaked out and shut down. Now he won't talk.

Naomi: Oh, and there's another thing.

Greyson: What's the other thing?

Naomi: He told me he loved me and I didn't say it back.

Parker: Awwww he said he loves you!

266

Summer: Don't take this the wrong way, but why didn't you say it back?

Naomi: I kind of ruined the moment, and then I wanted it to be like a really special moment.

Naomi: I don't know if he's upset about his family or me or a combination but he won't talk to me, so I don't know how to fix it.

Bailey: I'm sorry. And it's extra hard with things like this when they're on the road.

Parker: Do you want us to commiserate or do you want help?

Naomi: Both. But I think I'm at the point where I need help. It's only been like two days and I'm DYING.

Summer: I'd say fly out to see him, but I'm sure you can't with Liam.

Bailey: I'd happily help with Liam. I have school, but I'd have some time to stay with him.

Naomi: I can't leave work or Liam. So, I'm stuck here.

Parker: I have an idea!

Amelia: Why am I not surprised?

Greyson: Parker ideas are the best ideas!

Summer: They're the best ideas when they're run by the legal team first.

Parker: Ha ha.

Naomi: What did you have in mind?

Amelia: I can't wait to hear this.

Greyson: I volunteer to help with whatever you need!

Parker: Sadly, the FHL can't help this time. But how would you feel about a little help from the guys?

Naomi: If it would get Camden to talk to me, I'll do anything.

CHAPTER 22

Camden

I DO NOT WORK on it.

In fact, from the time we leave the next morning until our second game in a series against Omaha two nights later, I do the opposite. I continue to push aside any thoughts of my family, and now, I'm avoiding Naomi as well.

Despite winning tonight, the mood in the locker room is subdued. I'm not sure if everyone's just exhausted from back-to-backs, or if the dark cloud of my mood, which turned black the night Mike cut my hair, is spreading.

Maybe it's less of a dark cloud and more of an infection.

See? I am a little ray of pitch-black melodrama right now. I can't even stand the sound of my own thoughts.

Everyone gives me a wide berth. Even Coach barely said anything about me dropping gloves in the third period with one of their fourth liners who was clearly trying to provoke me. Fighting, something I rarely do, means five minutes in the box, putting strain on the other defensive pairs.

It was stupid. And now my cheek is swollen. I'm not sure I ever landed a blow. It's harder to land a punch on skates than one might think. Mostly, we held each other by the jerseys while taking wild swings. His connected. Mine didn't.

And I felt no better about it or anything else while watching my team play from my spot in the penalty box.

Knowing I need to repair things with my family and knowing *how* to do it are two different things. How can I pick up the phone to call when I stopped answering their calls years ago? Maybe they don't want to have me back in their lives. Maybe reaching out will make things worse.

All I know is that I feel like I've been pinned down under an avalanche of unwelcome emotions. I don't want to subject Naomi or anyone else to it, so I'm just … quietly imploding, I guess.

Or, as Mike said years ago—I'm fighting ghosts. Still.

Now, some brave soul pauses in front of my stall, where I'm still sitting in my gear.

A towel. Water dripping onto the floor. Bare feet, wet from the shower. One kicks me in the shin.

"Yo, Cole. Are you coming out to dinner?"

I glance up at Van with the kind of look that would wilt spring flowers. "Do I look like I'm coming to dinner?"

I expect him to scamper away, like everyone else has who's been subjected to me on this trip. But Van doesn't budge. He frowns and crosses his arms over his bare chest and the massive dragon tattoo he has.

"You look like you should come to dinner. You look like you need to come to dinner."

"And why would I need that?"

"Because you're acting hangry," Dumbo says.

"Hush," Tucker says, giving Dumbo a shove. "Don't poke the honey badger."

"I think the expression is don't poke the bear," Felix says.

"Yeah, but honey badgers are meaner than bears. I'd rather poke a bear."

"Maybe it would be best not to poke Camden at all," Logan says.

"Hey, Nikki. Have you got a Russian phrase about poking bears?" Van asks.

I try to tune them all out while starting to take off my gear. I'd like to get out of this building, get back to the hotel and ... wallow, I guess.

Actually, that sounds terrible.

For the last few weeks of road games, I had Naomi's texts and calls to look forward to. But the idea of opening the unread messages from her sitting on my phone fills me with dread.

Is it fair that I've been avoiding her since the other night? No.

Can I even give a good reason? Also no.

But am I still doing it? Yup.

"In Russia we don't say poke the bear," Dominik says. "We say jokes with the bear are bad. Or don't tease the dog when it's behind the fence."

"Huh," Van says, running a hand through his wet hair. "Kinda close, I guess."

Dumbo looks thoughtful. "The question becomes: Is Camden behind a fence?"

"And is he a bear, a honey badger, or a dog?" Tucker asks.

"I'm just a guy who wants to be left alone," I snap.

And so they do as I ask.

Which leaves me even more miserable than before.

They don't leave me alone for long.

I've almost fallen asleep when I hear a shuffling noise outside my door. Then the sound of someone swiping a card. The door swings open and a slice of light fills the room. It reveals several tall silhouettes before the door slams shut again.

I don't even have time to untangle myself from the covers before the first body lands on top of my legs.

"Ow!" a familiar voice says. "Watch my knee."

Grunting, I try to sit up and push Van off. "You're the one who jumped on me!"

Another person jumps on my chest, knocking me back, pinning my arms beneath a heavy body. "If you stop struggling, this will be over faster."

"Nathan?! Why are you—ow."

Someone turns on a phone light, blinding me. Then the lamp switches on. Aside from Van and Nathan, who are lying across my body, Logan, Felix, Eli, and Dominik are in the room.

"What is this?" I ask, trying to wiggle free.

This only results in Eli throwing himself on top of both Van and Nathan. Only, instead of being sideways, he's lying in the same direction I am, so his face is about a foot above mine.

"This," Eli says, "is a gift from Naomi."

"Somehow, I doubt that."

"He's telling the truth." Naomi's voice is in the room, and I realize Logan is holding up his phone with an active call. "I didn't ask them to do whatever it is they're doing."

"Assault is what they're doing," I grumble. "What did you *ask* them to do?"

271

"I asked them to get you on the phone since you've been refusing to answer my calls or texts."

"So, remember, this is your fault," Van says.

"Right," I say. "Can you all leave now so I can talk to my girlfriend?"

Eli grins down at me. "Nope. We've been instructed to stay for the conversation."

"You want to have a conversation with me while these guys are listening in?" I ask Naomi.

"I don't really care who listens in as long as *you* listen, Cole."

"Oooh, someone's in trouble," Van whispers from my legs. "She's pulling out the last name."

"Shut it, Vanity," Naomi says, and several of the guys start laughing. "Maybe all of you could also shut up? Respectfully," she adds.

I think I just fell in love with her a little bit more.

"Guys," Nathan says. "Be quiet. I want to get this done and go to sleep."

"The floor is yours, Naomi," Logan says. "Camden is listening."

"Along with the rest of you," I mutter.

Naomi jumps right in. "Camden, I owe you an apology. A big one."

I'm the one who owes her an apology. But I feel totally weird talking about this with all of the guys listening in. "I don't think that's true, but okay."

"It is true. When you told me you loved me—"

The guys break out into whistles and *ooohs* until Nathan yells, "I swear if all of you don't shut up now and *stay* shut up ..."

"You'll what?" Van challenges.

Nathan shifts, which makes Eli roll off of me and onto the

floor. I can't see what Nathan does to Van, but he howls in pain.

Someone starts banging on the wall.

"Enough."

This one word cracks like a whip through the room. Dominik is the one who said it, and I'm surprised to find that everyone actually listens.

"I promise this won't take long," Naomi says. "Camden, when you told me you loved me, I was completely shocked. In the best way. But I hadn't expected it. And then the whole car horn thing happened—shut up Van," she says just as he starts to chuckle. A few of the guys try to hide their laughter. I even find myself smiling.

"I felt like the mood was ruined, so I decided to save it for the right time," Naomi continues. "I thought I'd know when that was, and it would be really special."

"That's sweet," Eli whispers from the floor.

"It would have been sweet," Naomi continues, "but then I got wrapped up thinking about the perfect moment. The other night at your house I wanted to say it. Then I started overthinking, like maybe it wouldn't be the right time because you were upset. While you were struggling seemed like the worst time to tell you I love you."

She loves me.

I knew it, *have* known it, even if she hadn't said it out loud. I'm not sure this technically counts as her saying it. But it's an admission nonetheless, and one I desperately needed to hear.

I've been frozen since she started speaking in earnest, and not just because I'm buried under the combined weight of Nathan and Van. While it's an intensely vulnerable thing to be listening to this with so many people in the room, I'm surprised by the comfort they bring.

273

I'm not alone.

I haven't been alone, even if I've done my best for a long time to isolate myself. From my family, from my teammates, and from Naomi.

"I love you, Camden Cole," Naomi says. "And I was wrong to think there would be a perfect time to say it. I should have said it the moment I knew. Or at the very least, I should have said it when you told me. I love you, and I'm sorry I waited to say it."

"I love you," I say, fully expecting a whole bunch of ribbing from the guys. Surprisingly, they're quiet.

Other than Eli, who sniffles from his spot on the floor.

"Dude, are you crying?!" Van whispers.

"Shut up, Van."

When I glance at the phone, Logan's grinning. For once, it's not teasing but a full, genuine smile. And if I'm not mistaken, his eyes are bright with what look like unshed tears.

Is this something I have to look forward to? Will falling in love turn me into the kind of guy who cries at everything?

Possibly. Because a deep swell of emotion is building in my chest, and my nose starts to burn.

"I'm sorry for pushing you away," I tell her. "I have some things I need to deal with."

"I talked to Mike," Naomi says, and I suck in a breath.

"About my family?" I ask.

"No. I just asked him what I should do to fix things with us. He said I needed to chase you down. To not let you run. And as a person who excels in the figurative running away, I relate."

"He was right," I say. "Mike's right about a lot of things."

"I'll tell him you said that." I hear a smile in her voice, but with her next words, it disappears. "I don't want to run anymore, Camden. I want to put down roots, build something lasting. Forget about rental furniture and leases. I want that—and I want it with you."

I swallow. "I want that too."

"Good," she says. "Because sometimes, I might be the one running, and you might need to chase me down."

"I will," I promise. "I'll always come after you."

Eli sniffs, and Van chuckles. But then he sniffs too, and Nathan laughs. "I saw that."

"Saw what?" Van says defensively.

"A tear. You're crying."

"I'm just allergic to this comforter," Van says. "Or whatever they use to wash it."

"They don't wash comforters," Dominik says. "Not ever. Filthy. I saw it on *60 Minutes*."

"Ew!" Van yells, and someone starts banging on the wall again.

"That's only in the cheap hotels," Nathan says. "They use duvet covers in the hotels we stay in. They get washed after every guest."

"So you say," Dominik shrugs.

Nathan and Van finally climb off me. I sit up and stretch out my neck.

"Well, Naomi," Logan says. "Is that everything? Anything else to say?"

"Van," she says, and his head perks up. "Liam says to tell you that you had too many turnovers in the neutral zone tonight."

Logan laughs, and Van glowers. "It was only one time."

"Bye, Camden! I love you," Naomi says.

Now that I'm not buried under bodies and can literally see all the guys looking at me, it feels a little weird to say out

275

loud, but I do it anyway. "I love you too. See you when I get home."

Logan ends the call and reaches over to slap me on the back. "Way to show that emotional maturity. Good job."

"Does this mean you'll stop being such a grouch?" Van asks. "Nathan has claimed that role."

Nathan growls and lunges for Van, who ducks behind Felix. I almost forgot he was here since he hasn't said a word. But now, he nods at me and says, "I'm happy for you. And I'm sorry for … whatever it is that you've been struggling with."

He doesn't remind me that I still haven't shared as much as I need to with the guys. He doesn't need to. I'm very aware.

"What can we do?" Dominik asks. "Can we help?"

The reflexive answer is to tell him no, they can't help. To say that I'm fine. That I've got this.

But I swallow down that response and instead say, "Yes. I think I need some help."

It wasn't as hard as I thought it would be to admit it.

"Just tell us how," Felix says, even as Nathan grumbles, "I wanted to go to sleep."

I consider the thoughts that have been flitting through my mind for the past few days. Some, even longer than that.

"Eli, didn't you hire a live-in caregiver to help with your mom recently?"

"Yeah," he says. "You have help, though, right?"

"I do, but I think I want to switch up the arrangement, and I have some questions."

"Happy to answer any of them," he says.

"And who knows a good real estate agent?"

Felix lifts a hand. "Me."

I keep forgetting he owns the whole building where his loft is. "Great."

"I like his agent," Dominik says. "She's very helpful."

I'm not the only one who stares at him in shock.

"The Kid is buying real estate?" Van says.

Dominik shrugs. "What? It's a good investment. And I like it here."

"Anything else?" Nathan asks, and though he still looks irritated, he's also sincere.

I would love help with the hardest task—my family. But it's something I need to do on my own. Even if I should probably talk to the guys about it later. I know several of my teammates have had hard family issues and would probably be glad to talk.

My family is something I need to deal with on my own.

Actually ... maybe that's not true. But I'll have to wait until I'm back home and the person whose support I need most is by my side.

CHAPTER 23

Naomi

LIAM IS RECITING APPIES' player stats on the ride home from his first ever actual hockey practice, and I zoned out five minutes ago.

My sole focus is on trying to do math in my head. Specifically, I'm trying to estimate when Camden might actually get to my house based on flight times, waiting in baggage claim, the ride back to the Summit, and then driving to my house. That's assuming his flight isn't late and that he comes straight here.

So far, my math is either wrong, or he's going to get here after I'm asleep.

"Ugh," I groan, turning onto our street.

"What's wrong?" Liam asks.

"Nothing." It's just that spring is starting to show by way

of bright green leaves and flowers. The azaleas are nearly in full bloom, blazing even in the fading light of dusk.

It's beautiful, but I'm not in the mood for nature's cheer. *Read the room, nature. Blooming right now is just* rude.

It's been a full week, which feels longer because, after the state he was in when he left, no amount of phone calls, texts, or video chats could make up for not being with him. I know we're okay—the constant *I love yous*, now that we've both said it, reassure me of that—but still. It's felt a little bit like we've been in a prolonged fight.

I won't feel better until I am in his arms.

I won't be ready for any happy stuff—even celebrating the arrival of spring—until I see Camden's face again.

And then I do.

Because he's on my front porch, sitting in one of the new chairs I bought when the weather got above sixty-five degrees earlier this week.

Camden. He's home. He's *here*. And he's standing as he catches sight of my car, now speeding toward the driveway.

"Mom—the mailbox!"

Liam's warning doesn't come in time to save our mailbox.

I only clip it, but that's enough to uproot the whole thing. It topples over, spilling the mail I've forgotten to collect for a few days across the front lawn.

Who cares? *Camden is back.*

"I'll buy a new mailbox. Camden trumps mailboxes," I say as I throw the car in park, unbuckle, and sprint toward the porch.

Camden runs down the steps and I jump into his arms, grateful for a man whose job prepares him for full-contact hugs. My feet dangle above the sidewalk, but he's got me.

I unabashedly nuzzle into his neck, smelling him and

feeling the soft drag of stubble against my cheek. His hands tighten around my lower back, and his exhale sounds like one of pure relief.

"You're home," I whisper, blinking away tears that have surprised me. "By my calculations, it should have been much later."

"You were doing calculations to figure out when I'd be back?"

"Badly, apparently. But yes."

"Your calculations might have been correct." He pauses. "I asked if I could come back on an earlier flight. I needed to see you."

"Same." I squeeze him tighter, then press my lips to his ear. "I love you."

It feels so good to say it while I'm in his arms.

Camden pulls back, setting me on my feet as he cradles my face in his hands. "I love you, too."

A throat clears behind us.

"Can I hug Coach Cam now?" Liam asks. His tone is annoyed, but when I step away from Camden, I can see Liam's wide grin.

"Sure," I say.

I almost warn Camden that we came straight from hockey and Liam stinks, but then I don't. He's probably used to hockey stink by now. Liam can't be worse than a locker room full of adult men after a game.

My eyes get dangerously leaky again watching the two of them embrace.

"I missed you," Liam says.

"I missed you, too." Camden meets my eyes over Liam's head.

I lose the battle, a tear slipping down my cheek.

"Time to shower, bud," I say, trying to keep my voice

280

steady. "Make sure you dump all your gear in the laundry room so I can wash it. And let Panda out back, okay?"

Liam returns to the car for his bag, then smiles at us both before disappearing inside where I can hear Panda barking a greeting.

"I would have brought Panda out, but the door was locked," Camden says.

"I should get you a key."

"I'll get you one for my house, too," he says. "Although ..."

He stops, and though I have no reason to get nervous, I do. "Although what?"

"Let's sit."

I definitely don't like the sound of a sitting down conversation, but I follow Camden to the porch chairs. He grabs mine and drags it closer to his, making me laugh and cutting through my nerves a little.

"That's better," he says. He pulls his phone out of his pocket and starts talking as he looks for something. "I did a lot of thinking those first days when I was shutting you out. Which, again, I'm sorry about."

"You're forgiven. We talked about it, Cam."

"I know. I still feel bad that you had to call the guys to get me."

I smirk. "Or are you just sorry because of how they helped?"

"It was fine." He finds whatever he wants on his phone, but instead of showing me, he locks it and sets it on his knee before taking my hands in his. "I have some issues with my family that I haven't dealt with. Mike being here has made them bubble up to the surface, which ultimately, is a good thing for me."

He draws in a breath, and I squeeze his hands.

"I haven't talked to my family in a few years. When I went to live with Mike and his family, my mom got pregnant. A total surprise. They had twin girls. They both had some complications the first year, and they couldn't come out to see my games. Then they started forgetting our weekly calls, and I just ... felt like I'd been replaced."

"Oh, Cam."

"When I went home, all the dynamics were different. I didn't feel like I fit anymore, and I honestly didn't feel very wanted. I didn't have much of an emotional connection to my sisters, and my mom didn't understand. I think she was angry with me, and I was angry with them both."

"That had to be really hard."

"It was. But I've had a lot of time to reflect on it, and while I do think they could have handled things better, I was an emotionally immature teenage boy, used to everything revolving around me. I didn't handle it well, as Mike could probably tell you."

"Is that why you're so committed to helping him now?"

Camden nods. "I won't desert him when he didn't desert me."

This makes so much more sense. I mean, I know Camden is a great guy, the kind who would help someone in need. But having Mike live with him, paying for all the caregivers—that's more than most people would do.

"I don't think I've mentioned my mom to you," I say.

"I met your dad, but I think I assumed your mom had passed."

"No. She just decided she wanted a different life, one that involved academic pursuits and no children. My dad raised us." I hold up a hand when I see the look of concern on his face. "I really am okay with it now. She used to call every

282

Sunday and we'd have dreadfully awkward phone calls. Last year, I finally asked her if we could stop doing that."

"Do you ever talk?" Camden asks.

"Not on a regular basis. But when either of us calls or texts, it's because one of us wants to, which is better. It's not a great relationship, but I don't see it changing, and I want to invest in the people who really care about me and want to invest right back. It's not similar to your situation, but I guess I want you to know that I can relate on some level. And I understand the inclination to help Mike."

"Good. But this means he'll be with me long-term," Camden says. "And I know that could make things ... difficult for you. It means you're not just getting me; you're getting me *and* Mike."

"You're getting me and Liam," I point out.

"It's not quite the same."

"It's not exactly the same, no. But I would never ask you to choose between Mike and me. I like him, and so does Liam."

"Good. Because I've done some thinking." Camden turns his phone on, then flips it so I can see the screen. It's a house —a craftsman similar to this one, only larger. "I put an offer on this house."

I jerk my head up to stare at him. "What? You're buying a house? What if you get traded or something?"

"I talked to Coach on the road. He's been bugging me about signing an extension. If I want, I think the organization wants me to stay. At least for a while. And then ... we can see."

"We?"

"Yes, *we*. Whatever future plans I make, I want you to be an equal partner. Which is why I'm nervous about the house.

I know you want to end up back on Oakley, which I'm definitely open to. For now, with you and Liam settling in, this seemed like a good option. It was the only place I could find in all of Harvest Hollow that fit all the criteria, so I really hope you like it."

"What criteria?"

"Why don't you take a look while I tell you?"

I scroll through the photos of the place, which is absolutely stunning. Where my rental has been updated nicely, this one has been completely remodeled to create an open-concept floor plan that still retains all the charm and architectural details of the original build. And so much square footage. All of it beautiful.

"I needed a place with two master bedrooms—at least one of which was on the first floor. A few extra bedrooms, and a fenced backyard. As a bonus, it has a fully finished basement."

"It's amazing," I tell him, reaching the last two pictures. Camden points to the screen.

"That's the most important thing I needed, and only this house has it."

"A garage apartment?" I ask.

"For Jordan. I'd like him to be the only caregiver for Mike. A full-time, salaried position with housing included. So, I guess I actually come with two people, not one."

"Good thing I like both of your people. Did Jordan say yes?"

"He did. But he told me I was stupid for not talking to you first."

"About hiring him? Or about the house?"

"About both. He's right, but the agent said this house would go fast. Since it was the only one with everything, I don't want to wait."

"Things with us are still so new. You don't have to run things by me, Cam."

He scoots closer, perching on the edge of his seat as his brown eyes search mine. "But that's the thing—we're not so new. Not really. And I want to do more than run things by you. I want to make decisions together because I want a life with you. I wanted a house you'd love, a house with space for Liam to grow up, one with a yard for Panda." He shakes his head. "I want to marry you, Naomi."

My heart goes positively feral in my chest. A wild, unsteady rhythm. "You do?"

"Yes. But I'm not asking you that—yet. I have plans for it, but I needed to talk to you about all this first. Because our lives are both a little more complicated."

"Camden Cole, are you asking me if you can ask me to marry you?"

"Yes."

"Then, yes. You can ask me to marry you. Want me to tell me what I'm going to say when you do?"

His smile is slow and a little smug. "I feel pretty good about the answer."

"Yeah? Maybe I should make you sweat a little more."

"Please don't."

I laugh, feeling a lightness in my limbs. Like the cork popped on a bottle of champagne inside me, and now my blood is fizzy with joy. "Okay. I won't. I meant what I said on the phone. I want to put down roots with you. And I guess I can wait for an actual proposal. If you don't make me wait too long."

"How long is too long?" he asks.

I weigh my words, not wanting to sound desperate and also not wanting to hold back.

"Let's just say … if you had asked tonight, I would have happily said yes."

His eyes flare. "Good to know. Before that, two more things."

"Anything."

"First, I want to call my family." I can see the shift in his features and the nervousness written there. His hands shake a little, and I squeeze. "Will you sit with me while I do?"

My breath catches, and a warm wave of tenderness unfurls in my chest. Leaning forward, I place a kiss on his lips. I mean it to be soft and quick, but I realize as Camden kisses me back that we didn't kiss when I greeted him. My mouth seems bent on reminding me how remiss I was.

After a moment, I pull back, dizzy and breathless. "Sorry, I got a little distracted."

"You're not the only one," Camden mutters.

"I'd love to sit with you while you call. Anything you need. Did you mean right now?"

"I'm tired of running," he says.

"Then I'll be with you when you stop." I climb into his lap, handing back his phone as I wrap an arm around his neck. "You're really doing this now?"

He scrolls through his phone, and it makes my heart squeeze when I see he still has his parents on his Favorites list. "I don't want to. I'm scared," he confesses. "But I don't want it hanging over me any longer. I'm so tired."

I snuggle in closer, leaning my head on his shoulder. "I know. And I'm here."

For a moment, we sit there in the darkness. I hadn't realized that dusk fully fell while we were talking, and now everything is cast in the soft, forgiving light of a full moon. Camden stares at the phone in his hand for what feels like forever. Then he taps the screen and puts the phone up to his ear.

I can feel his breathing and heart rate both quicken, and I continue pressing closer, wanting my weight and warmth to reassure him as I let myself envision a future of moments like this—sitting on the front porch with Liam and Panda. I expand the vision to include Mike and Jordan, then picture us all having dinner in the house Camden showed me earlier.

It feels like a dream. Better than a dream. The kind of wish so good that I never could have imagined it becoming a reality.

I'm sitting close enough that I can hear a man's voice saying hello on the line. Camden clears his throat. "Hey, Dad? It's me. Cam."

I sit with him through the call, trying to hold back tears. It's an emotional call, though slightly awkward as Camden talks to his dad and his mom, who sobs so loudly I can hear her through the phone. Though Camden doesn't cry, at times, I can feel him shake a little, and I continue to hold him, pressing a hand to his chest.

At some point, Liam lets Panda out front, and he sits at Camden's feet, head in his lap.

When they finish, Camden sets the phone down and wraps his arms around me. "Thank you," he whispers into my hair.

"Anytime."

Panda, clearly feeling neglected, shoves his head in between us, demanding attention. Laughing, I scratch the dog behind his ears. He gives me a smile in return. Though it still throws me off to see a dog baring its teeth, it's a lot less scary than it was.

"Oh, hey—you forgot the second thing you wanted to tell me."

Camden chuckles. "Right. I forgot. Maybe I should save it for another night."

I pinch the area near his ribs that I know is sensitive.

"Fine," he relents. "The other thing I wanted to tell you is that with the new house, you have to promise you'll take better care of the mailbox."

He's still laughing when I wrap one hand around his neck and pull his mouth to mine.

EPILOGUE

Camden

Naomi is up to something.

How do I know? Because I am also up to something, and I see the signs.

There are phone calls she ends abruptly when I enter the room and furtive texts.

She's also been wearing an adorably smug look on her face all week, the kind that sing-songs, *I know something you don't know!*

Yeah, well—*same*. As she'll find out tonight. I'm not sure when I'll get to see whatever she's got up her sleeve, but I need to focus on my plans before I can think about it.

I check in with Parker as soon as I arrive at the Summit on game day. It's the first playoff game, and I'm not even nervous.

About *that*, anyway.

"Is everything set?" I ask.

She rolls her eyes. "Do you really doubt me, Cam? Of course. I've got seats and the suite. I'll handle getting everyone there. Naomi will go up at first intermission and won't suspect a thing until then. What about you? Are *you* ready?"

"If I feel like I'm going to throw up, does that mean yes?"

Her grin is huge. "Absolutely. You've got this."

I sure hope so.

Before the game, I'm completely in my head about it all, which is why I jump when someone squeezes my shoulder in the locker room.

I'm surprised when I look up and see Alec. He's around a lot, still giving out captainly wisdom and support. But I thought he'd be watching with Evie and Juno from the box I rented out for tonight. He's even wearing his old jersey.

"Planning to jump in if we need you, Cap?" I tease.

"Not quite," he says. Then he winks at me.

I'm not sure why, but between Naomi's secretive behavior and whatever Alec is winking about, I'm suddenly feeling a whole new level of nerves.

"Guys, hey!" Coach calls, and the locker room quiets. "As you might have noticed, Alec is here. He'll be calling our starting lineup, but before we get to that, I want to say a few words."

He clears his throat and rubs a hand over his head. "This is a very special team. And this has been a very special few seasons for me. Winning the Calder Cup last year was amazing and winning it this year will be the cherry on top."

The room erupts in cheer and chants. But Felix and I share a quiet look. I can see he's thinking the same thing I am—this sounds like a goodbye speech.

"No matter what happens next, I'm proud of you. For

your grit and determination, but more than that, for how you've become each other's family."

Van raises his hand. "Some of us became actual family, Dad."

Coach glowers at him. Van has been banned from referring to Coach this way while we're at official team things. Clearly, Van doesn't value his life.

But I'm still stuck on Coach's words—*no matter what happens next.*

What's happening next? What does he know that no one in this room seems to?

Except maybe Alec. Beside me, he is utterly calm. A knowing kind of calm.

"I've loved getting to see some of you grow up. Dominik —you've shown an enormous amount of character growth this year. I'm proud of you, kid."

The guys all clap, and Dominik's cheeks flush. He mutters something about how he used to act, switching to Russian for what sounds like calling himself a nasty name.

"And the twins—you've been a piece we didn't know was missing from our team. I don't think it will be long before you get your call-up. I know you'll be ready for it when you do."

Theo and Carter, who have been very vocal about their long-term NHL goals, look ecstatic and practically glow under Coach's praise.

"And the rest of you ... you're pretty okay too," Coach says with a smile. It fades faster than the guys' cheering. When he continues, his voice is much more somber. "One big change this year was losing our captain, so let's get Alec up here one last time."

Last time?

I mean, yeah—Alec is no longer captain. But he's been

very involved and often shows up to practices, conferring with the assistant coaches and our special teams coach.

Is Alec leaving Harvest Hollow? Is that why this feels like an ending?

With all the nerves I'm already feeling about later, I don't need an extra dose.

I tune out most of the lineup, which is as expected. My mind is racing through things that could go wrong later and on whether or not I'm reading into everything Coach just said. I can't stop wondering if all the tense conversations I observed over the past few months and the rumored visits from the AHL have something to do with his mood.

I'm dragged back to the room when Tucker says, "What about our other defenseman? You only called out one. Are we playing short tonight, cap?"

"I'm not your captain anymore, Tuck." And with that, Alec pulls his jersey over his head.

I'm not sure why it's so dramatic, but Dumbo gasps.

Alec grins. Then he turns to me.

"Your second D-man tonight is Cole—your new captain."

Everything goes dark for a moment. Not because I pass out but because Alec has tossed his jersey in my face.

I pull it off, taking in the pandemonium in the room. The guys, most of whom don't seem to share my shock, are on their feet, smiling and clapping.

This can't be right.

I turn the jersey over, prepared to throw it back and tell Alec he's lost it, when I see the name and number on the back. When I saw the C on the front, I assumed Alec was wearing his old jersey.

But it says Cole 11.

My mouth goes dry as I stare down at the letters stitched

on the back. The clapping and cheers fade into a dull white noise in my head.

They want *me* to be captain?

A hand touches my back and Coach sits down beside me, leaning close so I can hear him over the noise.

"I can see the doubt written all over your face, son, which only confirms my choice. Some men lead by sucking up all the attention in a room. Some keep people in line by scaring them into action. You have a quiet influence I'm not sure you even notice."

I'm set to argue, but he continues on.

"I've watched this year while you've battled whatever demons you've had. You fought, and these guys were ready to go into battle with you. I saw the turning point when you realized it was better not to do it alone. You are a strong, quiet leader who inspires men to be better. And the fact that you're too humble to realize it is another point in your favor."

Coach stands. I'm still speechless. He holds up a hand, and the guys quiet down. Then he turns, giving me a challenging look.

"Put on your jersey, Captain Cole."

I can't help but do as he asks. Whether I believe him or not—mostly not—I can see from the guys' faces that they share his unfounded faith in me.

And the last thing I'll do on a team is crush that faith.

I tug the jersey over my head, and when my head pops out, I'm smiling. The room erupts. Hugs, slaps on the back, someone tossing a ball of tape at my head. (Classic Van.)

The noise subsides, and Coach once more turns to me. "For your first act as captain, I've got a big responsibility for you. Normally, this is a decision I would make, but I want you to choose your alternate captain. You can take as much time as you need and it doesn't have to be tonight but—"

"Dominik," I interrupt. "I choose the Kid."

The room goes silent. Dominik's face looks as shocked as I'm sure mine did moments ago, and his pale cheeks flush. I can't explain all the reasons why, but I'm certain he's the right choice. Maybe, like me, he doesn't quite feel ready, but I have no doubt after watching him the last year that he'll grow into it.

Dominik is not smiling, but he has a determined look about him, and he gives me a nod. "I'll do it."

No one speaks for a moment, and then Van stands on the bench and shouts, "All hail Cole and the Kid!"

I'm not sure our locker room will be this loud even if we pull out a win tonight.

And only as we wind down the celebration to finish gearing up do I remember how much more I have to look forward to tonight.

———

Naomi

Camden is onto me. How can I be sure? I'm not. Not completely.

But he's caught me several times doing suspicious things and just ignored it rather than asking what I'm up to. And I'm the worst at hiding things when I'm excited, and this is one of those things that has had me grinning for a solid two weeks.

The package has been delivered, Jordan texts.

I snort and call him. "Look," I say when he answers, "we

can come up for a code name if you want to, but we are not referring to Camden's family as 'the package.' It sounds ... bad."

Jordan laughs. "Should I have told you that we're driving to the Summit now so everyone in the car can hear you through the Bluetooth?"

"Oh," I say weakly.

"Hey, Naomi!" Mike calls.

I'm going to murder Jordan. And I can't even threaten to do it because then Camden's whole family will hear me.

"Hello!" his mom says. She sounds a little distant, but I can still hear her just fine. She sounds like she's trying not to laugh.

"For what it's worth," Camden's dad says, "I'd vote for a code name like Eagle or Jaguar—something cool and tough."

Faintly, I hear the sound of Camden's twelve-year-old sisters in the background.

My stomach loops itself into another double knot of nerves. Talking to them all on the phone and on the occasional video call is not enough preparation for this surprise in-person visit. I might collapse in a monstrous heap of spent endorphins at the end of the night.

I pinch the bridge of my nose and force cheer into my voice while silently plotting ways to pay Jordan back for this. "Good idea, Mr. Cole."

"But I absolutely insist you have to use our first names. It's Scott and Kelli. Got it?"

"Yes ... Scott." When you grow up in the South, or anywhere with parents who still subscribe to Manners with a capital M, breaking the habit of calling adults Mr. or Mrs. is tough. Even when you're an adult yourself. "Jordan, what's your ETA for having the ..." I pause. "The Wolf Pack at the Summit?"

"Wolf Pack," Jordan says with another laugh. "I like it. The Wolf Pack will be there in twenty minutes."

"Great. Greyson is going to meet you at the back door and escort you all to the suite. I'll be down in my normal seats with Liam and Bailey until the first intermission. Then I'll come up with Liam."

"We can't wait to meet you!" Camden's mom says.

"I can't wait to meet you too! How was the flight?"

"The flight was good! First class was an unexpected surprise."

"You can thank Camden's credit card for that," Jordan says.

He assures me that Camden won't notice the charges, which would give away the surprise.

Since they moved into the new house with the garage apartment, Jordan has taken over more and more administrative duties for Camden. With Mike mostly needing companionship and not any kind of hands-on caregiving right now, Jordan has added on household duties like cooking and grocery shopping as well as managing some of Camden's business tasks.

Apparently, Cam doesn't ever look at his credit card statement—must be nice—and has an accountant who reconciles everything. Jordan has his own card for purchases, and he insisted we put all the flights on it—with upgrades to first class. It was a good call, though I wanted to vomit when he told me the total.

Jordan had only laughed. "I don't know if you are aware of this, but your boyfriend is doing just fine."

"I know, but I'm spending his money without permission. It feels weird."

"You're doing something really amazing," he'd said, his

tone changing to serious and sincere. "It's the kind of thing he wouldn't have done for himself, and he'll be thrilled."

I sure hope so.

When the puck drops, I can hardly watch the game because I keep glancing up at the box where Camden's family is. I can't see them or anyone else, but Jordan texted me that the Wolf Pack is in position.

"Mom!" Liam says, grabbing my arm. "Look at Coach Cam!"

Even though Cam is no longer Liam's Coach, that's the name he's been using, and no one's arguing about it.

Camden is doing his defense thing, sweeping a loose puck away from the goal and sending it up the ice to Logan. "What?"

"His jersey! Look at his jersey!"

I look. And see nothing.

Bailey leans close from my other side. She's become our game day companion, and one of my very closest friends. "Look on the front. Above the logo."

I see the C while she's still talking. "He's wearing the C today. I think Coach had him wear it a few games ago too."

"No, Mom—it's bigger. And look!" Liam points down to the program in his hand, which we hardly need to look at these days. In the program by Camden's name, he's clearly identified as captain.

"They made Camden captain!?"

Everyone is standing to cheer for the goal that someone scored—Eli, by the sound of Bailey next to me—but I'm screaming for Camden. As though he feels my eyes on him, Camden looks over to our seats and raises his glove. I wave and point to my chest and the spot where the C is on his. He nods, grinning, and then, it's right back to the game.

"Wow. He's made captain and his family is here—this is going to be some night."

Bailey laughs, then says, "It sure is."

———

As we're making our way up to the suite, an announcer says that there will be a slight delay due to some issues with the ice. I can see the ice crew down there with their shovels, the Zamboni waiting in the wings.

That will give me a little more time with Camden's family, and I'm not sure if that's a good or bad thing. Good, probably. They're wonderful, and I'm excited to have them here. But a little tiny part of me is terrified they won't like me or Liam or that Camden will be upset rather than excited by the surprise.

"Hey." Bailey pulls me to a stop just outside the suite while Liam bounds inside. Going to find the food, I'm sure. "You look like you need a minute. Just take a breath, okay?"

"Okay. Do you happen to have a paper bag? That might help."

"Not tonight. Are you okay?"

I nod. "It's just … a lot."

Bailey grins. "You're going to have a great time tonight, okay? Now, let's get you in there before we lose any more time."

I don't realize until I'm opening the door to the suite that Bailey has dropped back behind me, waiting in the hall. "Are you coming?" I ask.

I don't like the look on her face. It's too knowing, and I am distinctly aware something is definitely up even before someone practically tackles me in a hug.

"You are simply too slow, and I can't wait another second. Get in here!"

"Eloise?"

It is, indeed, Eloise. And true to her classic style, she's wearing a pink dress with tiny ice skates, sticks, and pucks all over it. "What are you—how are you—oh my gosh! You're here!"

She cackles and hugs me again. "I am, and I'm not alone."

Grabbing me by the shoulders, she turns me so I can see into the suite. It's a bigger one than we usually use—Parker said it was because the normal one was booked—and now I know why. What I think of as my entire Oakley family is here: my dad, Jake, Hunter, Merritt, Izzy, Sadie, and Benedict. Plus, Camden's family. And Gracie has Panda on his leash. Mike and Jordan are in the middle of it all, and every single person is staring at me, smiling.

I don't even realize that I've put my hands to my cheeks. "What is happening?"

Liam, who's leaning against Jake grins at me. "Coach Cam out-surprised you, Mom. That's what's happening."

He sure did.

The next few minutes are filled with joyous hugs, a few tears I manage to keep from overflowing, and so much laughter. Whatever nerves I had disappear. Meeting Camden's family feels totally natural, and they've clearly been integrating with my Oakley people. Izzy and Liam are eating with Camden's sisters, Panda at their feet, looking hopeful for handouts. Sadie is gesturing wildly while talking to Kelli, and Benedict, Jake, and Scott are having some kind of argument about the stock market.

Parker appears, hooking an arm around my waist. "Well?"

I give her a hug that I hope cracks at least one rib. "Of course, you were involved in this—playing both sides."

"Like anyone could keep me out of things like this. No one could pull off anything without my help," she brags.

"Yeah, well, next time, my big plan isn't going to involve you, and you'll be the one surprised."

"Try me," she says, and then suddenly, her eyes go wide. "Actually, there's one more surprise."

Someone behind me places hands over my eyes, and Parker holds me in place when I squirm. "Okay, now what? This night could not get any wilder."

"We'll see about that," Eloise, who must be the one covering my eyes, says.

Then her hands disappear, and I blink a few times. In only about twenty seconds, the room has been transformed. All the lights are out and little battery-operated candles are flickering, lighting up the room in a soft glow.

Camden stands right in front of me. He's not in his uniform, just the athletic shorts and shirt he wears underneath. He must have showered because his hair is wet and he does *not* smell like a man who just played a full period.

"What are you doing? Are you going to get in trouble? Oh, my gosh, hi!"

"I won't get in trouble if we make this quick," he says, and then his gaze goes behind me and his jaw drops. "Mom? Dad? Sarah and Elizabeth?"

"Don't mind us, son," Scott says in a whisper. "Just get on with it and we'll see you after the game."

"Well, there goes my big reveal moment," I mutter.

Camden's gaze returns to mine, and he grins. "You did that for me?"

"I did that for you."

"Wow. I can't—"

"Time," Parker hisses. "We can only buy you so much time."

"Right." Camden shakes his head, and then before I can even react, he drops to one knee, taking my hand in his. I feel like I'm about to melt straight through the floor and down to the sublevels, where someone will have to scrape a puddle of Naomi off the floor later.

"Naomi, I wanted your family to be here for this, and I also didn't want to wait until the end of the game."

"Which is what we *talked* about doing so you wouldn't have to rush," Parker mutters from behind me, and someone shushes her.

"I couldn't wait for two more periods of hockey to tell you that I love you and ask—Will you marry me?"

Behind me, several people sniff, and I find myself frozen, unable to respond, just staring at Camden. I have a sudden image of him the very first time I met him flash through my mind. Not on one knee, but crouched in Gator's Groceries, reading a label.

And then, like some kind of movie playing at high speed, I can picture a future together. Laughing with Liam, Mike, and Jordan, with Panda running around our ankles.

Standing along the beach on Oakley while Liam rides a wave in next to Izzy.

Kissing under a sky full of stars.

I'm startled back into the moment by a wet nose, nudging my hand. Panda whines, looking up at me then at Camden as if to say, *Answer the man before he has heart failure!*

"Yes," I whisper. "Yes, I love you, too, and would love nothing more than to marry you, *Captain* Camden Cole."

His smile tugs at something deep inside me, and I duck down to wrap my arms around him. He stands, lifting me with him as he does.

"I can't believe you did this," I whisper in his ear.

"I'm not done yet," he says back. Then louder, "Hey, Liam —you still have the ring, right?"

"You trusted Liam with the ring?" I hiss.

Camden laughs, and from beside me, Liam says, "You both trusted me with your secrets, and I kept them. So, don't come at me. Here."

Setting me back down, Camden takes the box from Liam, who gives us both hugs before joining Izzy and Camden's sisters. I had almost forgotten this whole room was full of people. People we know and love—but still.

I feel suddenly shy as Camden opens the box, revealing a ring with a massive turquoise stone.

"It's an aquamarine," he says. "I thought you might like a ring in your favorite color and—"

I cut him off with a kiss. He doesn't need to explain his choice—which is perfect—and he doesn't need to say another word.

Though I'm normally not into PDA, especially in front of my kid, I don't even care. Especially not when everyone around us starts to cheer.

Camden smiles against my mouth. "Just so you know—I should probably get back or I'm going to be in trouble with Coach."

We pull apart, and he hugs me, lifting me up off my feet. I hear a champagne cork pop somewhere behind us.

"Eh. You're the captain. What are they gonna do?"

"Good point," he says.

"Congratulations, Captain."

"Thank you. It's been a pretty huge day. Did you really fly my family here?"

"I did. On your credit card, though. Are you going to say hi?"

"I should—but again, I need to get back to my game. I'll be back after we destroy them. Also, my card is your card."

"Sounds good to me. Hey, Cam?"

"Hey, yeah?"

I lean close, my lips against his ear. "If I ever pull away, promise you'll run after me?"

"Promise. And you'll do the same for me?"

"Promise."

With one more kiss, he sets me down on my feet. And after quickly hugging his family, he practically sprints from the room. Parker shoos him out, but then pauses outside the suite frowning down at her phone.

I'm distracted by all the hugs and congratulations. Someone presses a glass of champagne in my hand and I take a quick swallow, the fizzy bubbles matching my current energy. My hand feels different with the ring on it, and I can't stop staring.

"He made a good choice," Benedict says, giving me a side hug. "Congrats."

"Thank you. I can't believe you're all here. Did you drive?"

Ben smiles. "Absolutely not. I chartered a private jet."

"Of course you did."

Down on the ice, the game has started up again. I'm about to grab Liam and see if he wants to go back down from our seats when Parker comes in. She looks, in a word, devastated.

"What is it?" I ask. "What happened?"

"I ..." She looks up at me, and her eyes are wild. "I don't want to ruin the mood."

"Don't worry about the mood. What is it?"

"I think the Appies are in trouble. The league is forcing

303

our owner out, which means ... I don't even know what it means."

Below us, the horn sounds as the Appies score a goal, and I wonder if Camden made it back on the ice.

Now, I'm also wondering if he'll still have a job.

"What can we do?" I ask, feeling my elation from the day's events starting to come back down to earth from wherever they've been hovering.

Parker forces a laugh. "Nothing. I mean, not unless you happen to know a billionaire who wants to buy a hockey team."

I almost laugh.

But before I can, Benedict steps forward and holds out a hand to Parker. "I don't think we've met. I'm Benedict King, and I just so happen to be a billionaire who might be interested in buying a hockey team."

Keep reading for a sample of Wyatt's book, If All Else Sails!

IF ALL ELSE SAILS

CHAPTER ONE: A QUAINT LITTLE MURDER COTTAGE

Josie

I am standing outside of what could best be described as a quaint little murder cottage, wondering if, instead of going on vacation with my brother, I'm about to die.

Jacob's cheerful recorded voice comes over the phone I'm pressing to my ear. Again. This time, I do what I almost never do because I'm not a heathen. Or a boomer.

I leave a voicemail.

"Jacob, hi. It's Josie—the sister you seem to be pranking right now. Why am I here? Where is here? I double-checked the address, but this cannot be the site of any kind of vacation. I did not pack to defend myself against a serial killer. Where are you? Call me back. You've got my number. Use it. Prefer- ably now."

I immediately follow up with a text, which reads CALL ME NOW in all caps with no punctuation. My brother will know the lack of a period or a neat row of exclamation points means either I've been kidnapped or I'm really and truly angry.

The message doesn't show a read receipt. It just sits there. Delivered.

Concern fissures through me. Maybe Jacob was in a wreck. Maybe he fell asleep at the wheel and drove right off one of the bridges on the way here. Maybe he's dead somewhere and my last message to him was full of snark and anger.

Or . . . maybe my mind sometime jumps too quickly to the worst possible scenario.

A less morbid and much more likely explanation is that Jacob got caught up working. Like always. He could have gotten a last-minute meeting with a big client. Or a potential client. An up-and-coming college football star poised for NFL greatness. Or a basketball player having a great year with endorsement offers coming in hot. He could have left the office late and gotten stuck in DC commuter traffic.

Or maybe he met a woman. Difficult, considering it's not quite noon, but I've found that, with Jacob's charm, anything is possible.

I know what my best friend would say. Toni would tell me I shouldn't have driven two hours to an unfamiliar address just because my brother held out promises of a fun trip together.

Never leave the house without your underwear or your boundaries, I can practically hear her saying.

But when it comes to my brother, I understand the concept of boundaries; I just can't seem to apply them.

I scan his text from yesterday, searching for any clues I might have missed.

The Super Summer Sibling Extravaganza is upon us! Pack a bag for warm weather and maybe swimming. Comfy clothes. Maybe one or two nice things, but this will be casual. Address in the next text. Don't look it up on Google Street View! TOMORROW AT 4 PM.

Yes—that's all the information he gave me.

And yes, after packing this morning, I adjusted the GPS to take me on the most scenic route from Fredericksburg to Kilmarnock, a small town on what's known as the Northern Neck. I even resisted the urge to look at the Google Street View, a decision I now regret. Because I definitely would have asked questions.

What if . . . he isn't coming?

"You're being ridiculous. He'll be here," I say out loud, like voicing it into the world will make my brother appear. He doesn't.

That doesn't mean he won't. But my worry expands, braiding with the excitement and nervousness of being in a new situation. While packing, I shoved down my anxious thoughts, stuffing them away like I stuffed half my closet into my suitcases—just in case.

Adventures are fun! I told myself while carefully rolling my shirts and lining them up in neat rows at the bottom of my roller bag. So are surprises! You are a woman who lives for excitement!

I didn't come close to convincing myself. But I packed. I came.

And now, as I stand on a driveway made of crushed oyster shells, baking in this sweltering oven of a June day, I wish I were back in my comfy but cramped apartment, working my way through my summer reading list. This year I've decided it will be composed entirely of books written by women—from the Brontës and Jane Austen to Toni Morrison and Madeleine L'Engle, whose young adult books I've always loved.

But no—I chose to leave the cocoon of home to find out what's behind Door Number Three. Which is apparently the sad little cottage in front of me, desperately in need of an extreme home makeover. Or a bulldozer. The siding, which may have been cream once upon a time, is now the color of a load of whites thrown in the washer too many times. Most of the wood trim is rotten. I'm no roof expert, but this one looks like it's one heavy rain away from collapsing.

If I squint, it's almost cute. More like it had been cute and is now disappointed by its owner's lack of upkeep. The front looks like a face—the windows its sad eyes above the half circle of frowning glass inlaid in the door.

The property, however, is gorgeous, with a swath of lush green grass fringed by pines on either side. The real star of the show is the glittering water behind the house, complete with a dock and a sailboat, which looks to be in much better shape than the house.

Parked near a structure that's somewhere between a stand- alone garage and a metal shed is an old Bronco. Definitely not Jacob's. He prefers his cars new and sleek and shiny. Lots of dollar signs and detailing involved. This SUV looks as though it's been restored, but that's not Jacob's thing either. I briefly wonder if the car's owner is inside the house watching me, but I see no sign of movement. The place has the abandoned vibe going on.

Abandoned but also the perfect hideout for a serial killer.

I give the sad little house a wide berth, walking toward the water as I swat away birdlike mosquitoes and wipe the sweat- stache off my upper lip. By the time I get there, my shirt clings damply to every part of me. The dock is sturdy, if a little splintered, the deep navy gleam of water almost inviting. Almost. A small dinghy motors past, driven by an older man with two little girls in pink life jackets. They all wave.

I wave back, like this is my dock. My sailboat. My little murder cottage.

The name painted in neat script on the side of the sailboat reads *QUINTessential*. The quint in all caps is likely some inside joke, because I don't get it. Frankly, it's a disappointing boat name. Aren't boats supposed to have clever names—like Nauti & Nice or Little Boat Peep or Signed, Sailed, Delivered?

I pull out my phone—still nothing from my brother—and take a few pictures of the water and then the boat. I stop just shy of climbing aboard. I've never been on a boat this size and I'm itching to explore. It's a little longer than the dock, just tall enough that I can't see much of the deck. I'm curious but not one for trespassing, so I turn and snap pictures of the back side of the cottage, which really should have more windows considering the view.

When I walk back across the lawn, three birds rocket away from a hidden nest under the cottage's sagging eaves. I come to an abrupt stop when a lacy curtain flutters in one of the windows. My heart leaps into my throat.

Is someone in there watching me?

I mean, it could be Jacob. He did send me the address. But he wouldn't be hiding in there. He would have run out and given me a bone-crushing hug—his specialty.

I also can't actually picture my brother stepping on the porch of this place, much less spying on me from inside.

As a cloud passes in front of the sun, I take another picture of the little house. You know—just in case it's evidence in the event of my disappearance or death.

The phone vibrates in my hand, and I don't bother with greetings when I see Jacob is calling.

"Tell me you're the one watching me from inside the creepy murder cottage."

He sputters a laugh. "The what?"

"You know—the sad little white house that's falling apart and might be haunted or home to a serial killer. The one whose address you sent me last night. The one I'm standing outside of, hoping it doesn't collapse when the wind blows."

"It's that bad, huh?" His voice sounds strained.

I close my eyes. Breathe in and out slowly for a few counts. Reopen my eyes just in time to see the curtains flutter again. "If you don't know the condition, that means you aren't here."

It also means he isn't the person inside watching me. I scan my surroundings as I take a step back toward my car.

"I . . . am not there."

Disappointment curdles all the happy hope I've been holding on to since his text last night. So much for the Super Summer Sibling Extravaganza. And any trust I had in my brother.

When I speak, my voice holds the icy depth of a walk-in freezer. "Jacob, whose house is this? And where are you?"

"It's kind of a long story."

"I've got the whole drive back home to hear it," I say, striding toward my car.

"Don't go yet," he says quickly.

"Give me a reason not to. A good one."

"The thing is," he continues, ignoring my questions, "I need

to call in a favor."

I squeeze my eyes closed. "A favor."

By my secret count—secret because you're not supposed to

keep records of wrongs by people you love—the favors are already stacked high on my side and somewhat lacking on

310

Jacob's part. We are as unbalanced as a single person on a seesaw. If anyone should be calling in favors, it's me.

Jacob is the gas giant at the center of our family's solar system. My parents and I don't even wait for him to ask us to jump or say how high. We just stay ready, knees bent and muscles flexed.

Is it a bit of a trauma response to Jacob coming this close to dying when he was twelve? Probably.

But even before that, he was the golden boy of the family. Almost losing him simply elevated his status. It also brought us all closer. And if we're a little lopsided in terms of who runs the show, there are way more toxic family issues we could struggle with. My parents have escaped his orbit the last few years after buying an RV, trading in my childhood home for something a little more manageable, and spending most of the year motoring around the country. I think they're in South Dakota right now. Or was it South Carolina? Possibly just the South. They're hard to keep up with these days.

Which might be the point.

In my older brother's defense, though he's a wee bit self-focused, Jacob is a decent guy. He's generous. Goofy. Bighearted. Able to make friends anywhere. Loyal.

Usually loyal.

"You see—"

Jacob's explanation is interrupted by sirens. I registered them

a few minutes ago, soft whines in the distance. But now they are loud, pealing cries. Two cop cars turn and speed down the driveway, kicking up clouds of dust behind them as they head straight for me.

"Any idea why the police are here?" I ask. He groans. "Oh no. He didn't. He wouldn't."

"He who wouldn't what?"

I've never been arrested, never considered running from the police, but find myself slowly backing away as the cruisers pull to a stop.

A swarm—okay, it's just two—of cops throw open the doors, leaping out like I am the fugitive they've been chasing for days. Not a confused elementary school nurse who might be trespassing as some kind of favor to the man formerly known as her brother.

One cop looks barely old enough to be out of high school, and the other has eyebrows so bushy they deserve their own zip code. They're thicker than his mustache, which is saying something.

"That," Jacob says, as the cops point what looks to be one gun and one taser at me, "is probably because of Wyatt."

Ah, I think, as the cops order me to drop my weapon— a.k.a. my phone—and put my hands up. Wyatt.

It all makes sense now.

———

Find If All Else Sails on Amazon or your favorite retailer!

A Free Sheet Cake Novella!

I've got a special FREE novella for you! This one takes place in my fictional town of Sheet Cake between The Pocket Pair (book #3) and book #4 but will act as a standalone or an introduction if you haven't read the series yet!

There are minor spoilers (mostly who ends up with whom) ... but if you're okay with that, you can sign up here! https://emmastclair.com/ante

ACKNOWLEDGMENTS

A massive thank you to Jenny for always reading and keeping me on track when I'm wavering. I LOVED writing this series with you and am so glad we found each other!

Thank you so much to Jordan Truex for being my early reader. You have been such a support and encouragement to me, and you really helped me in these final days! You are the best.

Thank you to Erica and Lindsay for catching some persistent typos!

Also, thanks to Jordan from @talkhockeywithme (go follow her!) for all the great memes and for the Dallas Stars tickets. Go Stars!

A NOTE FROM EMMA

When Jenny Proctor and I decided to write this Appies Hockey series together, we were barely hockey literate.

I distinctly remember having a moment of panic in May of 2023 when I realized that my first book, *Just Don't Fall*, was coming out at the start of September, and I might not get to see an actual hockey game live if I didn't go RIGHT THEN.

My husband was asleep beside me, and I bought tickets for a Texas Stars game in Cedar Park, two-and-a-half hours away for the following night. I then texted Rob: *Hey! I'm going to Austin tomorrow to see a hockey game. It's for work. Love you!*

Now, two years later, I am harboring a full-blown hockey obsession. Mostly with the Dallas Stars, but I actually follow hockey news and listen to daily podcasts about the NHL.

I even took a Learn to Skate Hockey class with my 12-year-old daughter. The young men teaching the class (*which was comprised of a few children, a few teen boys, and me—an almost fifty-year-old woman*) had no idea what to do with me.

(*For the record, my roller derby skills gave me a nice boost and I was good at almost everything but … stopping.*)

This final book is what I consider my love letter to hockey. I am Liam—filled with so many facts that no one wants to talk to me.

I have to actively try NOT to talk about hockey at dinners and basically any old event.

Thankfully, Jenny is equally as obsessed—only with the Carolina Hurricanes—so we talk hockey often.

I also joined a paid Discord server (hey, DLLS Diehards!) so I can talk to people about the Stars.

This book got to be the place where I infused that hockey love.

The sport is really unique, but what drew me in were the stories. Every team has its lore, and when I learned about how Joe Pavelski (the oldest player on the Stars at that time) opened his home to Wyatt Johnston (the youngest player on the team, drafted at 18 and coming from Canada to Dallas), I was SOLD. Pavs folded Johnny into his family, and you can see the mark this made on Johnston even now.

Those kinds of stories solidified my love of the sport, and they're what I wanted to capture in my books.

Jenny and I fell in love with this team and these characters. Their relationships and their care for each other. The way they support and chirp and struggle *together*. Even if you don't like hockey or sports at all, we wrote books focused around these characters and their relationships.

It was bittersweet writing this epilogue, and I love thinking of the guys playing on, even as Jenny and I move on to other projects.

Y'all, thank you for reading. Being an author is both rewarding and terrifying in equal measures every single day.

If you want to read more about these characters, you can check out the Oakley Island Series, which Jenny and I cowrote, or If All Else Sails. It's a standalone featuring Wyatt, a former Appie. You might just see some familiar faces there.

Happy reading, y'all! Thank you for being the best readers I could ask for.

-e

WHAT TO READ NEXT

The Appies

Just Don't Fall- Emma St. Clair

Absolutely Not in Love- Jenny Proctor

A Groom of One's Own- Emma St. Clair

Romancing the Grump- Jenny Proctor

Runaway Bride and Prejudice- Emma St. Clair

When Alec Met Evie- Jenny Proctor

As You Ice It- Emma St. Clair

If All Else Sails - a standalone with connections to the Appies

Love Stories in Sheet Cake

The Buy-In

The Bluff

The Pocket Pair

Sweet Royal Romcoms

Royally Rearranged

Royal Gone Rogue

Love Clichés

Falling for Your Best Friend's Twin

Falling for Your Boss

Falling for Your Fake Fiancé

The Twelve Holidates

Falling for Your Brother's Best Friend

Falling for Your Best Friend

Falling for Your Enemy

Oakley Island (with Jenny Proctor)

Eloise and the Grump Next Door

Merritt and Her Childhood Crush

Sadie and the Bad Boy Billionaire

Izzy and Her Off-Limits Love

The Serendipity- a whimsical romance (part of the Only Magic in the Building series)

ABOUT THE AUTHOR

Emma St. Clair is a *USA Today* bestselling author of over thirty books and has her MFA in Fiction. She lives in Katy, Texas with her husband, five kids, and a Great Dane who doesn't make a very good babysitter. Her romcoms have humor, heart, and nothing that's going to make you need to hide your Kindle from the kids. ;)

You can find out more at http://emmastclair.com or join her reader group at https://www.facebook.com/groups/emmastclair/

Emma is represented by Kimberly Whalen, The Whalen Agency.